FRAGILE CORD

ALSO BY EMMA SALISBURY

THE DS COUPLAND DETECTIVE SERIES

A PLACE OF SAFETY (Book Two)

ONE BAD TURN (Book Three)

ABSENT (Book Four)

THE DAVY JOHNSON EDINBURGH GANGLAND SERIES

TRUTH LIES WAITING (Book One)

THE SILENCE BEFORE THE SCREAM (Book Two)

FRAGILE CORD

Emma Salisbury

Book cover design by Aimee Coveney
Typeset by Coinlea Services in Garamond

ACKNOWLEDGEMENTS

For my family, for keeping eyebrows raised and eye rolling to a minimum. Most of the time. Thanks also to Caireen Harrison for her sharp-eyed editing, which kept me on the straight and narrow.

Can a story exist without someone to read it?

I hope you enjoy this book, I hope more than anything it makes you stop and think. You've been kind enough to purchase it, can you do me one last favour? Once you've read it would you post an honest review on Amazon.

Thank you.

Emma

'Where does one go from a world of insanity?
Somewhere on the other side of despair.'
T.S. Eliot

PROLOGUE

Tracey Kavanagh stroked her swollen belly absentmindedly as she reached for the drawing Kyle proudly held up for her inspection. It was three thirty on an uncomfortably hot day and the infant inside her shifted lethargically; the playground was full of red-faced mothers with excitable offspring and the sound of happy chatter reverberated around the red brick walls.

She swallowed hard as she studied Kyle's picture; her hands began to shake uncontrollably as an uneasy, anxious feeling worked its way through her chest. She could hear her heart pounding, the *thump, thump, thump* increasing its crescendo until it drowned out the babble from the children around her and startled her unborn child.

Her troubled gaze slid to the beaming face of her ruddy-cheeked son and in that moment she knew she must kill him.

CHAPTER 1

By the time the main exit doors of Hope Hospital's Accident and Emergency department were in full view Detective Sergeant Kevin Coupland had a cigarette clamped in his mouth ready and waiting for the lighter that was winging its way towards it like an Exocet missile. He glanced sympathetically at the bored looking receptionist logging in details of the walking wounded; mouth down-turned in disapproval as she keyed in descriptions of injuries sustained whilst half-cut, she didn't bother to return his smile. Three more strides and he was out into the forecourt, the end of his cigarette glowing as he dragged on it hungrily, glad to be free of the smell of piss and disinfectant and unpleasant stains on the waiting room floor.

Wild goose chase by the look of it, as far as he could see, yet an army of plods were still caught up at the scene. Three rapid response vehicles had been dispersed to contain the braying mob locked inside the wine bar in Swinton; several teenage girls had already been off-loaded to Salford Precinct Station for questioning in relation to theft, yet it wasn't the theft that had required urgent police attention; it was the savage attack that had followed it, setting everyone's teeth on edge.

Ricky Wilson, a self-employed builder and father of three, had been out with his family celebrating his wife's birthday when her hand bag had gone missing from beneath their table and a group of young girls standing nearby began to snigger. The rest of the details were hazy – opinions from Wilson's family, who'd only really begun to pay attention when the atmosphere turned sour – but when he'd challenged the girls they'd handed over his wife's bag quick enough - minus her purse.

It was a clammy Sunday night in a town fractured by unemployment and tempers frayed easily when thirsts were quenched with happy-hour shots – officers unlucky enough to work the weekend shift spent most of their time locking up drunks and breaking up fights. It was a tough eight hours, but there was a predictability about it. When the call came through that a man had been seriously assaulted on Swinton Precinct the officers responding thought at first it was a typical pissing contest, an altercation got out of hand, but all preconceived ideas flew from their minds when they rounded the corner that took them onto the pedestrianised square, saw that apart from the victim and his family, no-one else was in sight. No drunken bystanders braying at each other in the aftermath of a fight, no over-made-up women shouting the odds at passers-by, no underage drinkers pausing to gawp as they cut across the square to the decent kebab shop up along the top road. Both taxi rank and bus stop remained empty.

The only people to be seen were Ricky Wilson slumped awkwardly on the hard stone flags, his wife leaning over him stemming the flow of blood that leaked from his stomach with her jacket, their children stood around them, motionless. Cars continued their journey along Chorley Road, their headlights illuminating the figures on the ground, but none of them slowed down.

'Fuckin' great.' The first officer on the scene had muttered to his colleague as they'd approached Wilson. They'd been nearing the end of their shift, knew instinctively they'd be held up until the immediate area was secured. He looked at his watch and cursed, tried not to step in the blood pooling around the man lying by his feet. He'd turned back to his colleague once more. 'Better call it in,' he hissed, 'and where the fuck are the paramedics?'

In the hours that had elapsed Coupland had worked his way through the pissed and those aspiring to it at the bar Wilson and his family had been drinking in before the assault had taken place, the bar where his wife's bag had been stolen. The Sportsman was a concrete pub made to look better by giving it a theme. Football scarves and kits adorned the walls alongside signed photos of United players. A large TV screen was tuned permanently to the sports channel. There were two bouncers on the door. Both were dumpy and shaven headed. Black suits and open necked shirts, they wore ear-pieces to alert them to any trouble. Coupland stifled a smile. Having been in the bar a couple of times himself – all in the line of duty, of course – and recognising several punters whose collars he'd felt at one time or other, he wondered, just for a moment, the purpose of the doormen – to keep the undesirables out – or in?

Coupland's trip to the hospital had been in vain. His request to question the victim had been blocked by the consultant on call who informed him imperiously that his patient was about to undergo emergency surgery. The knife blade had pierced Wilson's bowel and if they didn't operate quickly, peritonitis would set in. Coupland attempted to speak to the man's distraught wife, Melanie, but a brief word with her told him he was wasting his time, all she knew was what she had seen – that her man fell down and didn't get up again.

One look at her now, huddled with her kids in the shabby relatives' room nodding at a male nurse who tried to explain what was happening, told him he wouldn't get much more from her tonight. The couple's children – a thickset boy with attitude and two shapeless girls – sat numbly either side of her, vacant behind the eyes as they stared at the nurse's moving lips until a defeated look settled upon them.

In the circumstances, the best thing he could do was give them some space.

Moving out from beneath the entrance canopy he stood away from the other nicotine addicts and positioned himself beside a low red-brick wall surrounding the hospital's perimeter. An NHS sign behind him directed visitors to the short-stay car park and his gaze followed the arrow to a bank of hastily crammed-in cars, abandoned by relatives too stressed about their loved ones to give a toss about leaving the car park later. He'd parked his own car around the corner in the long stay car park near maternity, although with hindsight he couldn't be any more certain the men who rushed there in the middle of the night weren't equally as stressed, despite the notion that the birth of your offspring was supposed to be a joyous occasion.

Overweight and fast approaching forty, Coupland had the kind of physique Russian shot-putters would die for – with none of the muscle. Hair still dark but starting to thin, and eyes that had seen more than they should. He sighed as he smoked to the end of his cigarette and threw it down onto the pavement, grinding it into the tarmac with the toe of his shoe, wishing for the millionth time that getting rid of scum could be as easy. Mindless scum that preyed on a hardworking man as he enjoyed a night out with his family. He thought about going back inside to question Wilson's family, reckoned that he'd get no sense out of any of anyone until Ricky came out of surgery and his condition was better understood. The family were in shock; their statements could keep – for now.

As he strode towards the long-stay car park he passed four storeys of ward windows, blinds drawn tightly against the ink-black sky. The lamplight from each nurses' station gave off a forlorn glow.

Hope Hospital. He thought of the patients tucked up in their beds, the sick and the dying lined row upon row and he wondered how a hospital could derive a name that conjured up the opposite of what Wilson's family must surely be feeling right now, staring at Styrofoam cups as they waited for the kind nurse to come back and translate the surgeon's words.

As he turned the corner of the maternity ward he located his car easily enough and opened the driver's door. Two vehicles up from him a man dressed in jeans and an inside out tee shirt leaned against the bonnet of a modest saloon car, weeping; the label of his tee shirt stuck out beneath his hairline as he bowed his head into his chest and his shoulders heaved.

'Boy or girl, mate?' Coupland called out to him with as much interest as he could muster given the time of night and the circumstances of his own visit to the hospital.

The man's head shot up, watery eyes glistening in the summer moonlight. His words came out in a breathy sigh:

'A boy.'

He nodded at the proud new father. 'Congratulations, you must be very happy.'

'Over the fucking moon, mate,' the man replied, beaming. 'Over the fucking moon.'

Coupland snorted. 'Just you bloody wait, pal, a few more years and you'll have your work cut out for you.'

'You've kids yourself then?'

Coupland nodded, 'A daughter.' Pause. 'She's sixteen.' He said it on an outward breath, as though no other explanation was necessary. A number summing up the attitude, the mood swings, the sheer resentment of having a dad who gave a damn, let alone one in the force. But then came the involuntary smile, the chest puffing up as she came into his mind's eye, the sheer bloody pride. 'She's doing Drama at college,' he added, mock modesty implying she was the next Dame Judy at the very least, 'spending too much time studying the scrotes on the course if you ask me.'

He shook his head. Words were not his strong point; he'd joined the force at a time when all he had to do was sign his name to get taken on. He'd never found the vocabulary to express how his daughter made him feel, the sheer bloody enormity of it. 'She'll be the death of me,' was all he muttered, grinning, as though that prospect was preferable to the endless other ways of leaving this world behind.

In many ways, he supposed, hope was relative. How you saw it depended on where you were standing at any given moment, and for this new father, emotionally wired over the birth of his son, the world, right now, in the car park of Hope Hospital's Maternity Ward, was full of it.

*

When Coupland pulled into the hospital car park for the second time less than twelve hours later he found the spaces near maternity were taken, that he'd have to make do instead with the empty bay near the Sexual Health Department, always the last to be taken as no one wanted to advertise their visit to the clap clinic. It was funny how even in the blistering heat – the temperature in the shade was an uncharacteristic twenty-eight degrees, only there wasn't much shade – anyone entering that particular ward kept their baseball caps jammed firmly over their faces. It was a ward where eye contact was never made, where the patients were known only as numbers, and appointments were not always necessary. He'd been out with a clap nurse once, or genito-urinary medicine to give it its Sunday name. Didn't last long. Always felt like he was undergoing an examination every time he got undressed. And the stories she told were enough to turn him celibate.

Coupland made his way to the High Dependency Unit where Ricky Wilson had been moved following surgery. He'd not regained consciousness. His wife, Melanie, who'd stayed by his side through the night, now sat on a foam-backed settee in the relatives' room surrounded by a multitude of brothers and their wives, whether hers or her husband's, Coupland couldn't be sure. She was still wearing yesterday's clothes; blood had caked onto the lines around her knuckles and along her hairline where she'd leaned in close to Ricky, keeping him going while they'd waited for the paramedics to arrive. Her blouse and the knees of her trousers were ruddy brown, where the contents of her husband's stomach had spilled out onto her.

All eyes were upon Coupland as he entered the room; there was a collective hush as the family strained to hear what the stranger in a suit had to say.

'His mam's in with him now.' Melanie volunteered, as though she felt the need to explain why she'd moved from her husband's side, away from the tubes and wires that were keeping him alive, the constant beeping of machinery that signified he wasn't out of the woods yet.

The congregation separated like the parting of the Red Sea to make a path for Coupland to approach her. He held out his warrant card as he did so. A whisper went around the room, passing on he was a copper.

'You got the bastard who did it yet?' a faceless voice shot out at him, and he shook his head slowly, looking for the voice's owner without success, settling his gaze on Wilson's wife. Mid-forties, a head-turner on better days, he thought. Eyes large and expressive; lips just the right side of full. Today she looked haggard, eyes hollowed from crying, lips pursed into a worried line.

'It's early days yet, Melanie,' Coupland said gently, 'but it's essential I get a statement from you as quickly as possible.' He paused before adding: 'We'll need to complete an e-fit of the attackers for circulation and that works best when your memory's fresh.'

With every word he uttered Melanie seemed to sink further and further into her chair until Coupland found himself talking to the top of her head. There were clots of Ricky's blood in her scalp; matted along her parting. Two women sat either side of her – sisters-in-law, it turned out – both called Margaret. They'd been propping her up, holding onto an arm each to stop her from collapsing while their men paced the room, wild-eyed and dangerous, making threats against the animals who'd done this to one of their own.

The Margarets stared at Coupland as he spoke, gently letting go of Melanie at the same time, exchanging their physical support for vigorous nodding and rubbing of her arms, mindful not to touch the splashes of blood.

'He's right Mel,' said the prettier Margaret, *call me Mags*, 'they need your help to catch 'em.'

The other Margaret, who preferred her Sunday name, was a plain, older woman in her mid-fifties. She bounced her head in agreement as she rose to her feet, patting Melanie on the shoulder like an obedient dog. 'I'll go and fetch you some clean clothes, love, you'll feel better once you've tidied yourself up a little.'

Melanie hiccupped capitulation and moved her head in a jerking movement that Coupland took to be a yes. The plain Margaret's shoulders lifted a little before she slipped out of the room, relieved at the prospect of a short respite from the desperate family gathering.

Without the physical support of her sisters-in-law Melanie seemed to jackknife in on herself, her skeleton reduced to marrowless bone. Her head bent forward as though searching for something by her feet. She spoke into the space between them. 'We've been together since we were seventeen,' she informed him, 'never had a night apart.' Her accent was harsh, old Salford, over emphasising the 'a's so that it sounded as though they'd never had a night *apaaart*. Coupland nodded, sat down in the now vacant seat beside her, fishing around in the breast pocket of his shirt for his note book and pen.

'If you could start from the beginning, Melanie,' he coaxed, 'from the point where you'd noticed your bag had gone missing…'

*

When Coupland left the hospital two hours later, Wilson still hadn't come round. The detective had looked in on him lying unconscious, a ventilator tube in his mouth, the black concertina bag inflating and deflating beside him. A drip was attached through a cannula to the back of his hand. He looked lifeless, as though he'd already left them.

Wilson's brothers continued to pace the relatives' room and swear as though performing a religious chant, a ritual capable of warding off evil. Every so often they'd lose it completely and slam their fists onto the coffee table, spilling coffee cups and startling Melanie from her bedside vigil, everyone hoping silently that the frayed tempers would disturb Ricky, rouse him from his coma so he could tell them all to *shut the fuck up*.

The medical staff were growing increasingly concerned. The doctors, having done as much as they could, gave the family as wide a berth as they could while everyone held their breath. There was nothing more anyone could do now but wait.

The sun shone brightly overhead as Coupland located his car, passing the subdued Sexual Health patients smoking outside as they waited for the number they'd been allocated – a cloakroom ticket drawn from a recycled tissue box – to be called. Each stood several feet apart, stealing furtive glances at the person closest to them whilst trying to look nonchalant, as though waiting for a friend. Just then the automatic doors to the clinic opened spewing out a middle-aged man who stared at the ground all the way to the sheltered bus stop. Coupland looked away, fighting the temptation to compound his guilt by gawping.

Coupland's shirt clung to his back like a second skin. He pulled at his clothes, undoing another shirt button in response to the unrelenting heat. He'd kept his jacket on while he'd interviewed Melanie out of respect, but now, free of the restrictions of his own sense of protocol he shrugged it off, rolling-up his shirtsleeves before climbing into his car.

Just then a woman passed by, holding the hand of a small boy. The woman was flushed, the overhead sun an increasing irritation compounding her discomfort; the boy complained of being thirsty. Pulling impatiently on her son's hand the woman cajoled him with the promise of his favourite juice but could he *just walk a little faster?* The exchange reminded Coupland of his own childhood, how it seemed to consist of a series of promises and deals: sweets if you eat your greens, stickers following a trip to the dentist, a present from Santa if he was a good boy. Life was a series of reasonable barters, something to strive for, but achievable and seemingly fair.

Maybe it was the job that had made him a cynic, but he couldn't help feeling sorry for the boy, his mother teaching him one set of rules, the school of hard knocks eventually teaching him another. He thought of Ricky Wilson's children keeping a vigil by their father's bed. They'd discovered the hard way that life wasn't perfect.

That fairness doesn't come into it.

Ever.

CHAPTER 2

The woman stood with an expression of open incredulity at the scene of destruction before her. The room had been ransacked, every drawer upturned, the contents strewn across the floor in a mindless, haphazard way. Piles of clothes lay crumpled, trodden underfoot amid the debris that represented their lives.

'I'm sorry, mummy.'

Detective Constable Alex Moreton looked long and hard at the seven-year-old boy in front of her and not for the first time wondered how such a perfect little person could create so much devastation. Ben was small for his age; his mop of unruly hair and fragile features usually protected him from much of his mother's wrath, but on this occasion he was not to be so lucky.

'For pity's sake, Ben,' she bawled at him, exasperated, 'look at the state of your room! I want it tidy before you leave for school this morning.' She could but live in hope. Padding back to the bedroom she walked round to Carl's side of the bed, shaking him awake.

'C'mon love, I need you up keeping an eye on His Nibs while I go for a shower. I want to go in early.'

Six foot five with a head of dark curls, Carl was an adult version of Ben. Correction, an adult-*sized* version of Ben – she still wasn't convinced about his maturity. With strong broad shoulders and a boyish grin, he had a way of looking at her that exasperated yet excited her at the same time – on most days anyway. She looked at his sleep-filled features doubting he'd even heard her. It was all right for him, she thought, he worked from home, didn't have to contend with the rush-hour traffic to get to the other side of town. He worked for himself as a freelance web designer, didn't have to show willing like she did every morning, making sure she was in early and one of the last to leave, just to prove she was committed. His days were relaxed and flexible, so he got to spend more time with Ben too – another sore point. Her job paid the bills though and Christ knows they needed the money, and she did enjoy her work – most of the time anyway.

'Mmmm…' Bleary-eyed and hair tousled, Carl looked up at her, laughing at her serious frown. A whiff of sour morning breath rose up to greet her and she tried not to wrinkle her nose.

'Come back to bed,' he said sleepily, 'we could do that thing we keep talking about but never have time for anymore… can you still remember what to do?'

A smile played on his lips as he lifted a hand to her breast, his thumb circling her nipple through the fabric of her dressing gown. Tempting though it was to climb back into bed, his timing was way off beam. Right now she had something more important on her mind than a roll under the duvet. After recently sitting her sergeant's exams she was waiting on tenterhooks for the result. She'd been studying for the exams when she and Carl had got back together, hell-bent on proving herself in the force. Everything had seemed so simple at the time: promotion would mean respect; the extra money would come in handy too. The direction her career was heading had been clear-cut. Her job, even the cases she dealt with had a commonality that comforted her – she caught bad guys and put them away – end of. Or at least that's how she explained it to Ben when he asked her what she did every day. He loved that she was a police lady, as he called her, and he loved to listen to her stories from work, none of which remotely resembled the truth, but lying to protect loved ones was a skill every cop had to learn early on in their career – it went with the territory.

Stepping into the bathroom she checked her appearance in the mirror. Foundation would conceal the circles under her eyes but nothing would hide the hardness that had settled around her mouth, the cynicism that looked back, shaking its head at her. There was no escaping it, the job had aged her. Not so much in a physical sense; she still worked out at the gym three times a week, lifting weights to keep her muscles toned and pounding the treadmill to improve her stamina. It was more her state of mind that had changed, the way she now looked at the world. It had taken its toll, staring into the darkest corners of the human soul every day, detesting what stared back.

Showered and dressed in a sharp new suit she'd bought during the mid-season sale she kept her make-up to a minimum, her one concession to extravagance a red designer lipstick she'd bought in Kendals last Christmas which she wore every day to justify the price. With a final glance in the mirror she walked through to the kitchen where Carl was overseeing Ben, making sure he didn't put too much sugar on his Weetabix, Coco puffs resigned to the back of the cereal cupboard as babyish. 'Can we watch cartoons?' Ben asked hopefully, looking up at his father first, then turning to his mother.

'Ye-'

'No!' Were the opposing replies, until Carl, catching Alex's disapproving look, backed her up.

'No way, Tiger! Let's concentrate on your breakfast and getting ready for school, eh?' Ben's shoulders drooped as he chewed his cereal deliberately slowly. Alex looked at him sternly before squeezing round the table to plant a kiss on the top of his head.

'Don't sulk just because you didn't get your own way,' she scolded him.

'But I thought that was the whole point of sulking,' Carl quipped, dropping his eyes when Alex levelled her gaze at him. She hated it when he tried to be funny in front of their son. What he saw as a bit of fun she viewed as a lack of respect, challenging her authority. Carl scowled as he poured them both a coffee, banging mugs onto the counter top and deliberately slopping milk onto the table. Ben giggled. Avoiding her eye, Carl mopped up the mess with his sleeve. He looked over the top of the cereal box at Alex, taking in the new clothes.

'You look great.'

Blushing, and feeling a bit mean for being short with him, she smiled. 'Now I've taken the sergeant's exams I thought it was about time to start dressing the part too. Let the buggers know I mean business.'

Carl's face fell.

'*Ally*,' he said quietly, aware that seven-year-old boys had the uncanny ability to tune into Adult Conversations at sixty paces.

'Mmmmm?' She responded absentmindedly, taking a sip of her coffee as she read the morning paper's headline: *Man critical after a family night out.* The article showed a holiday snap of the victim relaxing on a bar stool beaming into the camera. He was wearing a sleeveless t-shirt; sunglasses perched on the top of his head. The picture had been taken a few days into the trip, bright pink skin just beginning to turn brown.

'…so that's a yes then?'

Shit.

Alex had missed what Carl was saying, the hopeful tone in his voice alerting her to proceed with caution. If she was committing herself to something she wanted all the details first. Trying not to glance at the clock on the wall – he hated it when she clock watched at home – she looked over at Ben who was following the conversation with interest, a mischievous smile playing on his lips.

'Go and brush your teeth, love,' she instructed him, wincing as he scraped back his chair and walked slowly to the kitchen door, trying to eavesdrop a while longer.

'Hurry!' she urged, openly glancing back at the clock and seeing it was twenty to eight.

She turned back to Carl, who was waiting expectantly for her reply.

'We could do with a night out,' he prompted. 'Mum and Dad'll have Ben for the night. We can go to one of those fancy wine bars on the top road.'

'Don't fancy this one,' she said pointedly, holding open the newspaper so he could see the article about the man who'd been stabbed outside a local bar on Swinton's precinct.

'It can be anywhere you want. Let me wine you and dine you, then take you to bed…'

Ah.

Now she understood.

'Carl, we talked about this already—'

'No *you* talked. Threw up a handful of reasons why another baby's out of the question…' His voice trailed off and he looked at her, willing her to help him out a little. Her silence spurred him on.

'You'll be running out of excuses, soon.' He hurled at her before getting up from the table, clearing the plates away noisily.

It was obviously his turn to sulk.

'Look, it's not that I don't want another baby, Carl,' she countered. 'It's just that, well, how can we afford it, what with your income being unpredictable?'

It was true enough. Since he'd returned from his voluntary work in Africa he'd had a string of low paid jobs that he'd quit after a few weeks, all for a variety of reasons, but basically because he hated the thought of being tied to a desk somewhere, joining the commuter line each morning that snaked into Salford Crescent and exited ten minutes later at Manchester Piccadilly, pouring out from the confines of the station like worker ants. 'I'm sorry Ally, but I get stifled driving a desk.'

Alex's face was impassive as he said this, her mind wandering, counting the different ways the predators she came into contact with stifled their victims. Carl's voice broke into her thoughts: 'It's why I put myself back through college, Ally, set up the consultancy…so at least I can still pay my way.'

The casual hours fitted around Ben's schooling too, and while Carl'd never make a fortune, it provided him with money he could call his own. The truth of the matter was that if they both wanted another baby they would manage. Alex constantly baulking at the idea had been an unspoken area of tension between them for some time. Until now.

'Is it me?' he blurted out. 'Do you not want another child with me?' Behind him, Ben hovered in the doorway, soaking up the atmosphere like sponge fingers in a trifle. He looked from Carl to Alex, his brow furrowing at the raised voices.

Every time Alex looked at her son her heart filled with love, pride – and dread. He was the centre of her world, was there really space for another child in their lives? She couldn't imagine loving anyone as much as Ben. Her feelings for Carl were different, not a lesser love, she was sure of that, just impossible to compare. Her love for Ben was unconditional, blind. Having a son made her understand the mothers who shielded grown men during police raids, giving them false alibis and turning up religiously for prison visits no matter what they'd done. Mothers had the capacity to stand by their sons long after their fathers had walked away to create new lives and new offspring that didn't bring shame and disappointment to their door. Mothers stuck by the sons they'd been given, for they still saw the boy and not the man. The enormity of such unconditional love overwhelmed her; did she really have the capacity for more?

She pushed back her chair, picked her car keys up from the kitchen counter. 'I've got to go.'

Carl looked up at her with surprise.

'But you haven't finished your coffee.'

'I'll get one at work.'

Ruffling Ben's hair as she passed him in the doorway to let him know everything was okay, she checked her appearance in the hall mirror before leaving their small Victorian semi and climbing into her old Fiesta parked on the tarmac drive.

As she turned the key in the ignition Alex replayed their conversation. She couldn't begin to tell Carl the conflicting thoughts that were darting round her brain right now; all she knew was that a night of alcohol-fuelled passion was the last thing she needed.

Pulling up outside the newsagents on the corner of their road she left the engine running while she ran inside the shop to buy a packet of mints, popping one into her mouth and crunching determinedly before slipping back into the car, indicating, then pulling out into the flow of slow moving traffic making its way towards Salford's city centre. The coffee Carl made her had been too strong, had left a distinctly bitter taste in her mouth.

CHAPTER 3

Coupland moved across the CID room acknowledging the detectives already present. His bum cheeks had just made contact with his chair when an authoritative voice set them off twitching uncontrollably.

'Need your report on the stabbing within the hour, Sergeant.'

DCI Curtis didn't wait for a response, moving on instead to his own cramped office to sift through the witness statements gathered at the wine bar where Ricky Wilson had been celebrating before his attack. Coupland bit back a retort about knowing how to do his bloody job, preferring to keep his arse out of whipping range for now. His attention was grabbed by a commotion going on in the corridor. An incident room was being set up in the side room next door; two uniforms were manoeuvring a table through the door, Chuckle Brothers style, negotiating the legs through the narrow space. 'Need a hand Jim?' Coupland called to the larger of the two men. A message coming from the officer's radio obliterated part of his response, 'cough' being the only word Coupland could catch.

He'd gone home for long enough to shower and change, quietly, without waking Lynn. A sister at the Neonatal Intensive Care Unit at Hope Hospital, she'd just come off a double shift, would castrate him in a heartbeat if he made the mistake of waking her. A half-hearted shave had left clumps of stubble under his chin. He'd needed caffeine, but not so badly he'd risk clattering about in the kitchen, he was in major bad books already. He sat now nursing a vending machine latte, the plastic-tasting liquid doing nothing to revive his enthusiasm at the prospect of trying to decipher his own handwriting. Things hadn't been great between him and Lynn recently but, with luck and a prevailing wind, normal marital relations would be resumed again sometime soon. His fingers started to skip along the computer keyboard at the prospect of this, a smile starting to form on his lips. He could but live in hope.

Alex Moreton walked purposefully down the recently decorated corridor, picking an imaginary piece of thread from her jacket lapel as she turned to enter the lions' den. Her confidence had grown in line with her ambition over the last couple of years; there was no doubt in Coupland's mind she was destined for great things.

She waltzed into the CID room, twirling around in a suit he hadn't seen before to the sound of wolf whistles and catcalls, before getting down to the mundane tasks of the day. She accepted the attention of her colleagues now in the way it was intended: the universal piss-take was the great leveller of them all – given to anyone who looked as though they were trying too hard – turning up in new clothes or with salon-cut hair. Even Coupland's visit to the dry cleaners earned a round of applause. They hadn't seen the light or anything, and the men still liked to chance their arm – Coupland himself told jokes that would have him hauled up to Complaints if Alex ever decided to get arsey, but she had her own armoury of deadly bloke jokes and wasn't afraid to use them.

Giving in to his thirst Coupland got up from his seat and headed back down the corridor to the drinks machine for his second drink of the day. The message above the coin slot instructed: *Please use correct money as no change given.* He dug around in his pocket for coins just as Alex popped her head into the corridor, asking if he'd shout her a drink. Finding several fifty pence pieces Coupland held up the coins like an exhibit in a trial.

'No problem.' He offered, 'What do you want?'

Alex knew the odds on getting her first choice was slim. The black coffee had run out weeks ago and the tomato soup – which had been replenished – now tasted like Bovril. She was content to relegate her choice of beverage to fate.

'Cheers Sarge, I'll have anything.'

'Tea? Cappuccino?' Coupland enquired, his questions met by a disinterested shrug of the DC's shoulders. '*Bovril?*' he persisted.

No reply.

He turned in time to see Alex already had retreated into the CID Room, arms out, palms facing upwards as if saying *whatever*.

Coupland understood. He fed his money into the coin slot before punching a series of random numbers. 'Not like we'll be able to taste the difference anyway…'

'Did you get dressed in the dark this morning?' Alex shot at Coupland as he handed her the brown coloured liquid the machine had grudgingly spat out moments earlier. His suit was the usual off-grey, pilled at the sleeves ensemble he climbed into most mornings, but today the shirt was more skewed than normal and clashed angrily with the tie knotted tightly at his neck. An expanse of tripe-like flesh hung proudly over the buckle of his belt.

'I did as a matter of fact. Trying to keep on the right side of Lynn.'

'Things any better now?'

Coupland hesitated. He didn't like bringing his private life into work, didn't even keep photos of his family on his desk, as though their proximity to the bastards he came in contact with would somehow taint them. But then he'd blurred the lines between work and home when he'd gone for a drink with a civilian call handler who brought bunny boiling to a whole new level.

'She still doesn't believe nothing happened.' Coupland shook his head, as though he was the injured party. 'Can't understand why Adele would've come round to the house if there wasn't more to it.' He shrugged. 'Thing is, neither can I.'

'Perhaps her guide dog had lost his sense of smell.'

'Ha bloody Ha. And you wonder why I don't bother saying anything.'

Alex flushed. 'Sorry, but let's be honest here, you were flattered that someone else with a pulse actually fancied you. Can you honestly say things wouldn't have progressed if Lynn hadn't found out? Seems to me she's right to be upset.' It seemed to Alex that Adele Gunnell was loopy in the head for looking twice at Coupland in the first place, but then there was no accounting for taste. Luckily the telephone operator had been on a fixed term contract that hadn't been renewed, but she'd still managed to cause Coupland maximum embarrassment and, more worryingly, had left a fracture in his marriage he was desperately trying to heal.

Coupland scowled. 'I get this at home.' He dropped his voice as officers filed into the room for morning prayers. 'I don't need it here too.'

He looked around the assembled team. As well as Alex, DCI Curtis had joined them for the briefing, along with DCs Turnbull and Robinson, two detectives who'd worked together so frequently they appeared to Coupland as a single unit. A harmless enough duo, they could be relied upon to carry out tasks assigned to them, not sharp enough to get anyone's backs up. They'd assisted Coupland in collecting statements from the wine bar the previous evening and following up overnight leads.

The assault had attracted media attention, hence the DCI's appearance that morning. Happy to keep a low profile during the briefing – his forte leaned more towards handling PR – he raised his hands towards Coupland in mock surrender, conveying the message *Pretend I'm not here.*

Those who had been assigned to the assault case outside the wine bar, Turnbull and Robinson included, sat to one side of the briefing room, those who'd been left to pick up the slack – burglaries, muggings, an allegation of rape at the local comprehensive and drug dealing at the Science Faculty at the University – sat on the other, Alex sat in the centre of the room. It wasn't unusual for rivalry to form during an investigation, and though he'd never seen any negative impact on the team morale long term, he had thought about getting the officers to participate in some team-building exercises, although copious amounts of alcohol at the end of a shift seemed to do the trick. However, while HR insisted on sending him on coaching courses, he felt duty bound to put some of it into practice. He mulled the idea around his head for a while, deciding if he had a To Do List, he'd certainly place it at the top.

Curtis nodded at Coupland to begin the briefing. He'd been the first senior officer on the scene and the room quietened as he stood to update the assembled team.

'Two of the girls brought in for questioning in relation to the theft of Melanie Wilson's bag have been arrested,' he began, 'the others released without charge.'

'Who's the duty solicitor?' Alex asked him.

'Lewisham.'

An uncomfortable silence settled on the room, each man

struggling with his own thoughts and for a moment nothing could be heard but the clearing of throats and the shifting of buttocks as officers stared uneasily at the floor.

'I didn't know he was back.' Alex muttered, ashamed she hadn't been in touch, trying to think when she'd last spoken to him.

'I'll call in on him,' Curtis replied, equally shame-faced, 'check how he's doing…' His words hung in the air like a terminal diagnosis. Sensing that everyone was desperate to return to comfortable ground, he motioned for Coupland to continue.

'The events following the theft of Melanie Wilson's bag are still hazy. According to the girls accused of stealing it, Wilson became aggressive towards them even when the bag had been returned.'

'Hardly surprising, since they'd kept hold of his wife's purse – and mobile phone,' Turnbull observed.

Coupland concurred. 'That's the kind of logic we're dealing with. Wilson – in their view – continued to badger the girls, until he and his family were asked to leave by the management – which they did – quietly enough according to witness statements, and surprise, surprise, no one saw or heard anything more until Wilson's son raced into the bar shouting that his old man had been attacked and that someone should phone for an ambulance.'

'None of the family have a mobile?' Robinson asked, a sour-faced Geordie with nicotine-stained hands.

'Melanie's was stolen, they couldn't get a signal on Ricky's, and the kids had been told to leave theirs at home so they wouldn't spend the evening texting their friends – the night out was meant to be quality time.'

'Not the most salubrious of places for a family night out,'

Curtis chimed, 'is Wilson a regular?'

'Not so much, Sir, according to the staff,' Coupland replied. 'There's a restaurant next door, Italian, the Wilsons had started off in there, had called into the bar for a nightcap. It was on their way to the taxi rank.'

Curtis nodded. 'CCTV?'

'I'm on it,' Turnbull chipped in.

'There's a known criminal element that frequent the bar,' Coupland added, 'which might hinder the investigation if the regulars become afraid of talking to us.'

'Aye, that'll be right,' interrupted Robinson. 'I mean, normally they're queuing up to talk to us, eh?'

Coupland shrugged in response. 'Fair enough, but I reckon it's more than that. I was stone-walled everywhere I turned last night, like there's some kind of bloody conspiracy.'

'Probably is.' Alex spoke up. 'It's a close-knit town. The problem is everyone knows everyone else. No-one wants to be the first to start talking.'

Curtis nodded, made a couple of notes onto a pad of paper, began assigning tasks to the officers congregated before him. He turned to Coupland. 'Go back over the information you've already uncovered,' he instructed, 'run it through the usual checks, see if any familiar names come up.' Once more Coupland bit back a smart-arse answer. He'd spent the best part of his career putting senior officers in their place only to be assigned the shittiest tasks or take the fall when things went pear-shaped. He couldn't help it – blurting out what he thought rather than filtering his comments was an affliction as uncontrollable as Tourette's – but it had held him back, put lead weights round his ankles when he'd tried to climb the greasy pole of Inspectordom. He watched the detectives file out behind Curtis, keen to return to the sanctity of his spreadsheets. A Salford Grammar boy done well, Curtis was more amenable to the obligatory brown-nosing that was expected of the overly ambitious. Unlike Coupland, he attended all the right meetings, played the right sports, laughed louder at the Assistant Chief Constable's jokes.

As far as Coupland was concerned, Curtis was welcome to the paper-shuffling and attendance at endless committee meetings required of the upwardly mobile officer. He'd found over the last couple of years that since his career halo had slipped, he enjoyed the job much more. Christ, occasionally he even felt as though he made a difference. Moving up the food chain took you away from all that. Removed you so far from the streets that victims became statistics, tiny points on an axis rather than significant people in their loved one's lives. But Curtis was no fool. Middle-thirties and battle-scarred, he knew the only way to earn the respect of his men was not to get involved too closely, so he kept himself in the loop, close enough to know what was going on, but at a safe enough distance not to get shit on his shoes if it went belly up.

The overhead light panels flickered above Coupland, causing him to squint. During a recent refurbishment the designers had replaced much of the strip lighting with eco-friendly, mood-enhancing natural light panels, designed to reduce stress. The result was the feeling of working under a giant solarium, without the benefit of improving your tan. Much worse was the fact that they worked on sensors, automatically dimming when no activity could be picked up in a room, causing officers slumped over keyboards catching up with emails to wave their arms frantically like they were having some form of seizure if they wanted the lights to come back on.

There had been uproar when someone from HQ, an accountant, Coupland suspected, had suggested fitting these lights into the interview rooms. When Coupland had read the memo he'd nearly choked on his bacon roll, advising anyone who'd listen that the day they made interview rooms stress free was the day he'd hang up his size elevens.

'What next, eh?' he'd spat accusingly. A piece of masticated bread mingled with ketchup had stuck to his front teeth, making him look as though he was suffering from advanced gum disease. 'Rubbing lavender on their bleedin' temples before an arrest in case reading them their rights upsets 'em?' As usual he'd gone off half-cocked but there wasn't a single officer who disagreed with him. Thankfully common sense had prevailed in the form of Curtis, who'd quashed the suggestion once and for all, proving he wasn't so far removed from reality that he'd forgotten what it was like trying to extract the truth from a lying bastard.

Coupland sat back in his chair, allowing himself a moment's contemplation. He'd begun reading through Melanie Wilson's interview notes; he tried now to return to his original train of thought. It was pitiful really how, as a supposedly intelligent species, we took in so little about our surroundings, tending to ignore all our senses. Melanie had barely been able to recall the time of the attack until her son reminded her they'd been heading out for a taxi when the midnight bus that stopped by the junction had appeared at the traffic lights. Ricky had marched after it, shouting to the others that if they shaped themselves it'd save him the cost of a cab.

Coupland supposed it was the shock, the sheer incomprehension that followed when something happened that wasn't supposed to happen, that skewed people's perspective. In the end all he'd been able to establish was that the assault had been carried out by two men who appeared out of nowhere, literally coming out of the shadows to carry out their attack in silence, and by the time Melanie had realised what had happened the attackers had simply merged back into the darkness. It was a calculated, deliberate assault. Whoever had carried it out intending to use minimum effort to inflict maximum harm.

Coupland rubbed at a tendon at the base of his neck, rolling his shoulders forward and back. It had been several hours since he'd had anything to eat, wondered if he should chance the vending machine soup. His stomach rumbled like distant thunder and he remembered Lynn had a Zumba class tonight so it was make do on toast.

His desk phone buzzed once, sharply, reminding him of the sound made in the board game, *Operation.* Caller display informed him it was the DCI.

'Sir?'

'A moment of your time, Coupland. Press office want me to prepare a statement.'

'He's not dead yet, Sir.'

Shit. When, oh, when would he learn?

'I'm on my way.'

*

'Come,' Curtis beckoned, remaining in his seat as Coupland approached his desk. 'Sit down.' These were instructions Coupland found easy to comply with; he wondered if the rest of the conversation would go as well. Curtis flicked through the report Coupland had given him before the morning's briefing.

'Nasty.'

Coupland winced at the understatement, hoped Curtis referred to his Thesaurus before he went in front of the press. Curtis's office was small but tidy. Framed photographs of his family lined the walls, each one a picture of domestic harmony. 'Press'll be all over this,' Curtis continued, absentmindedly straightening his tie as he spoke. 'Gang-related?'

Coupland shrugged his shoulders. 'Too early to say, Sir.'

This seemed to irritate Curtis, as though he'd already prepared his statement and would now be forced to re-write it.

'Early indications suggest this wasn't gang-related.' Coupland attempted to clarify the situation. 'Just a case of a family being in the right place at the wrong time, I suppose.' Curtis considered this. 'Even so, press'll have a field day,' he observed. 'Any news on the victim?'

'Still in a coma.'

'And witnesses?'

'E-Fits being taken as we speak.'

Curtis nodded his approval. 'Keep me appraised of every development,' he instructed before dismissing him, pen poised, ready to write the sound bites he'd be spouting in front of the camera should Wilson take a turn for the worse.

'Very well, Sir,' Coupland muttered into the void.

*

'How did you get on with the CCTV?' Coupland called out to Turnbull when the officer returned to the station.

Turnbull pulled a face. 'Nothing out of the ordinary. Coupl'a dealers doling out their wares, local kids, attend the local high school when they have to. And no,' Turnbull butted in before Coupland had the chance. 'They didn't see nothing, didn't hear nothing – wouldn't say nothing even if they did.'

'That it?'

'Cameras are pointed down the side street and back alley, nothing front of house – the security guys are there for that.' Coupland scribbled something down on his desk pad and picked up his car keys.

'Where you off to?'

‘Food first. Not eaten since last night, stomach thinks my throat’s been cut. After that the hospital.’

Topkapi was situated on the main road running through Pendlebury, about 400 yards from last night’s assault. It had a dining area that consisted of one chipped Formica table and four nailed-down chairs. No one used the table to eat on; instead it had tolerated several hundred backsides leant against it over the years while food orders were given and punters waited for Styrofoam trays filled with meat covered in sauces never seen outside a kebab shop. ‘Usual, Osman,’ Coupland called out to the shop owner, ‘all the trimmings, mate.’ The Turk nodded and set about the rotisseried lamb like a serial-killing tribesman in some war torn country. The polystyrene tray contained slices of donner, some shish, cubes of chicken marinated in chilli oil. Coupland stabbed at the pieces with his plastic fork, as though identifying each mouthful before attempting to eat it.

‘You see anything unusual last night?’

Osman shrugged, ‘Punters coming in sober, minding their manners would be unusual. Last night was fairly normal – two kids arguing about something on a mobile phone, one couple having a full blown domestic while they waited for their pizza, a young girl had her hands full propping up her mate who’d been dumped by her boyfriend.’ Osman sighed. ‘What is it about the English that a night out isn’t complete without someone bursting into tears?’

Coupland thought of his own family get-togethers, the state his sisters got into when they were on the wrong side of a bottle of wine. ‘I know what you mean.’

‘Even so, it wasn’t as busy as usual, but I suppose the attack would have put people off staying out.’

Coupland wasn’t so sure; he’d attended major incidents

where onlookers arrived with thermos flasks in tow. 'We might be a nation that cry when we're pissed but we love a good gawp,' Coupland sniped, patting his pockets for change.

Osman waved the gesture away. 'On the house.' Coupland nodded his appreciation.

'How's the guy doin' anyway?'

'Clinging on by his fingernails.'

Osman paused as though considering this image. 'Aren't we all, Sergeant Coupland?' he asked simply. 'Aren't we all?'

*

Coupland slowed outside his home on the way to the hospital. He wouldn't pass it on his normal route but a detour was in order while he agonised about calling in. Lynn's shift at the hospital wouldn't start for another couple of hours, there'd be time enough for them to talk before Amy came home, neither of them wanting to expose her to more raised voices. He pulled up at the kerb and lit a cigarette for courage.

One stupid mistake. That's all it had taken to send his marriage into free fall. Not a day had gone by that he didn't look in the mirror and cringe. He'd never meant to hurt Lynn, yet all it had taken was 10 minutes of flirting and he'd scampered after Adele like a dog with two dicks. Lynn was convinced that they'd slept together, refused to believe his protest that it'd been one drunken kiss. Even so, she'd countered, it was obvious he'd been tempted, that if the opportunity had presented itself he would've happily shagged her. The annoying thing about Lynn was that she always had a point. If he'd thought of a good enough excuse to get a pass out for the night he'd have gone back to Adele's without a care in the world. And now? Now he was banged to rights anyway: a wife convinced he'd been unfaithful, and a mounting resentment that if he was doing the time he might as well have committed the sodding crime.

He stared up at their bedroom window as Lynn pulled back the curtains. She looked out onto the street below, her gaze settling on his car. If she was surprised he was parked out front she didn't show it, her eyes found his and seemed to lock onto his soul. He'd been about to open the driver's door when his phone rang, breaking the silence. He was tempted to leave it, but he'd asked to be kept informed of any change in Ricky Wilson's condition. He picked up his mobile and grunted a reluctant greeting.

The control room operator's words sent his heart sinking to the pit of his stomach. He scribbled the call-out details into his pocket book, reading it back in the vain hope he'd misheard it. He rubbed the inner corners of his eyes with his thumb and forefinger, already focussing on the carnage he'd been summoned to. He threw his cigarette out of the driver's window and started the ignition, looking once more to where Lynn had been standing watching him from their bedroom window.

She was gone.

*

It used to be said of certain women – I remember my father saying it – "she's a good little home-maker". But can you *make* a home? Or even make yourself at home? Isn't home some place you have as a child, and spend the rest of your life running from…?

- As if, Blake Morrison.

CHAPTER 4

The house was set back from the road, obscured from view by a bank of Leylandii planted years before the current owners had moved in. Mock Tudor in design, it had a solid oak front door flanked either side and above by leaded windows, with an adjacent detached garage. The circular driveway had space for several vehicles. Today, it accommodated easily the two private ambulances and squad cars that were parked outside.

A child's bicycle lay abandoned at the side of the house, silver racing stripes glinting in the sunlight. As Coupland approached the front door he noticed that the uniformed constable on the doorstep looked about twelve years old, making him wonder briefly whether he'd ever looked so young. Over the years a cautiousness had set in, an over awareness of the frailty of life – a general acceptance that he was passing through, that in the grand scheme of things what he tried to achieve on a daily basis would amount to sod all. There were positive days of course, days where he knew he made a difference, but as he walked towards the house of horror, as it was already being dubbed, he found it nigh on impossible to recall any of them.

The front door was open; being dusted for prints along with all the other entrances to the property, although early indications suggested this was just a formality. Inside, he found himself standing in a large square hallway, high ceilings for a modern house, black and white tiles on the floor. Light spilled softly into the hallway from a partly opened door. Following the light Coupland made his way along the hall, passing family photos that smiled down at him from every angle. He found himself in the kitchen, a modern, spacious room displaying solid white units and granite worktops.

Brightly coloured magnetic letters spelled out *Kyle*, *Doctor*, *Bank,* on a large fridge-freezer beside several photographs: a man and a woman with a small child at a theme park; the same small child dressed as an elf during a school play; in another he was blowing out candles on a train-shaped cake, cheeks puffed out like two rosy apples. A notice-board over the kitchen table had a list of emergency numbers; a shopping list with Billy Bear ham underlined, and a notice for a school fair at St. Michael's in two weeks' time.

It was a busy kitchen; one where meals were made from scratch and the gravy didn't come out of a jar. A sweet smell of baking hung in the air, a grocery bag lay half unpacked on top of one of the units. A recipe for lemon meringue pie lay beside it, the ingredients ticked off one by one.

Through a doorway leading out from the kitchen there was a large mud-room containing a washing machine, dryer, and three pairs of Wellington Boots and a pair of trainers lined neatly in a row. A child's easel stood in the corner; beside it a small table held a jar of cloudy water, a plastic moulded pallet with an assortment of colours squeezed from tubes of expensive-looking paint.

The artist's pad on the easel was blank. Coupland looked back at the cloudy water in the jar and to the paintbrush beside it, streaked with dried paint. Moving closer he saw that the top sheet from the artist's pad had been crudely torn off, tiny fragments of it remained on the uppermost gummed edge of the pad. A strange feeling came over him as he stared at the blank sheet of paper trying to imagine what the child had been painting. He thought at first he was sickening for something, until it dawned on him he just felt plain sick.

'Sarge?'

Startled, Coupland swung round to find himself facing Alex. He nodded, trying to assimilate what he'd been thinking with the reality of the situation.

'Have you been here long?'

'No,' he replied hesitantly, 'I just wanted to get a sense of the place, before…' He inclined his head towards the floor above, where they both knew that any sense of how the family was before would be wiped out with just one glimpse of the hell awaiting them.

'The victim's name is Kyle Kavanagh, Sarge,' Alex informed him, 'his mother's name is Tracey.' He noticed she referred to the word *victim* in the singular, yet two bodies were waiting upstairs.

'Where's the husband?' he asked. Alex inclined her head in the direction of one of the furthest rooms leading off from the hallway. 'He's in the lounge – sorry, sitting room, as they call them around here. There's a PC with him, Sarge, and the family GP's on his way over.'

'How is he?'

'*How do you expect?*' She answered hotly, the flush creeping up her neck giving lie to the calm exterior she'd shown when she first approached him. The confidence she'd exuded earlier at the station had all but evaporated. Instead, he found himself looking at a hollowed-out version of Alex. 'How long have you been here?' he asked, searching her face for clues as to what he could expect to find in the rooms above.

'Long enough,' she replied in a voice that seemed to escape from somewhere inside her, then, more to herself than to anyone who might have been in the room with her, 'Long enough…'

Coupland stared at her, wondering what she'd seen that had dimmed the light in her eyes. 'They're waiting upstairs for you…' Alex urged him, swallowing quickly, concentrating on the glare of his brightly coloured shirt. 'They're ready to take the bodies away.' Coupland's shoulders sagged as he made for the door leading back into the kitchen. He paused, raising his eyebrows briefly at Alex who had made no move to follow him.

'I'll wait down here, Sarge, if it's all right with you.'

Her voice sounded choked, as though something was caught in her throat. She'd been in the vicinity when the call came in, had been one of the first officers on the scene, when there'd been a flurry of hope that at least the unborn child could be saved. Coupland paused:

'Will you be—'

'I'll be fine, Sarge,' she cut across him, raising a hand to her mouth as though fearful any noise it made would give her away. She held her other hand out in his direction, palm outwards, as if to say *back off*. He nodded, turned and headed back through the kitchen towards the hall, towards the staircase and the first-floor landing.

It was a big house.

Too big now, Coupland thought.

His feet felt heavy as he climbed the wide staircase. An uneasy feeling rose in his chest and it came as no surprise when he heard, moments later; Alex's choked-back sobs fill the air.

At the top of the stairs his feet touched padded carpet. A long, galleried landing led to several rooms to the east and west of the house. At the front of the structure, a large central window dominated the wall, letting in sunlight and providing a spectacular view of the valley across to Irlam. The forensic team were silently packing away equipment, each man and woman focussing on a different zone, a different place, anything other than what they'd actually been working on.

No one spoke.

Harry Benson, the Senior Pathologist, made a point of glancing at his watch as Coupland approached, his disapproving mouth puckered so tightly it resembled a fully clenched rectum.

'If I'm keeping you from something…' Coupland barked, then stopped short as he caught sight of the look that flickered across Benson's brow, the fatigue in his eyes caused by sheer disillusion. These cases were the hardest to fathom, the ones where the crime was committed by those meant to protect. Benson turned to a colleague, issued a series of instructions before heading towards a room at the rear of the house, beckoning for Coupland to come too.

The detective swallowed hard in an attempt to brace himself as he followed Benson into the large family bathroom, to the oval-shaped bath where Kyle Kavanagh lay naked and motionless. The boy's fair hair was plastered to his scalp; droplets of water were still evident on his face and body. His fingers and toes were prune-like from being in the water so long. Coupland was aware of other images coming into view: bottles of children's shampoo and bubble bath lay at angles around the perimeter of the bath. Had they been knocked over during the scuffle as the child splashed and kicked to stay alive? The shampoo was one of those that claimed to be gentle on the eyes, Coupland wondered if it would be as gentle on the lining of the lungs.

A laminated poster of the planets was blu-tacked to the wall.

Benson pointed to bruises that were beginning to form

on the boy's shoulders, 'Where she held him down…' he explained, demonstrating mid-air with the heel of his palm, showing how the boy's mother had applied pressure to keep him below the water's surface just long enough for him to drown. Coupland sucked in his breath as his imagination took over. He pictured the frightened child, wondered if he'd called out for help. He felt a jolt of terror charge through his body as he imagined the boy's feeling of betrayal when he realised what his mother was doing, still not believing it even as she did it. Loving her anyway.

'Alex okay?' Benson asked over his shoulder as he pointed at barely visible finger marks on the boy's upper arms. 'She's one the same age, hasn't she?'

Coupland nodded, grunted a yes in the direction of the medic's back. There'd been a hint of a relationship between the surly pathologist and the DC back when she was in uniform, might have been serious too, if her son's father hadn't come back on the scene.

'See here?'

Benson pointed to the pressure marks on both arms, looked back at Coupland as he waited for a response. Coupland grunted again, moving his head up and down vigorously as if to emphasise he *could* see, when in actual fact he barely glanced towards Benson's pointed finger. Instead his eyes kept creeping towards the boy's peaceful face, a face that earlier would have shown an eagerness for life, a desperation to learn, to *live.* Reluctantly he allowed his gaze to follow the trajectory of Benson's pointed finger; saw the abrasions on the boy's upper arms. 'Where the father tried pulling him out…'

Without another word they moved back onto the landing, Benson raising his eyebrows as he motioned towards his assistant, indicating the child could now be moved. Both men stood silently, looking around until they found a place on the landing wall they could focus on. A framed picture of the boy as a curly haired toddler caught their attention. It had been taken at Disney, one of those meet-the- character photo opportunities. The boy wore a plain tee-shirt and short dungarees, chubby legs rolled over the top of his ankle socks as he stood knock-kneed for the camera, his scuffed leather sandals turned into each other as he beamed at his mother, his arms wrapped around an adult size Minnie Mouse. Coupland studied the happy scene as he cleared his throat.

'When did he...?' he asked, unable to finish his sentence.

'A couple of hours ago.'

It was as if they'd been struck by an affliction that prevented them from saying the word death or anything alluding to it. Like they were taking part in some bizarre game of charades where they had to second-guess each other's sentences.

'And the mother…?'

'Through here…'

The master bedroom had been tastefully decorated in shades of cool blue; fitted wardrobes surrounded a king size bed. The sun streamed through the large central window, its rays bouncing off a carefully placed crystal that hung in its middle, catching the light and transforming it into coloured beams like a miniature laser show. To the side of the window a dressing area complete with dressing table and large vanity mirror led through to an en-suite bathroom. In the mirror's reflection Coupland could see a corner bath, an assortment of bath products arranged around its edge. Confused, he turned to Benson. 'Where...?'

'Far side of the bed…' And so their fractured word game began again.

With a jolt Coupland saw the top of the woman's head

jutting out from behind the neatly made bed, tilted forward as if in prayer. He almost expected her to turn around, disturbed by the strangers standing in her bedroom doorway, to ask them what the hell they thought they were doing. Except she wasn't able to turn, nor would she be able to ever again.

His immediate thought when he stepped towards her was that she looked like a puppet on a string. A rope of some kind had been secured to the bedstead; the other end of it had been tied around her neck. Coupland turned back to Benson for clarification. 'I was informed it was sui—'

'—It is.'

'I don't get it, she—'

'—She has a noose around her neck, Kevin,' Benson said sharply, 'and the pressure of the cord has cut off the air supply to her lungs and brain, what bit of that is hard for you to take in?'

Coupland stared at the semi-kneeling body of Tracey Kavanagh, the angle of her torso as it slumped forward putting pressure on the taut rope. He was unnerved by the fact he was unable to see her face, could only see the crown of her head, a central parting in her dark hair, which hung down like a curtain obscuring her forehead and eyes from view. What bothered him most was the fact both her feet – indeed her knees – were on the floor. There were no restraints on her arms or legs, nothing inhibiting her freedom. The colour drained from his face as realisation dawned:

'But she could have stood up at any time.'

'She didn't want to, Kevin.'

She was fully dressed; a cheesecloth maternity dress was bunched up around her knees, exposing the back of white calves that were beginning to show signs of mottling. Benson provided a voiceover:

'When Alex arrived at the scene she checked for signs of life. Although the mother was dead she hoped there was a chance to save the baby. She lifted the woman's head to remove the pressure of the ligature from her neck, tried breathing air into her mouth. She thought that if she could prevent the brain from being starved of oxygen, there'd be a greater chance of the foetus surviving…Only it was obvious to the paramedic and the emergency doctor who responded to the call that the life of the foetus – and the mother – had been extinct for some time.'

'*Jesus.*'

A cold draft blew through the room lifting the hairs on the back of Coupland's neck as he pictured Alex fighting to keep the woman's unborn child alive. He let out an involuntary shiver. 'I thought the whole point of hanging was to step off something and dangle by the neck – that you hung from a height until your body was starved of air – eliminating any room for second thoughts.' He stepped closer to the woman, lifted the hair at the nape of her neck so that he could see where the noose had been tied. The knot was just beneath her hairline, easy enough to reach if she'd changed her mind.

'In many ways it mirrors a traditional hanging,' Benson informed him, 'by which I mean the body dangles from an overhead rope. The rope mark – as you can see here—' he pointed to the line just visible beneath the ligature, 'is characterised by an upward slant. Garrotting, or a faked suicide, would leave a horizontal line.'

An image of her lifting her arms behind her head came into view, tying the knot precisely, allowing no margin for error. Coupland looked up at Benson, 'It must've taken a hell of a lot of willpower to fashion a noose and then use it in such a way that she could stand up at any time she wanted.'

'Or desperation.'

Both of them remained silent, then Benson said: 'Cases of asphyxiation where the victim could simply have stood up to save himself or herself, are, for the most part, quite rare. They tend to be associated with autoerotic or unusual partnered sexual practices,' he folded and unfolded his arms as he said this, giving the impression he wasn't entirely comfortable with this line of thought, 'but the intent is never to actually die.'

Coupland recalled a similar incident involving an Australian rock star at the end of the nineties, half remembered reading interviews with the singer's close friends who claimed he'd never intended to die, that something that evening had gone terribly wrong. At the time he didn't get it, the need to push life to the furthest limit. He wasn't so sure he was any nearer to understanding it now.

'You think that's what happened here?'

Coupland wasn't convinced, whether because unusual sexual predilections didn't fit with his image of the cosy family scene he'd encountered downstairs he wasn't sure. There certainly didn't appear to have been anyone else in the bedroom with her – no other belongings – other than her husband's – certainly no evidence of sex play. Given what she'd just done to her son, Coupland surmised, suicide seemed the most probable cause. The shake of Benson's head implied the pathologist thought the same. Crouching down onto his haunches so that he could see her face, Coupland found himself staring into eyes that bulged out of their sockets like some grotesque animation. Her swollen tongue protruded through her mouth. He felt the displacement of air as Benson crouched beside him.

'A suicide hanging causes death in several different ways, Kevin: Pressure on the jugular vein and carotid artery, which result in a lack of oxygen reaching the brain… Pressure on the vagus nerve causes breathing inhibition… which in turn causes asphyxia, because the breathing passageways are obstructed by the tongue and glottis, which are pushed into the pharynx.' He paused, as though mentally checking he'd included the most salient points. 'I'm certain all this will be confirmed when I open her up.'

Benson's words set Coupland's teeth on edge, yet he knew the pathologist wasn't being insensitive. It was his job to cut people open and rummage inside their bodies, to identify the reason for their death, in the same way it was Coupland's job to get inside their *heads*.

He walked over to the bedroom door, to where the photographer stood kicking his heels in case he was needed again. These cases were never as straight-forward as they looked, and this one…

'You've taken shots of the knot and the angle of the rope?' Coupland called out to him. The man nodded, piqued, he knew how to do his bloody job.

'And the knot where she secured the rope to the bed?'

He nodded again.

The DS scratched his chin, moved his hand down to the base of his neck and then up to just under his jawline as though his shirt collar was chafing him. He rubbed the area of skin from ear to ear absentmindedly as he looked back into the bedroom at the rope securing Tracey Kavanagh to the bed. Benson watched him from inside the room. 'Are we done here?' he asked. Coupland waved him away impatiently, pointing to the photographer's equipment lying by his feet, half packed away.

'You got a video recorder in there?'

The photographer nodded, knelt down to unclasp his case while Coupland motioned with his hands for him to come back into the room.

'Here,' he motioned for him to approach the body, 'I want you to record me releasing her.' He paused, thinking for a moment, 'I'm going to cut the rope either side of the knot, both on the bedstead and around her neck so they're preserved for testing, but I want to be sure we've captured how this rig-up looks from all angles, so I can replicate it later. Got that?'

The photographer nodded, tried out the camera from different points in the room until he was happy with the view through his lens. To get the shot of Coupland cutting around the knot on the bedstead was easy enough – he took up position at the foot of the bed, using the zoom lens to home in and capture the detail as Coupland worked a knife to cut through the rope's thread. In order to capture the clearest image of the Detective Sergeant cutting the rope either side of the knot behind Tracey's head he had to crawl along the length of the bed while Benson lifted her hair.

'Closer.' Coupland kept repeating this instruction until the photographer was near enough to the woman he could smell her shampoo, its unmistakable fragrance catching in his throat. The brand was a popular one. He would never be able to smell it again without gagging.

CHAPTER 5

Angus Kavanagh sat rigid on the oversized settee, staring blankly at Coupland as he introduced himself and DC Alex Moreton. Angus was medium build; square-shouldered with closely cropped fair hair. Pale blue eyes looked up from under patrician brows, his lashes barely visible. His skin was pale too, reminding Coupland of the cream you used to get on the top of fresh milk before government health advisors turned such things into a guilty pleasure; today's cartons contained a watery imitation that didn't even taste like it came from a cow.

There was a slight tremor in Angus's hands and two spots of colour flashed across his cheekbones, which Coupland put down to shock. Even so there was an air about him, a self-assurance that hinted at a privileged upbringing, making him look older than his thirty years. The information the uniformed officer who'd stayed with him had gleaned was sketchy; he'd spent more of his time restraining him, preventing him from bolting back upstairs to his wife and child than finding out his personal details and that of his family. Even now the officer bounced on the balls of his feet, ready to lunge if the poor bastard made another move to dash out of the room.

Coupland flicked through the officer's notebook. Angus had been married to Tracey for six years; Kyle attended a local independent school. They were happily married – Coupland noticed the PC had underlined *happily* several times, as though there were degrees of happiness and each line represented a different level. Angus and Tracey, going by the number of lines, were extremely happy. They had no financial worries, no problems within their marriage, and Kyle was doing well at school.

'Can I get you something, Angus?'

Alex crouched down on her haunches so she was at the same level as Angus, the way an adult would try to make themselves appear non-threatening to a distressed child. He seemed incapable of moving his head, had stared at their middles all the while Coupland told him how sorry they were, asking if there was someone they could call. The PC had poured him a shot of something he'd found in the kitchen, and Angus nursed it now in his hands, swirling the liquid round and round in his glass without taking a sip.

'Can't face it…' he whispered to no one in particular. His eyes were puffy and red-rimmed and his nose looked as though he'd blown it several times in succession.

'How about I make us a nice cup of tea?' Alex soothed, smiling at him sympathetically as she slipped from the room. Coupland knew it was an act, that she was using all her reserves to stay in control, digging deep to retain a professional exterior in front of him. He knew that she, like himself – like all of the officers called out to this house, for that matter – would wake up one day, maybe tomorrow, maybe the day after, or maybe even a long time after that, and her heart would weigh a little bit heavier for working on this case. It was the price they would pay for doing what they did for a living, and there was as much chance of any of them moving on to do something different as there was of night deciding not to follow day.

With Alex gone the room lapsed into silence. A carriage clock sat centre stage over an Adam-style fire surround, the second hand tick-tocking its way around the gold face oblivious to the fact that for this family time had long since ceased to matter. A leather armchair faced towards the centre of the room. Coupland moved it closer to Angus and sat down.

'Angus,' he began, 'had anything been troubling Tracey recently?' He was now in Angus's eyeline, could see the fog that had descended behind his eyes as he tried to make sense of what he'd stumbled upon upstairs. 'Was she taking any prescribed medication for depression?' The cogs in Angus's cloudy brain turned slowly as he computed the detective's questions.

'*Here we go.*' Alex bustled back into the room carrying a tray laden with a matching teapot and cups, a jug of milk and a sugar bowl. The crockery was one of the expensive ranges in the window display at Kendals – Denby, Coupland thought – beyond his price range anyway. Alex busied herself with the milk and sugar, talking aloud as she took on the role of mother, prising the glass out of Angus's hand and replacing it with a cup of hot sugary tea.

'Drink it down,' she instructed him, 'like Watney's Brown.'

They watched as he did as he was told, sipping the liquid slowly at first, then, as it began to cool, taking larger and larger gulps until it was gone.

'Angus isn't a Salford name,' she twittered, filling the void, then poured tea into two more cups, passing one to Coupland and taking one herself before remembering the PC and gesturing to him. He moved his head reluctantly to indicate a 'no,' peeved at being the afterthought, carried on bouncing on the balls of his feet, albeit more slowly now.

'I was born in Scotland.'

Both Coupland and Alex snapped their attention back onto Angus, who seemed to have emerged from his trance-like state.

'My parents and sister are still up there,' he said, 'I left the fold when I came to study at Salford uni. Met Tracey, never went back.'

He was well spoken, Coupland thought, recognising the universal plummy public school tone in his voice. There wasn't much of a Scottish accent, though, more an inflection, a genteel hint of a brogue. There was a Scot at the station, IT support or some such title which basically meant he came round unplugging the terminals and plugging them back in whenever anything went wrong. Rebooting them or whatever. Everyone called him Scotch Jim. He hailed from Glasgow and his accent was thick and guttural and when he was pissed he chanted *Flower of Scotland* and showed everyone his arse. When he was angry his words all rolled into one and no one could really understand what he said but went along with him anyway so as not to cause offence. Angus's accent was softer, more upper middle class.

'Whereabouts in Scotland?' Alex asked him.

'Edinburgh.'

Ah…

'Beautiful city,' Coupland commented. He'd never been, but had seen enough Hogmanay shows over the years to think it warranted a visit one day. Angus nodded, distracted; the hall stairs creaked as body bags containing Tracey, then Kyle, were carried outside to the waiting mortuary van. The PC moved soundlessly towards the door ready to be on hand if needed. Angus moved his head as he followed the sound, pushed himself to his feet and shuffled unsteadily to the large bay window in time to see the van doors open and swallow up his family.

'When can I see them?' His voice rasped as though it hurt when he spoke, and his breathing became ragged. Coupland could see the horror of reality starting to set in, that apart from the mortuary and the funeral home, Angus would never see Tracey or Kyle again. Certainly not in the way he was used to – laughing and joking and very much *alive*.

'Later. I'll take you later, Angus.' Coupland replied, 'In the meantime I need you to help me put together a list of Tracey's movements today, where she'd been, who she might have spoken to. A list of her friends, relatives, anything that can…' He could tell he was losing him; his eyes had become dull again, his skin took on a waxy pallor as though he was going to be sick.

'Where d'you keep your address book Angus?'

Alex was back on her feet again, walking out into the hallway opening all the adjoining doors until she found what she was looking for. A small room, used as an office, containing a large oak computer desk and leather chair at one end, a small settee and coffee table at the other. A computer screen sat on top of the desk, beneath it the computer's hard drive, a printer perching precariously at one end, beneath a wall-mounted phone. A small shelf displayed a dozen CD ROMs and several paper clips. A pile of taxi receipts and expense forms were weighed down by a leather-bound Filofax. Alex picked it up and hurried back to Angus.

'Is this it?' she asked him, holding it aloft. This time she sat beside him while she waited for him to respond. When he moved his head in the tiniest of nods she flicked open the fastener with her thumb.

'Here, let me go through it with you…'

While Alex worked though the names and addresses of friends and family with Angus, Coupland wandered back out into the hall, keen to get a better feel for the place. He glanced inside each room for signs of something amiss, or even signs of *anything*, for that matter. The presence of something – or the absence of it – that would help him on his mission to find a reason. Filicide, where a parent murders their child, causes shockwaves right through to the family's core, spreading out into the community. For most people it was inconceivable, an aberration, an act against humanity. When that parent goes on to kill him or herself, it leaves more questions than answers, as those left behind struggle to come to terms with betrayal *and* rejection, to find meaning in their loved one's final words and actions.

It was not unusual for someone on the brink of suicide to make preparations; to tidy their home, to make sure their insurance and finances were in order. Many saw it as leaving nothing to chance, a clumsy way of trying to minimise pain. This was the reason that they left a note, to absolve blame and explain their impatience to move on to another world. Tracey had left her home spotless, but there had been no note, only a ticked off shopping list on the kitchen work-top and a to-do list for the school's summer fair. Coupland's gaze swept each room looking for a hint of discord: a solicitor's letter threatening court action maybe; torn up photographs or forgotten shards of smashed crockery lying on the floor; tell-tale dents in the walls, but there were none.

Moving from room to room he surveyed every living space, each one a picture of suburban calm. Yet something troubled him, niggling away at the base of his skull, and he tried to focus on it now as he headed back through the kitchen to the mud-room he'd found himself in earlier. Muffled voices wafted through from the hallway but he stayed put. If he were needed Alex or one of the uniforms would come looking for him.

Despite the circumstances of his visit he liked this room; the large windows ensured the maximum exposure to natural light, and looked out onto a vast well-stocked garden that suggested a gardener rather than any green fingers on the part of the owners. To the side of the room an external door led into the garden; a heavy-duty doormat and boot scraper lay in readiness for the debris and muck that comes hand in hand with small children. This was the kind of home he would have liked for him and Lynn, all that space for a growing family, for Amy and the brothers and sisters they had hoped for her but had never arrived. Despite its *Grand Design* scale Tracey had turned it into an oasis of security and love.

Was it really a charade?

And if it wasn't, what could have happened to make her wipe out her own flesh and blood?

As Coupland turned from looking out through the patio doors he found once again he was facing the little boy's easel, which had been angled to look out into the garden. He tried to imagine what the boy had been painting – the rockery perhaps, or the large sunflowers that swayed in the welcome breeze? He felt the cogs turning in his brain, alerting him to the fact that something wasn't quite right. Retracing his steps into the hallway he took the stairs two at a time before cutting across the landing, opening every door until he found a room painted in primary colours with a bed the shape of a racing car standing pride of place in the centre.

Every little boy's dream.

A miniature wardrobe and chest of drawers stood against a wall, a pit-stop sign had been stencilled onto the toy-cupboard doors. On the far side of Kyle's room, beneath the window, was a small desk. On top of the desk was a ream of blank A4 paper and a wooden pencil case with a sliding lid. Coupland had owned one himself as a small child, hadn't realised they still made them. He walked over to the desk and picked up the pencil box, sliding open the lid to find half a dozen charcoal pencils, neatly sharpened. Turning it over in his hands he found a message carved on the underside of the box: *To Kyle, Merry Christmas, love Grandma and Grandad, XXXX.*

After taking a final look at the empty walls he hurried back down the stairs and into the sitting room where Angus slumped back against the settee. Alex, Filofax open on her knee, already making the first of a series of calls.

'Shit,' Coupland muttered under his breath as he took in Angus's vegetative state. 'I take it that was the doctor, then. What's he given him?'

'Something to deaden him from the neck up,' Moreton answered. 'Why?'

'Nothing,' he muttered. 'It'll keep.'

CHAPTER 6

Coupland returned to the station ahead of Alex, who'd stayed on at the Kavanagh house long enough to help a groggy Angus stumble across to his neighbour's home while forensics completed their examination of the property. She'd called Angus's father on the phone – a quietly spoken courteous man, deeply shocked at the news. He'd informed her that he and his wife would catch the next available flight from Edinburgh, promising he would call her when they landed.

'But how did it happen?' he'd asked. Alex had skilfully evaded his question; doubted she'd continue to be so lucky. 'We can't be sure yet…' she'd said blandly. 'We're going to have to carry out tests before we can be certain… I'm confident we'll have more information by the time you arrive.' There'd been a moment's hesitation, and she'd found herself holding her breath in case he asked her for anything else.

'Very well then,' he'd said, deflated, and before she could lie any further to him she heard the click of the receiver going down, followed by the dialling tone.

Without breaking pace Coupland headed toward the bank of interview rooms in search of Roddy Lewisham, the duty solicitor representing one of the young girls accused of stealing Melanie Wilson's bag – the proximate cause, it seemed, of Ricky Wilson's attack. Either that or it was a coincidence, only he'd learned over the years to distrust *those.*

There'd been no further news from the hospital – which meant at least Ricky hadn't deteriorated, but a couple of hours had passed and the clock was ticking. The description of the assailants he'd managed to get from Melanie during his visit to the hospital was being circulated amongst the press and handed out to drinkers in all the bars along Chorley Road, close to where the incident had taken place. It wasn't a great description – it had been dark and everything had happened so quickly, one minute they were heading for the bus stop and the next minute two figures with baseball caps lurched towards Ricky. The men were white – she'd seen white hands holding the knife, white faces beneath the rim of the caps, but other than that she hadn't given them a lot to go on. With any luck Ricky's description could fill in the blanks.

As Coupland drew level with the interview rooms furthest along the corridor he passed a policeman leading two girls back to the cells. Medium height, they were both heavy-set with bulky shoulders and hefty thighs beneath white track-suits. Fake Ugg boots despite the clement weather. Both girls sported the Salford knuckle duster – a bank of gold sovereigns on every finger – and a selection of hollow gold chains hung around their wide necks. Dirty hair was scraped back from their faces into ponytails secured high on each girl's crown with an elastic band.

Behind them one interview room lay empty; the next one along had the door slightly ajar and Roddy Lewisham leaned into the door jamb, his back facing the corridor as he conferred with a colleague who was seated at a small table scribbling into a legal pad. Coupland cleared his throat, waited for the solicitor to turn around.

'Kevin!' Lewisham exclaimed, his eyes softening at the corners when he saw who it was. They weren't friends exactly, they didn't bother socialising outside work, they were bound by something much deeper. It had been Coupland who'd found

Lewisham's daughter the night she'd been murdered, who'd punched Lewisham hard enough to knock him out cold so his last memory of her wouldn't be distorted by the way she'd been found, posed like a mannequin for the gratification of her killer. Instead it was Coupland who had the image of her corpse seared into his brain, her sightless eyes wide open in fear. He hadn't been able to spare Lewisham much, but at least he'd spared him from *that.*

When Coupland first met Lewisham he'd had a fearsome reputation as a defender of the indefensible. Officers cringed when they heard he'd be representing their suspects, knew that they'd be in for a rough ride. After his daughter's murder he seemed smaller somehow, a reduced version of his former self. These days he just went through the motions.

'How's it going with those two?' Coupland inclined his head in the direction of the holding cells where the girls had been taken.

'They're admitting the theft but nothing else,' Lewisham replied. 'I'm handling the younger girl's charge. My colleague here,' he nodded towards the seated man, 'has the pleasure of representing her friend.' He smiled ruefully as he said this, as though he'd got away with the lesser of two evils. 'If you think they had something to do with Wilson's assault you'll need to find the evidence fast, otherwise they'll walk.'

Coupland mulled over Lewisham's words. 'We're working on it, but the truth is no one else is coming forward to say they saw or heard anything. It was your average boozy weekend night, the bar was five people deep and leering room only, yet no one saw a thing. Swinton's a small enough town, you know as well as I do that someone's covering up for the attackers, and to a man, everyone in that bar that night will have known who did it, even if they didn't see it with their own eyes.'

It was true. Carrying out an assault was seen by many as an act of strength, a demonstration of power to be bragged about in drinking circles. Someone, somewhere was wearing this particular badge of honour, and others – many others by now if past performance was anything to go by – knew who it was.

'I appreciate that, Kevin, but you can't hold the girls on supposition,' Lewisham countered.

'No.' Coupland paused. 'I understand that... Look, let me see what we can turn up by the end of the day, and if that doesn't pan out then we'll go back to square one.' He turned to go, hesitated; he hadn't sought Lewisham out just for an update on the case.

'Listen, I was going to grab a coffee before I go over to the hospital to check on Wilson's progress. Only I need a decent cup, one that comes in a mug I can hold without burning my fingers and froth on the top that doesn't resemble someone's spit. Fancy joining me?'

Lewisham laughed. 'We're going out then?'

Coupland ached because he knew it was forced, that humour was part of the armour the bereaved wore to protect others from becoming entangled in their grief. Lewisham excused himself from his colleague and accompanied Coupland back along the bank of interview rooms, past the CID Room where everyone looked up as they went by, raising their hands to wave, relieved that Roddy was with someone, someone else who would ask him how he was doing, if he was keeping well. They'd ask after him next time, once they'd plucked up the courage.

'DCI Curtis was looking for you,' the desk sergeant called out as they went by the front desk, and Coupland raised his hand as though holding back the news.

'You've not seen me,' he shot back, and the officer nodded, carried on shuffling his papers.

The station was built facing onto the pedestrianised shopping area of Salford Precinct, sending out a clear message that law and order was a central part of the community once more. There might not be a policeman on every street corner, but each time the residents did their weekly shop the station building situated between Job Centre Plus and the Marks and Spencer seconds shop would be a reminder that Greater Manchester Police considered community relations a priority. As he exited the building Coupland took a sharp left, ducking into a tea-room across the vehicle-free street that served proper milky coffee without the fancy prices the American coffee chains charged for calling it a latte.

The tea-room was small and clean and decorated like an elderly person's front room. There were ornaments along the windowsill and upon the shelves were pot shire horses. Oak beams and a bridle attached to the wall gave it a country feel. The owners had put in net curtains to obscure the view of teenage mothers congregating in the square to enjoy their mid-morning can of cheap lager and the hairy-arsed plods who drew straws to move them on, dispersing them anywhere so long as they kept out of sight when the Top Brass came to visit.

They gave their order to the waitress and settled into companionable silence as she set about the coffee machine before bringing two frothy cappuccinos their way. There would never be a better opportunity to broach the subject Coupland had been working up to. He cleared his throat as he looked into the lawyer's troubled eyes. Lewisham was a solid-framed man with broad shoulders and a misshapen nose honed from years on the rugby field. Dark, neatly-trimmed hair framed a face so sad the skin clung to his jaw as though his facial muscles had stopped working and he had neither the will or the motivation to get them moving again. His eyes were hollow caverns surrounded by shadows. He looked defeated.

'So, how are you, Roddy?' Coupland began.

Lewisham didn't take sugar but stirred his coffee anyway before scooping the froth onto his teaspoon and licking it off. He set the spoon back down on the table with a clatter and sighed.

'Jesus, Kevin, why spoil a perfectly good moment?' he answered in such a tone Coupland wished he could take his question back.

'It's not mandatory to ask, you know,' Lewisham continued. 'You won't be failing in your duty as a mate if you just want to come out and have a coffee and not follow it up with a dissection into my pitiful existence.' A range of emotions flashed across Lewisham's face as he spoke: sadness, bitterness, anger, all rolled into a defensive layer that protected him from the outside world. 'I'm doing just fine,' he summed up half-heartedly.

'Bollocks.'

They glared at each other for a moment, until Lewisham shrugged. 'Okay,' he said, blowing out his cheeks, 'you sure you want to hear? Only it's not exactly *It's a Wonderful Life…*'

Unblinking, Lewisham laid bare his emotions like they were exhibits in a trial determining his level of sorrow. 'I wake up every morning as though I'm coming round from some terrible nightmare, that the last two years have been a cruel dream that bears no resemblance to reality. I cherish that moment, because it's those few minutes of misplaced hope that give me the strength to face the rest of the day.' He paused, picked up his coffee cup, blew across the top of it before taking a sip.

'I walk across the landing to Siobhan's room, which my psychiatrist tells me to keep closed so that I'm not drawn into remembering her. He thinks it's time that I "picked up the threads of my life". Ha!' His laugh was sharp and rasping, like a smoker's cough. A bitter look flashed across his face and his mouth twisted as he spoke. 'He talks about threads when the reality is there isn't even a microfibre of my life left. Not as I knew it. To lose your wife to cancer is unlucky, to have some mad bastard throttle the life out of your only child is twisting the knife a bit, eh?'

Coupland could only nod in response. Whenever he was with Lewisham, the man's grief weighed so heavily on his shoulders that he was struck dumb by his own inadequacy, incapable of uttering any sort of useful platitude. He hoped that listening helped, that even if he had nothing useful to say just sitting there and nodding would ease his friend's burden, if only for a while.

'So, I go into her room,' Lewisham continued, 'after all, it's my fucking house, and if I want to go in there I will. And for a while the world is all right again. Her makeup and jewellery is still scattered across the dressing table, her school uniform hangs over the back of a chair. It's all as she left it; she had no reason to tidy it away, did she?' His voice cracked. 'She thought she was coming back.'

How could either of them have known that everything she did that day would be for the last time?

Coupland looked away, not because he was embarrassed by his friend's emotion, but fearful that his own, unchecked, would get the better of him and discourage Lewisham from opening up any further. 'There are so many memories in that room. It's like… it's like she's still in there. Can you imagine how that feels?'

Coupland was not a superstitious man, but he pushed any thought of Amy from his mind. To place his living breathing whirlwind in the same freeze frame as Roddy's daughter might tempt fate, and the thought of anything happening to her made his throat constrict. He could feel Lewisham watching him, searching his face for understanding – acceptance, rather than rejection – of what he'd just said.

He gave the tiniest nod.

'And then I leave her room to go downstairs,' Roddy continued, 'but the house is so quiet… so I turn on the T.V. and the remote control is exactly where I left it the night before, not halfway down the back of the chair or kicked under the table, and it hits me like a fist that she's gone.'

He paused, as though mulling over what he was going to say next, deciding to say it anyway. 'I want to see her again so badly, Kevin, but the only way I can be with her is if I leave *this* world behind.'

In the days following Siobhan's murder Roddy had overdosed on the medication he'd been prescribed to help him cope. On release from hospital he was transferred to a psychiatric unit in Cheadle. At first he'd been kept on suicide watch but, after a while, either because the doctors felt they could trust him or that they couldn't protect him forever, they let him go.

'Does it not get any easier?' Coupland ventured, guessing the answer.

'During the day I'll be doing something completely inconsequential and I'll be reminded of her… only now I find myself forgetting how she looked or how her voice sounded, as though my mind is somehow relegating her to the past before I'm ready… and I feel guilty and frightened that one day I'll forget her altogether. I mean… I know I should let her go, that she isn't in this world anymore, but she's in *my* world, and that should count for something, right?'

Coupland faltered. He was out of his depth and conscious that for the last twenty minutes he'd done nothing other than imitate a nodding dog. He knew about pain but none of the antidotes – apart from the alcoholic kind, and in the long run that brought a completely different kind of pain. At least Lewisham had taken a leave of absence, returning to the legal practice on a part-time basis.

The theft charge at the wine bar in Swinton was the first case Lewisham had handled at Salford Precinct since he'd come back to work. Returning to the scene where his daughter had met her killer had been an unconscionable milestone, but he'd done it, and Coupland took this as a sign that he was on the road to surviving Siobhan's death, that her killer hadn't claimed Roddy as a victim too.

If he'd been a demonstrative man he'd have reached out to comfort him, place a well-meaning hand on his arm or shoulder, but he'd grown up a regular recipient of his father's belt, leaving him unsure how to interact physically with another man. He cleared his throat and pulled back his chair, calling out for the bill in a voice so abrupt the waitress and Lewisham looked at him strangely.

CHAPTER 7

The first thing that struck Alex when she returned home that evening was the noise; the chaotic babble that marked out a family home. Carl was in the front room, engrossed in an action film where Matt Damon saves the planet, the sound of gunshot and TV explosions spilling out into the hallway. In the kitchen the washing machine spin cycle competed with the tumble dryer's hum in providing a soundtrack to their lives she'd been completely unaware of. Upstairs Ben's voice could be heard calling down for a drink.

An appetising aroma wafting through from the kitchen told her Carl had cooked them something special and she found herself contrasting her home to Tracey Kavanagh's:

The silence.

The smell of pain and sorrow.

*

'Hey, I didn't hear you come in.'

Carl appeared in the doorway, making her jump. He wandered over lazily and planted a kiss on her cheek before going over to the sink to pour Ben a beaker of water.

'I've only just got back,' she replied stiffly, trying not to picture Angus Kavanagh returning home to a house of slaughter. Carl held the plastic tumbler out to her.

'Do you want to take this up to His Nibs?'

She shook her head.

'I'll get a shower before I look in on him,' she answered.

The case had left her feeling contaminated; Tracey Kavanagh's perfume had permeated her clothing while she'd held her close to breathe air into her lungs. She could still taste the woman's saliva in her mouth. 'Need to get changed,' she muttered to no one in particular.

Alex inclined her head in the direction of the stairs. 'How's he been?'

'*He's* been great,' Carl began, 'which was more than can be said for the client I went to see.' He pulled a face, made a circle out of his thumb and forefinger on his right hand, moved it back and forth in a gesture that implied his client liked to amuse himself in private on a regular basis.

Alex smiled in sympathy.

'You know, Ally,' Carl continued, 'you wouldn't believe the bloody day I've had…'

His voice trailed away as she climbed the stairs, unfastening the buttons on her suit before shrugging her clothes onto the bedroom floor. In the bathroom she made straight for the shower, standing beneath the bullets of water as they kneaded her scalp, easing away the tension. She closed her eyes, breathed in lavender soapsuds, leaned back against the cool tiled wall until the water began to run cold.

You know Carl, you wouldn't believe the day I've had either…

Shivering, she stepped out of the shower, drying herself roughly on an oversized towel before throwing on an old sweatshirt and jeans. She towel-dried her hair, staring into the mirror to see if the day had left a visible mark on her body as well as the scar on her soul. She closed her eyes, tried to focus on happy thoughts. Stepping into Ben's room, her spirits soared at his sleepy smile when he saw her approach his bed. Lifting the covers she slipped in beside him, held him close as she breathed in his little boy scent – buttery toast and Play-Doh.

He was warm. *Alive.* She clung onto him like a limpet, pushing all bad thoughts out of her head. Blinked away images of Kyle Kavanagh in the bath, cold and bruised and dead.

Was it possible to look into the eyes of your child and see how he'd turn out? Sometimes, when she studied Ben, she'd glimpse the man that he'd become. It was there in his face, in the set of his jaw. The turbulent teen; the faithful friend; the apple of her eye. This transition into manhood was already creeping up on them and soon, before she was ready, the hugs he gave her now would drop away, and sooner than she'd like he'd stop holding her hand to cross the road. One day he would shrink from her touch and grunt answers to her questions, but would he have changed so much where it mattered? The thought of him no longer needing her was terrifying. She gave him a squeeze, nuzzled into the nape of his neck.

'You're squashing me,' he chided before falling asleep. She kissed him on the top of his head then quietly slipped out of the room.

Her new suit lay on the bedroom floor where she'd discarded it. She picked it up, placing it carefully onto its hanger. She pulled off threads from the carpet that had stuck to the skirt, straightening creases, brushing make-up from the lapel. She wondered if the fibres were from Angus's clothing when she'd pulled him away from his son; if the make-up was Tracey's.

It was a beautiful suit.

Expensive.

She never wanted to wear it again.

CHAPTER 8

It was probably the point when the pathologist folded the baby's face forward to expose its skull that Coupland hoped he'd seen it all. That once this was over, nothing else could ever shock him. Surely, he thought now, as he looked as the stretched skin and tissue that had once been Tracey's Kavanagh's unborn child, nothing could be more disturbing to watch than the examination of an innocent, snuffed out by his mother before he'd taken his first gasp of air.

The hospital mortuary was a large dank room with tiled walls. A corridor behind double doors led off to the fridges where the dead awaited their final inspection alongside cadavers donated and stored for the medical school. There was a stone sink, a metal trolley laid with surgical instruments, and a set of weighing scales perched on a work surface beneath a wipe-clean board. In the middle of the room stood a rectangular metal table upon which lay the un-named baby of Angus and Tracey Kavanagh.

The palms on Coupland's hands began to sting, and when he looked down he saw that he'd been clenching his fists so tightly his fingernails had cut through his skin, leaving a trail of bloodied half-moons. He looked over at Alex standing on the other side of the table, raised his eyebrows at her, silently signalling his concern:

Are you okay?

She nodded.

A thousand unspoken questions passed between them:

How could she?

What was she thinking?

What kind of a woman could do this?

What kind of a mother…?

Alex's stricken face told him she thought there was more she could've done, as though Tracey and Kyle's death were her fault because she hadn't arrived in time to stop the young mother taking their fate into her own hands. Despite knowing it would be futile, Coupland had tried to reassure Alex that she could've done no more but she was determined to beat herself up. Back and forth they served and volleyed each silent question, and they continued to parry like this until Benson opened the baby's skull with a saw, began his inspection of the brain.

Jesus. This time Coupland found himself unable to meet Alex's eye. *Surely it didn't get more soul destroying than this…*

It had been hard enough to stand through Kyle's post-mortem, and afterwards he'd stood in the car park smoking his way through a packet of Silk Cut listening to the vitriol that poured from Alex's mouth as she used words he'd never heard her utter before to describe her feelings towards the young mother that was now Tracey Kavanagh, deceased. There'd been no stopping her, so he'd resigned himself to listening to her barrage of anger as he mentally prepared himself for the next examination.

It was better in a way, he thought, that she vented these feelings while she was at work, rather than take them home. He blew out his cheeks, shaking his head in disbelief. Christ, since when was *he* an expert in relationships? He lit a fresh fag from the dying embers of the last one while he searched for an answer to *that.*

It wasn't that he disapproved of Alex's antagonism towards Tracey Kavanagh; in many ways this case was too personal for his DC to deal with objectively. Tracey was no older than Alex. Both were attractive young mothers with their lives ahead of them. Watching Benson dissect Tracey's corpse had been a grim reminder of Alex's own mortality. It wasn't something anyone came to terms with easily. It was just that, having sat through the young woman's post-mortem and the removal of her foetus for further investigation, Coupland felt drained.

He'd stood by watching Benson, togged up in his surgical gown and gloves, lean over the woman's body and rummage wrist-deep inside her womb, working a sharp knife to release her unborn child. He'd tried to train his gaze so it stayed on her face, her alabaster skin contrasting sharply with long black hair, sightless eyes gazing up towards heaven or wherever the place was that people went to when they left their body by their own hand, but it was impossible. The sound of blood sloshing into the gulley beneath the table soon drew his eyes downwards, back towards the open cavity and the sight of Benson examining Tracey's baby before placing it into a metal basket at the end of the table.

It had been hard enough watching Angus Kavanagh crumple at the sight of his wife and child laid out before him, nothing but useless platitudes to offer him as he wept beside their bodies. No longer capable of either opinion or thought, Coupland wanted to be done, to be out of there. The smell was beginning to get to him too.

Severed organs and disinfectant.

What he really wanted was to hold Lynn tight, tell her that he loved her, that he'd never stopped, that he was an idiot all right but he was her idiot. She'd been late home last night from her exercise class, told him she'd stopped off for a drink with the girls. By the time he'd followed her to bed she was spark out, or pretending to be.

Had he lost her already?

Pushing the thought right out of his mind he focussed on the present, just in time to see Benson remove the baby's tiny brain so he could weigh it. At this point Coupland dipped his head and stared at his shoes, noticing they'd lost their shine.

Turnbull was making headway. During the immediate hours following Ricky Wilson's assault he'd ordered the pub landlord to lock everyone indoors to prevent anyone from leaving the premises before they'd been questioned. It had been a painstaking task, made worse by the amount of alcohol consumed and the fact that half the punters had been off their faces. He'd drawn a map of the wine bar and labelled every table, identified each drinker with a number and marked down where they'd been sitting or whereabouts near the bar they'd been standing when the assault had taken place. Over the last couple of days he'd cross-referenced each statement, corroborating with each drinker – or as much as was possible under the circumstances – who'd they'd been sat with or near, and whether anyone remembered someone slipping in or out of the bar during the minutes leading up to Ricky Wilson getting stabbed.

At first, he'd blamed the reticence of the crowd that evening on a general unwillingness to get involved, the universal *can't be arsed* attitude of the public in general. It had gnawed at him, that a local man could be attacked in front of his family, and instead of outrage he'd come across a gutless acknowledgement that these things happen, as long as they happen to someone else. But now he had second thoughts, had reason to believe it was more than that. He'd run routine checks on the names of the drinkers he'd interviewed from that evening; the majority of the regulars were pretty unremarkable. Nothing out of the ordinary: possession of controlled substances; speeding fines; driving without insurance; nothing there to concern him at all. But then he'd looked more closely at the staff…

CHAPTER 9

"The body of a six-year-old boy and a young woman thought to be his mother were found dead in their home on the outskirts of Salford yesterday evening. A Police spokesperson has advised that they are not looking for anyone else in connection with this investigation."

The news bulletin was brief and raised more questions than answers; answers Coupland wasn't sure they'd ever uncover. After the post mortem he and Alex had returned to the station to determine what preliminary investigations needed to be completed before preparing a report for the coroner's office. The officers assembled in the CID room were irritable and jumpy; no one liked cases like these, everything about them represented a waste – of life, of resources, of their own bloody energy. Danger was supposed to lurk in dark corners, to jump out when least expected, not manifest itself in the one thing that embodied security and love – a mother.

'Tracey had returned home from the school run,' Coupland began. 'She'd stopped off at the local supermarket on the way over to school to pick up groceries. The time on the till receipt tells us that she went to the supermarket straight before school – it's about a ten-minute drive away – and that she was at the check-out by 3.20pm, time enough to drive from there to school to pick up Kyle before returning home.'

Coupland's voice was professional, devoid of emotion. Which was the exact opposite of what he was feeling. The catalogue of Tracey's actions leading up to her suicide was grotesquely powerful, each word like a hammer blow to the stomach and he watched the officers around him flinch, shifting around uncomfortably for there was nowhere to vent their anger. No evil bastard to hunt down.

'Her husband found their bodies when he returned home just before five pm.' Coupland looked around the room; to a man he could see they were thinking the same thought:

What had it been like for Angus Kavanagh to come home and stumble upon carnage like that?

Each officer imagining him or herself in Angus's shoes, opening the front door to their own homes…Robinson sat frozen, head bowed. Turnbull, grim-faced, had turned to stone. Coupland was unable to think of anything to lift the men from their thoughts, yet he could see he needed to bring them back. 'By the time Angus found them,' he emphasised, 'both Kyle and his mother had been dead for some time.' He aimed this comment pointedly at Alex, who was seated to his left, to emphasise that she could have done nothing more for this family, that her conscience was clear. Several pairs of eyes turned in her direction as she studied a file in front of her; she glanced up to see approval and sympathy in equal measure. Forcing her lips into a smile, she acknowledged Coupland's gesture.

She looked pale and drawn, he thought; nothing a decent night's sleep couldn't fix. He doubted anything could be done for the dullness that remained behind her eyes.

'When are Kavanagh's parents arriving?' he asked.

'Tomorrow afternoon,' she replied. 'I said I'd pick them up from the airport, get a chance to suss out their opinion of their daughter-in-law privately before they go and see their son.'

Coupland nodded. 'okay. Can you pay a visit to the school? Find out what impression the other mothers had of Tracey, *and* the father for that matter.'

'I've still got the names from their address book to go through,' Alex reminded him, 'do you want me to carry on with that?'

Coupland nodded once more. 'Might as well, we need to get as complete a picture of this family as we can.' He paused. 'I'm going to go back to speak to the husband, find out more about him and his business.' He pictured the PC's notebook with the word *happy* underlined several times. 'I want to find out how rosy everything really was in their garden.'

'But it was a suicide, yes?'

He heard the hope in Alex's voice, her desire that this was a cleverly constructed murder laid bare for everyone to see. Mothers did not kill their children. 'C'mon Alex,' he said evenly, 'you know the statistics.' It was true enough; despite the uproar every time a paedophile snatched a small child, the grim reality was that most child murders were committed by a family member, a close one at that.

So much for Stranger Danger.

'There was no sign of a break in, nothing stolen, in fact the house was a picture of calm.'

'Calm before the storm,' Turnbull observed grimly.

'In a way, yes,' Coupland replied, then, turning back to Alex: 'There are no unaccounted-for fingerprints, but most damning of all is the fact the bruises on the boy's shoulders match his mother's hand-span, and she was found with a noose around her neck that she had to lean into for it to work.'

For the benefit of those who hadn't been at the scene Coupland began to describe the way Tracey had hanged herself, pointing to the photographs on the wall behind him. 'Tracey was discovered in a kneeling position on the floor, she'd tied a rope around the top of the bed's headboard – and the other end round her throat – then simply lowered herself to the floor, asphyxiating without breaking her neck.'

'Jesus, that's a pretty hard thing to do to yourself,' someone at the back of the room muttered.

'As opposed to the stepping off a stool and dangling by the throat variety?' Coupland shot back. 'Both bloody drastic if you ask me.'

'At least she had a choice in the matter,' Alex interjected, still reeling from the sight of Kyle lying at the bottom of the bath; of the foetus with its skull rolled back. 'Or are you all forgetting that?'

Alex sighed, *cases like this…* She shook her head vigorously, angry with her train of thought. What the hell did she mean, *cases like this*? There was no normative behaviour here, she reminded herself, this was something way off the charts. She remembered a novel she'd read in her teens, Anna Karenina by Tolstoy, the opening line: *Happy families are all alike, but an unhappy family is unhappy in its own way.* The words had always struck her as poignant, but now… now they struck her as prophetic. Tracey's crime – for that's what it was – was unthinkable. Yet, the reaction to it bordered on bizarre. If an intruder had broken into the Kavanagh's home, wiped out the mother and child in a frenzied attack, there'd be outrage. Newspaper headlines would bray for the killer's blood. Children would be kept indoors, their parents suspicious of every stranger, waiting for news that the monster had been caught before letting them play out once more.

But what, in reality was happening? Oh, there were headlines all right, newsreaders quick to separate the perpetrator from the crime as though uncomfortable with the *situation*, in the same way that people avoid eye contact with the disabled. Everyone – her colleagues included – seemed content to skirt over the fact that a terrible crime had been committed.

It was a bit like incest. People know it goes on but choose to ignore it. By the volume of cases their division referred to social services there were significant numbers of children at risk in their own homes, yet precious little was visibly being done. Why was it that the braying public, who could normally be relied upon to demonstrate their anger at the most heinous crimes, chose not to recognise this killing for what it was?

Alex surveyed her colleagues around the room, feeling a detachment that hadn't been there before. If a woman killed her neighbour's child there'd be uproar, but her own? She didn't mean the battering mothers, the women who lashed out in cruelty or anger; theirs was a publicly reprehensible crime, the bruises and broken bones logged on the front pages of the national papers like a scorecard. No, it was the suburban murders, carried out with the minimum of fuss or pain, that baffled her, and the quiet acceptance that came with it. Was this apathy because parents viewed their children as their personal property, to do with as they wished? Free to harm their own but woe betide a stranger try to? She shook her head, unable to accept that thought. It occurred to her that, for a nation of animal lovers, the collective treatment of our children came in a poor second.

Exasperated, Alex tugged at her short hair. *Feeling like this isn't going to help anyone*, she reasoned. Certainly not Angus, who'd need all the help he could get to put his life – or what was left of it – back on track.

She closed her eyes and exhaled slowly, counting down as she did so.

'Maybe Tracey was mentally ill?' Robinson suggested.

'No,' Coupland informed him. 'According to the family GP there were no medical problems. She'd never consulted him about depression, never suffered from the baby blues, and all was going well with the pregnancy.'

'We have to consider her choice of suicide,' he added. 'In overdose suicides it's not unusual to find that the person actually took smaller doses of pills at earlier points in time. In suicides where the victims cut their wrists, you frequently see 'hesitation cuts' – shallow cuts done prior to a cut that's fatally deep. It's like they're working their way up to the actual event. In this case Tracey chose to hang herself – a method that normally leaves little margin for error. There's no report of any previous suicide attempts in her medical records. What that says about her state of mind I'm not sure.'

Turnbull spoke next: 'Couldn't the fact her feet were still on the floor, allowing her body to absorb the hanging, mean that maybe this *had* been a form of suicidal lead-up, but one that had gone badly wrong? It would explain the lack of suicide note, if she hadn't intended to kill herself.'

'And why stop off on the way home to buy ingredients for a pie you have no intention of eating?' Alex joined in hopefully.

'If she was that efficient,' Robinson cut in, 'maybe she was thinking ahead and filling the freezer for her hubby?' The officers around him groaned into their chests; sometimes his logic functioned on another level.

'Robinson may not be too wide of the mark.' Coupland's voice rose to counteract the babble that was erupting around the room. 'Most suicides like to leave their house in order, try to forward plan as much as possible. Every room in the house was spotless. She was, in many ways, preparing her exit.'

A memory from long ago floated to the fore of Alex's mind. 'Years ago when I was a student I'd taken a summer job at an insurance brokers. I remember serving a customer who'd called into the office to renew his motor insurance. Pretty unremarkable in many ways. He had two daughters a couple of years above me at school, I couldn't recall their names, knew them only to nod to. The man had been friendly enough when I'd asked after them, thanking me for my help before he left. Later that evening he parked in a secluded spot in woodland close to the town, secured a hosepipe to his exhaust before feeding it through the driver's window and starting the engine.' The room remained quiet. 'I'd never quite understood his motive for paying his insurance renewal until now; perhaps he'd settled *all* his debts before he killed himself. Preparing *his* exit. Trying not to leave his daughters with anything to worry about.'

'Apart from his suicide, of course,' quipped Robinson. Coupland blinked slowly, trying to fathom how much a person could take before they reduced themselves to nothing. When he looked up he saw that Alex was watching him. She raised her eyebrows.

'Did you notice anything strange about the house?' he asked her. She frowned in concentration as she pictured herself walking through every room.

'In what way?'

'Well, the Kavanaghs are a good-looking couple, beautiful house, yeah? Big cars, a picture-book lifestyle…'

'So?'

There was something about Angus and Tracey's set up that didn't fit Coupland's mind-set of what a normal family home with young children should look like. He didn't have a clear picture of what seemed wrong, just an impression. His own home-life was hardly like that of the Waltons, but still… He thought of the miniature tornado that had been Amy when she was small, the chaos she left in her slipstream. How they'd thrived on it. He frowned at the memory. Had she been the glue that had held them together? What was going to happen to them if Lynn couldn't bring herself to forgive him? He blinked the thought away.

'There was something odd about the walls – something was missing?' He moved closer to Alex, sure she would have noticed it too.

'I can't remember, I'm sorry. Seeing the boy and his mother like that… it threw me off balance for a while.'

'I know.' He mulled his question over for a moment then answered it for her. 'Pictures.'

'Pictures?' Alex frowned, unable to make the connection.

'Pictures.'

'You mean photographs? There were loads of them, on virtually every wall…'

'Precisely, which shows that Angus and Tracey loved showcasing their family.'

'Right….' She still wasn't getting it.

'There was an easel in the mudroom, kiddy-sized paint pots and a jar of water. Upstairs, there were reams of plain paper in the boy's bedroom, expensive charcoal pencils on his desk – so I figured he must have liked to draw a lot – yet I couldn't see one single painting on any wall; not one drawing, not even a scribble. Nothing. Now why was that?' They batted it round for a couple of minutes, but other than adding it to the list of things to ask Angus there was precious little time to speculate any further.

'I hate this part,' said Alex.

'Me too.'

They were in the in-between stage of cutting a path through clues and facts, nurturing ideas and weeding out lies until the truth took root. It was anyone's guess whether it was possible to ever really put a case like this to bed, to be satisfied that there were no suspicious circumstances at play.

Alex was reminded of a novel by Priestly she'd read as a child: *An Inspector Calls*. During a society celebration toasting the engagement between the offspring of two wealthy families, the festivities are interrupted by a surprise visit from a police inspector. The questions he asks relating to the case reveal that they all had secrets linking them to the suicide of a young woman.

Apportioning blame.

Isn't that what it came down to at the end of the day?

The officers dispersed as Coupland delegated tasks, until only he and Turnbull remained in the room. He'd asked the DC to stay behind, wanted to pass on Lewisham's concerns. 'Saw Lewisham yesterday,' he began, casually enough.

'Yeah?'

Coupland's shoulders sagged a little as he blinked away the image of Lewisham's murdered daughter, of the crushing realisation that they hadn't got to her in time. It was impossible whenever he thought of Siobhan not to make comparisons with his own daughter, Amy, and something inside him contracted.

'You know,' Turnbull began, shaking his head, 'I don't know how he—'

Coupland swallowed his impatience and wafted his hand as though swatting a fly. 'He doesn't have much choice, does he?' he reasoned. 'Anyway, I didn't want to talk *about* Lewisham, just wanted to pass on his concern regarding your suspects for the theft of Melanie Wilson's bag—'

'Save your breath,' Turnbull butted in. 'Had to let 'em go.'

'Not enough to charge them, then?'

'Oh I'll charge 'em all right,' Turnbull sneered.

'For theft?' Coupland persisted, 'Or do you have something more...?'

Turnbull sighed, he was frustrated with his progress as it was, didn't need it rubbing in. 'Jesus, if I'm being backed into a corner then I'll just do 'em for theft, but there's more to their guilt than nicking someone's purse and mobile phone. According to one of the night shift boys they've been brought in before,' he explained. 'Seem to make a habit out of nicking women's handbags, only their victims have so far refused to press charges.' He pursed his lips so tightly it looked as though his mouth had been sewn up.

'Someone's providing them with muscle,' Coupland suggested, 'but why?'

Turnbull paused. 'There's something just not quite right with all this… they're willing to admit their guilt for taking Melanie's bag but I'm convinced they're doing it to avoid me delving any deeper and discovering what else they're covering up.' He sighed, summing it all up: 'They're telling more bleedin' lies than a politician at election time.' He shook his head in frustration. 'Those two know more than they're letting on.'

'That's the nature of our client group,' Coupland replied dryly. *They all know more than they ever let on.* The knack was extracting the bits that mattered, the bits that made a case stick. 'How's the rest of the investigation?'

Turnbull pulled a face. 'I couldn't understand why everyone I spoke to kept clamming up,' he said. 'Granted, no one wants to be the one to point the finger in an assault case, especially where knives are concerned, but I wasn't even getting the time of day. None of the record checks I carried out threw anything up – just your low level criminal activity – nothing to arouse suspicion.' He paused, slipped his index finger inside the gap where his shirt had pulled out of his waistband to scratch just below his navel.

'Turns out it isn't the punters I need to focus on – but

the bloody bouncers. There's two in particular – James Brook and Daniel Horrocks, friends since their truanting days, both employed at the wine bar, both have a string of offences behind them including serving eighteen months at Strangeways for violent disorder. On the evening of Ricky Wilson's assault they'd intervened in the fracas over his wife's bag, and when it started up again later – when Wilson realised Melanie's purse and phone were still missing – it was Horrocks who asked Wilson to leave. It always struck me as odd that they didn't eject the girls.'

He paused. 'What if they were in on it together? Now *that* would explain why I'm not getting any contradictory statements from the regulars in the bar – if these guys had anything to do with Ricky's assault, then no one'd want to point the finger at them. They were well placed too – out of sight all the time they claimed to be on the door. The bar staff were busy pulling pints and serving shots and once the punters were inside getting tanked up, no one would actually be keeping tabs on the security staff, would they?' He spat out the word *security* as though he'd bitten on a turd.

Coupland considered Turnbull's comments, giving them serious thought. He was on edge. The smell of the mortuary was embedded in his nostrils. In his stomach. The one person he could talk freely to, who never judged him, was barely speaking to him at all. 'How many work on the door?' he asked.

'There's four on each night,' Turnbull replied. The finger beneath his navel had been working in a circular motion, was now moving side to side. 'Two on the front door, two roaming. If the guys on the door need to take a dump they have to radio the other two requesting cover before they can even think about dropping their trousers.'

'And of course they're all backing each other up?'

'Precisely. I've questioned them all – and at the time of Wilson's attack, Brook and Horrocks were on the door.'

'But they didn't see or hear anything?'

'You've got the general gist of it,' Turnbull answered wryly.

Coupland's smile was a disappointed one; he hated assuming the worst of people and being proved right. It was the part of his job that gave him the least satisfaction. 'So what now?' he asked.

'I'm going back to the hospital to see if I can get anything more from Wilson's family, something that might corroborate this,' said Turnbull, 'but first I'm going to pay Horrocks and Brook a home visit.'

'I'll do it,' Coupland offered. He was in the bloody mood for it.

Turnbull smirked. 'You sure about that?'

'Why, where do they live?'

'Not so much where, in fact they both live on the same road, it's just that after release from prison both suspects went back to live at their parents' home.' Coupland's heart sank. Often, the most challenging part of dealing with thugs wasn't putting up with their abusive behaviour or the constant threat of violence. The biggest hurdle, he found, the absolute pain in the arse, was dealing with their mothers.

*

'Hey little man, how's it going?' Alex looked around her as she spoke into the phone, relaxed into her chair when she was sure she wouldn't be overheard. She wanted to get through as many of the contacts in Tracey's Filofax as she could before calling it a day but first she wanted to hear Ben's voice, find out what was going on in his little world.

Such was the way of things, she observed, that when a man

called his family he was applauded for being a good father, yet when a woman did the same thing she was accused of not being able to separate her professional life from her domestic responsibilities. It was unfair, but it was a fact of life that went way beyond the force, with thousands of women facing the same inequalities every day. It was better to just get on with it, she reasoned, her problems were no different from anyone else's. She guiltily pushed the thought out of her mind that Emmeline Pankhurst, who'd grown up in Salford, would be turning in her grave at such a passive attitude, reminding herself it had never been her intention to change the world, just to earn a decent enough living for her family.

She smiled as Ben's sing-song voice tumbled down the line to her.

'Daddy took me to McDonalds after school,' he told her triumphantly, the way kids do when the more gullible parent has succumbed to their constant demands.

'*Did he now?*' Alex raised her eyebrow in disapproval, then chided herself. She couldn't be in two places at once, she wouldn't be home for a couple more hours – at least Ben had been fed, although she used the term loosely.

'Have you read your reading book to Daddy yet?' she asked him hopefully. There was a pause while he considered his answer.

'Daddy said I can do it after the cartoons.'

Cartoons before schoolwork? She tapped her short fingernails on the desk-top. 'You know you should read your book to Daddy before you settle down to watch the television, Ben,' she said firmly, scratching at an ingrained coffee-ring. She listened to his heavy breathing down the phone line, detected an impatient sigh as she pictured him glaring at the device that brought his mother's instructions to him even when she wasn't there.

'*I'm* not watching the cartoons,' he muttered indignantly. 'Daddy is.'

CHAPTER 10

Coupland stared along the row of terraced pebbledash houses that looked out onto Pendlebury Road and squared his shoulders. There were no other cars parked along this stretch of road; the majority of tenants relied on buses when they needed to go into town, everything else could be obtained from the concrete precinct that separated the single row of maisonettes from the Tattersall Estate. That is, if you didn't mind walking through groups of off their face teenagers intent on taking the piss no matter what.

Coupland's hand lingered on the car door handle longer than was necessary, checking and rechecking it was locked; yet still he didn't move. Instead he scanned the windows of the neighbouring houses. This was the part he hated, the time wasting foreplay before the main event. Pound to a penny he'd been seen pulling up, that right this minute size ten feet were pounding upstairs to a small back bedroom before he'd even turned the engine off.

The woman who answered the door glared at Coupland for a full ten seconds before speaking. No one wore a suit around here, save for the filth or the debt collectors, and by the look on her face neither were welcome in her home. Her eyes raked Coupland as she made her assessment, her gaze settling on his hard-earned belly.

'You'll be a copper then?' she accused him, when she finally decided to speak.

She had a bitter, staring face, and when she sneered her

lips pared back to reveal nicotine-stained teeth at angles with each other like neglected tombstones in a cemetery. Two rows of lines beneath her eyes hinted at sleepless nights worrying about what her boy was up to and, more importantly, who he was up to it with. Hollowed out cheeks gave a haggard appearance framed by short brittle hair, an uneven parting revealed a scalp stained auburn from a home colouring kit.

'Jimmy Brooks' mam?' Coupland asked, already knowing the answer. It was the same old dance, just with different partners.

The woman sighed. 'What's he bleedin' done now?' It wasn't a question really, more the exasperated response of a put-upon mother. Coupland tilted his head and held out his hand to pacify the woman. 'Nothin' as I know of yet, luv, I just need to ask you some questions.'

'Me?' That threw her. She folded heavy arms across a body that had long since lost its shape and now resembled a lumpy sack. She regarded Coupland with open hostility. 'What d'ya wanno ask me about?'

Coupland took a breath before he answered. 'The assault on the precinct on Sunday night, luv. I've reason to believe—'

'He was workin',' she cut in. 'He didn't do it.' Her reply was automatic, ingrained over a lifetime of blame being laid at her door. First her old man, now the boy.

He wasn't there.

He didn't do it.

Same game, just different players.

'Look,' Coupland glanced up and down the street; word would be spreading like wildfire that he was there, so he tried to minimise the damage this would do. 'Can I come in?'

'A'll not 'ave a copper in my 'ouse,' she informed him. 'So say what you've got to say, then piss off.'

'Everythin' all right, Sheil?' a hardboiled voice called out from somewhere to Coupland's left, and before he knew it they'd been joined by a tank of a woman, hell-bent on joining in the conversation. Danny Horrocks's mam, going by the house number she stomped over from and the way his luck was petering out. Christ, he thought, as he gave her the once-over, she brought a new meaning to the word hefty. Hard-faced too. One of those women who could pee standing up. He'd seen enough of them do it – after hours in bus shelters and shop doorways and stare you down while they did it. One of those women who if they told you to shift you just kept on walking, didn't ask why. Everything about her looked mean, from the set of her shoulders to the face flattened from a lifetime of brawling. Hooded lids drooped over flint-like eyes. She stared hard at him now, and as she did so every one of her features looked to him down-turned, as though God had put her face on upside down for a joke, only forgot to change it back again to its rightful position. Coupland cursed silently; Jimmy's mother had been difficult enough on her own, now she had reinforcements he'd be pissing in the wind.

Sheila turned to her ally, told her the copper'd been asking about the assault on Sunday night. A calculating look crossed the other woman's face as she stared long and hard at Coupland. 'You'll be asking after our Charlie an' all then?' she asked him, a hint of malice in her eye.

Coupland sighed. 'I take it there's not much point, eh?' he replied, weary now. He nodded at the woman whose doorstep he was standing on, keeping him at arm's length like he was a Jehovah's Witness. 'I'll come back another time, Sheila,' he said, and he made to head back towards his waiting car, but not before hearing the sour one mutter: 'Don't bother.'

*

The CID room was deserted. It was the transitional time, the in-between hours when those without families piled into the pub and those with families piled into the pub before returning to loved ones, but Coupland remained at his desk. Given the trouble it had landed him in in the past a swift half was no longer an option and with the best will in the world the thought of going to home to a frosty reception didn't appeal, so he stayed put, not yet ready to return to the apocalypse that was his marriage.

Savouring the silence he replayed the recording the photographer had taken of the cutting and removal of the cord around Tracey Kavanagh's neck. He'd managed to get a close-up shot of the knot behind her head, and Coupland could see his own hands moving swiftly to sever the rope either side of the knot before bagging it for later. The camera then panned backwards, taking in the wider scene. At the time Coupland had been so wrapped up in his own tasks, cross-referencing each knot with the location it came from, that he hadn't paid attention to what else had been going on around him. Now, alone in the silence of the CID room, he was able to observe the pathologist as he handled Tracey once she'd been freed from the rope, and in the moments afterwards, when Coupland had moved away. Benson seemed to hold onto her longer than he needed, as though willing her back to life. It was probably the pregnancy, Coupland reckoned, that made it so much harder. A life slain before it even had a chance to gasp air. He watched now as the video showed Benson lowering her carefully, almost reverently, onto the floor, before laying his hand on her stomach and closing his eyes. Coupland remembered how at the time he'd seen the pathologist crouch down beside her, and he'd presumed he was continuing with his examination. But it occurred to him now, as the camera zoomed onto Benson's bowed head and moving lips, that he wasn't checking her for further injury.

He was praying.

Both knots lay in separate evidence bags on the desk before him, already tested for DNA. He picked up the one that had been cut from behind Tracey's neck, slipping it out of its plastic cover, running his fingers along the twisted strands. A wave of sadness swept over him as he reconciled the smiling family captured in the photographs on each wall in the house with the forlorn figures laid out in Benson's laboratory. Different people reacted to pitfalls in their lives in different ways. There was no right and wrong, no way to second-guess them. Maybe in Tracey's own mind her actions made perfect sense. A solution to a terrible problem. But what had been the problem?

The rope seemed to beckon him, taunting him to place it around his throat, and he did so, tightening his grip until his knuckles turned white, feeling the searing sensation of rough fibre against skin. In that moment he knew without doubt that Tracey Kavanagh had *intended* to kill herself. He closed his eyes, imagining her determination. Breathless, overcome with panic, pain… and then nothing. His eyes shot open and he found himself gasping for air, his hands clutching at the rope until it fell to the floor and there was nothing to grab onto, nothing but his own skin. He slumped forwards in his chair, cradling his head in his hands as he tried to understand what made Tracey certain she was making a bad situation better. He waited for his breathing to return to normal, though little could be done for his emotions, which seemed to be running all over the place.

The overhead light panel snapped on, a vacuum cleaner hummed in the distance, invading his thoughts. 'Enough,' he said aloud, scraping back his chair. He stumbled over to the AV unit and switched it off, his legs unsteady, then scooped the knot back into its plastic cover before returning it to his desk and locking the drawer.

*

'Where's your mum?'

'Dunno.'

'What time did she go out?'

'Dunno.'

Coupland resisted the urge to yank the earphones from Amy's ears, reminding himself he'd have had the same response if they'd been sat across from each other at the dinner table where MP3 players and mobile phones were banned. Amy simply couldn't be bothered to speak to him.

She was lying across her bed, thumbs speeding across the keyboard of her mobile phone like they'd taken on a life of their own. An incoming beep and the grin that met it told Coupland some boy was on the warpath, accessing his daughter by invisible means. Lighting up her face in a way Coupland hadn't managed since she was five years old. How the hell could he compete with that?

Amy's smile faded when she saw him in the doorway, her face adopting the look that signified if he was in the doghouse with her mother, he was in the doghouse with her too. He was unsure how much Lynn had told their daughter, but the semi's thin walls combined with the radar skills of teens – when it suited them – would have flagged up something was seriously wrong between her parents.

'Shall I make us some dinner?' he asked, his voice all over the place as his throat constricted at the sight of her. A beautiful, confident young woman. Ready to cut him down with one cruel remark. Better that than the alternative, he told himself, grateful for small mercies.

'Mum made me something before she went out,' Amy replied belligerently, as though the idea of eating with him was preposterous. Shoulders sagging, Coupland returned to the kitchen weighed down by guilt and anger in equal measure. He opened the fridge door, half hoping there'd be a plate of something covered in cling film, an indication that Lynn might not want to share a meal with him but she didn't want him to starve either. The shelves were empty. It was as though she'd cleared the fridge of food just to make her point. A solitary bottle of milk stood in the fridge door, a mouldy piece of cheddar on the cheese shelf.

Sighing, Coupland picked up the cheese, pinching off the green bits with his forefinger and thumb. The bread bin contained a stale loaf, which toasted would be bearable, and in the cupboard above the kettle he located a half bottle of brown sauce. He went into the dining room, returning with a generous glass of whisky, and set about making dinner for one.

CHAPTER 11

The CID room was empty bar Alex who'd spent the morning on the telephone working through the last few names in Tracey Kavanagh's Filofax, that she hadn't been able to get through to the night before. She was hunched forward in her chair, cradling the phone to her ear with her shoulder while doodling onto a pad on her desk. Flowers and concentric circles, cowboy hats made out of a sideways number eight. A tortured tree. She was nodding into the phone, doodling into her notebook when Coupland entered, glancing briefly in her direction. He walked quickly on, as though not wanting to draw attention to himself, patting down the back of his hair and dabbing at the corners of his mouth with his middle finger and thumb.

'What's up with you?' she called out as he moved around the room like a bear with a very sore head.

'Leave it, eh?'

She could smell his boozy breath from across the room. Retrieving a packet of mints from her bag she ventured over to his desk where he was rifling through his top drawer, pausing when he found a packet of paracetamol, pushing two tablets from the blister pack before dry swallowing them.

'Suit yourself,' she retorted, 'but there's no reason to shoot yourself in the foot. If Curtis gets one whiff of you you'll be suspended.'

Coupland slammed his drawer shut and took the proffered mints. 'Top girl,' he said sheepishly.

Alex patted her jacket pocket for change. 'I'll shout you a coffee,' she informed him, 'while you decide whether or not you want to talk about it.'

She returned with a black coffee and a chocolate bar to make up for the fact the vending machine had run out of sugar, placed them in front of him like a Druid offering up a sacrifice.

'Sorry I snapped,' Coupland mumbled. He had a dejected air about him: eyes red rimmed through lack of sleep, breath reminiscent of a drayman's apron. 'I think Lynn's seeing someone,' he said quietly, unwrapping the chocolate bar and breaking off a chunk. Breakfast so far had consisted of a Silk Cut and the previous night's untouched coffee reheated in the microwave. He popped the chocolate into his mouth, politely offering Alex the next chunk, which she declined.

'What makes you say that?'

'Last night she didn't come home till midnight. Seemed to think it was funny that I might have been worried. Refused point blank to tell me where she'd been, or who she'd been out with.'

It certainly didn't sound like Lynn, Alex thought, Coupland's wife hardly ever went out on her own. They were a close family, doing everything together, certainly when Amy was small. Now of course, their daughter was at the stage where she preferred the company of her friends, and Coupland was getting used to having Lynn all to himself in the evenings once more.

'Maybe she's trying to rekindle her social life,' Alex suggested. 'You know, so it doesn't always revolve around you.'

He considered this. 'So why now?'

'You're kidding, right?'

'So it's a punishment?'

'Not entirely, maybe she reckons not always being at your beck and call will make you value her more…' Alex shrugged. 'Maybe she's just trying to make you jealous.'

Coupland snorted. 'It's working then.'

'Have you talked to her?'

'Have you tried having a sensible discussion when your partner's half cut and you've been working towards it yourself for the best part of the evening?'

'Didn't go well then.' It was a statement not a question. There was something inevitable about the outcome of a mid-night row, both parties tired and unwilling to concede a point, neither ready for the proximity of bed and the premature intimacy it brings.

'Look, you need to talk to her, but not when you're both exhausted. Can't you go away for a couple of days, neutral territory? Might even relight old fires?'

'You're joking. She's avoiding being in the same room as me.'

'A meal then; book somewhere as a surprise. Surely she can't wriggle out of that?'

'Maybe not.' He gulped the remainder of his coffee, nod-ding as though he'd come to a decision. 'Okay,' he shrugged, 'I'll sort something out… Any luck with the address book?' he asked, moving on to a more comfortable topic.

'Well, yes and no. Many of the names are Angus's business associates – people Tracey and Angus had gone out with occa-sionally to secure a deal, rather than close friends,' she replied.

'I'm going through everyone listed though.' She paused. 'Just hadn't realised there were so many.'

'What about old work friends, school even?'

'Well there's the thing,' Alex said acidly, 'Mommy Dearest wasn't too hot on the social front.' She looked away quickly, ignoring the look Coupland shot at her. 'People vary when it comes to keeping in touch,' he reasoned. 'You can't read too much into the fact she wasn't some sort of social butterfly.' Some people gathered friends from cradle to grave; the friends they were pally with had attended the same school, sat a few desks along from them in the same class. Coupland was on the other end of the spectrum, shedding acquaintances like a snake sheds its skin, counting his friends on one hand. Lynn was his best friend.

Until now.

'Only recent acquaintances seemed to be listed,' Alex continued. 'Committee members on the PTA, that sort of thing. None of them described themselves as pals either, just a small number of mums who shared the school run, baby-sitting circle, that sort of thing.'

Out of all the names she'd contacted so far, those that knew Tracey tended to have children in the same class, but that was all they really had in common. They'd earned their place in her address book because they were the parents of Kyle's friends, rather than acquaintances of Tracey's. None of the mothers that Alex spoke to could say they *knew* Tracey, she certainly hadn't confided in any of them. It wasn't that they hadn't tried to include her either, several were keen to stress they'd invited Tracey into their homes whenever she came to collect Kyle after school, but she'd always declined.

'They thought she was a bit stand-offish,' Alex concluded.

While Alex had been talking Coupland had finished off the bar of chocolate and tossed the wrapper into the wastepaper basket in the corner of the room. He laid his hands palm down on the top of his desk, splaying out his fingers.

'What about her family?' he asked, without looking up. 'Parents? Brothers and sisters?'

'A brother she's estranged from. Both parents are dead.'

He opened and closed his fingers, as though checking they still worked.

'Sounds as though she was pretty isolated, then.'

Alex wondered if she'd heard him right.

'You mean, "Sounds as though she was pretty isolated" as in "Reasons to justify wiping out your kids"?' Her voice trembled as she spoke; she hoped he hadn't picked up on it. Coupland looked at her sharply. 'If this case is too much…' he said harshly, startling them both.

'It isn't!' she protested, dragging her fingers through her hair and wiping an eye with the heel of her hand. The back of her eyelids began to sting. Gingerly Coupland got to his feet. His stomach rumbled. He felt nauseous, the chocolate sitting uncomfortably on last night's scotch. He belched bile into his mouth then swallowed it away. He glanced around the Goldfish Bowl, which was now beginning to fill up. 'Let's take a walk,' he said. 'I think we could both do with lining our stomachs.'

They headed back along the corridor towards the main reception area, where they made a bee-line towards the new canteen. After fishing around in the pocket of his jeans for change he bought two mugs of coffee and two bacon barmcakes, Alex asking for the lid of her roll to be dipped into the bacon fat. As vices went it was pretty harmless, she justified, and he couldn't argue with that. They sat in silence for a moment as they ate, Coupland mulling over how much of his job now was about managing other people, not just solving crimes. It was obvious, he supposed; he wasn't a one-man band, couldn't be everywhere and do everything at once, and though at times he found it hard to believe there were officers out there just as dedicated, and experienced – in fact more so – than him, he had to face the fact he wasn't indispensable. It made sense that his role was about passing on his experience, mentoring, coordinating. Made him realise he didn't want to go any higher though – *not,* he reminded himself ruefully, that it looked like that might ever be an option.

The brown coloured liquid that masqueraded as coffee seemed to be doing the trick. His stomach was settling, accepting without resistance his tentative mouthfuls of bacon. He'd not taken his eyes off the acne-ridden youth who'd served them, was confident that only coffee, water and milk had entered the cup, although the angry spots up both the boy's arms were worrying. He shifted his seat so the offending limbs were out of his eye line as he concentrated on keeping his breakfast down, and turned to face Alex. He understood her anger, he just worried she was unable to channel it. At least focussing on her for the moment stopped him dwelling on his own problems.

'Sometime they're just shitty cases,' he observed, using his finger to mop up brown sauce that'd dribbled onto the table from his roll.

'They're *all* shitty cases. That's my point.'

'Are you saying we're not treating this one seriously, then?'

She shook her head. 'No, it's not that.' She scrabbled around for the right words, plunged headlong in anyway. 'Just not *as* serious.'

As she said it she realised it had come out like a criticism, as though she was knocking the way he'd been handling the investigation. She held her breath, waiting for the rebuke.

'Alex, it's not a case of treating an investigation like this less seriously – c'mon, half the team including yourself have got families. But treating it differently – yes, I mean, we already know who the killer is, it's more about filling in the blanks.'

'But why?' she persisted. 'So we can justify her actions?

How far back will we have to go to find the moment we're looking for, the exact moment that we can point to and say *Yeah, that's the reason she did it.*'

Her voice had risen slightly, the canteen was almost deserted and the staff behind the counter were watching them with interest, the spotty boy scratching his arms absentmindedly.

Coupland shook his head vigorously, found it no longer hurt. 'You're missing the point, Alex,' he said. 'We're not looking for reasons to justify her actions – that's not our job – what we're involved in is the removal of doubt. The *how* and the *when* and an attempt at the *why,* so her family and the community can be reassured that she *did* in fact commit the crime and it's not an elaborate murder. And yes, the reasons behind it help reassure the rest of us it's not catching.' He glanced once more at the pock-ridden youth, frowning. 'That if the wind changes direction one day we're not all going to go out and do the same thing that she did.'

Alex looked unconvinced.

'You studied Psychology, didn't you?' he asked as he finished the dregs of his coffee.

'Not so as you'd notice,' she replied, pushing her cup away, unfinished. 'I was only there long enough to write my name inside the course books.'

'More than I ever did.'

Coupland wondered whether he should take her off the case. He thought again. Ricky Wilson's assault was tying up the bulk of his officers; he didn't want to start messing around with the teams this late in the day.

'I don't think this is so much about the way we perceive the case, as the way *you* perceive it,' he said as gently as he could. 'Maybe you'd find it helpful to talk this through with someone more experienced in this field? One of your old professors, maybe?'

Alex reacted as though he'd leaned across the table and squeezed her breast. 'Well if that isn't the most longwinded way of saying I should get my head looked at,' she stormed, 'I don't know what is.' She stomped to her feet, sending him a withering look not unlike the one Lynn had given him when he'd asked where she'd been the previous evening. He listened to Alex's footsteps as she tap-tapped across the polished floor, groaning inwardly for thinking he could help.

He stood and turned to push his seat under the table, noticed he still had an audience. The canteen staff had all but pulled up a chair to watch the both of them and they smiled back at him now, enjoying his discomfort. He singled out a plump middle-aged woman, smirking as she wiped enormous hands on a tea towel.

'Tables need wiping,' he snapped, then pointed to the pimply youth, 'and get him to cover up those bloody arms.'

CHAPTER 12

After fishing around in his trouser pocket Coupland located the key to his desk and unlocked it, pulling the rope Tracey Kavanagh had tied around her throat out of the top drawer, still inside the evidence bag. He held the plastic packet gingerly by the edges, reluctant to hold it for too long in case his senses went into overdrive again.

'There's an element of hanging that strikes me as being completely cold-blooded.' He paused, glancing at Alex, who'd turned up at his office door minutes earlier apologising for her outburst, assuring him that she was all right *really*. Her makeup was smudged around the eyes, as though she'd swiped at it with her hand, and she'd looked a little shaky while she'd stood in front of him waiting for a response. The fact was she was a bloody good cop and he needed her on the case as much as she needed to stay on it, exorcising her demons, so he'd asked her to stay. He'd wanted her to look at the ligature Tracey had used in more detail. She'd flinched only slightly when he'd brought it out of his drawer, and her reaction reminded him sharply that she was already far more familiar with the noose than either of them cared to remember.

'What I mean is that, unlike throwing yourself from a bridge, you have to gather the equipment you intend to use, assemble it, check that it works. Hanging isn't a knee-jerk reaction to a crap day.'

There was a sharp knock on the open door, the police photographer waited in the doorway until he'd been given right of entry.

Coupland beckoned him with his hand. 'All set?' he asked.

The man nodded in reply, setting down the case he was carrying onto the office floor and lifting out a collapsible tripod and video camera, which he expertly assembled in a matter of minutes. Coupland turned back to Alex. 'I wanted to record the motion required to undo the knot, so we have a reference that may come in useful later on.'

He lifted the bag containing the tied rope, tipped it so that the contents fell onto his desk before nodding towards the cameraman.

'Will we be able to rewind it as it plays?' Alex asked, 'played backward it'll show us how the knot was tied surely?'

Coupland smiled and shook his head. 'It doesn't quite work that way, but at least we'll be able to see how each loop was constructed, so that we can be absolutely certain that Tracey could have physically created this ligature.'

'Are you saying she might not have done it to herself after all?'

Coupland sighed impatiently. 'No, that's *not* what I'm saying.'

During the post mortem Harry Benson had showed them that there'd been no scraping or friction marks on Tracey's skin beneath the rope, which there would have been if the knot had been tied under her chin, then twisted until it was in position behind the back of her neck to make it *look* like a suicide.

'She had an accomplice, then?' Alex persisted.

'I'm not saying that either. Stop trying to put words into my mouth.'

Alex shot Coupland a filthy look.

'Look, I didn't mean to jump down your throat.' He smiled weakly. 'I just need to be absolutely certain that she was capable of tying the noose where she was. *Could* she tie this knot while holding her hands behind her head? I don't even know what type of knot it is.'

'It's a bowline knot, Sarge.' They halted their conversation and stared at the photographer who'd finished assembling his equipment in silence and now stood behind them, waiting for their attention. Coupland squinted at him, mentally working his way through the list of civilian personnel. 'Sorry,' he said, embarrassed, 'I can't remember your name.'

'No one ever does,' the man said, flushing. 'It's Johnson, Sergeant.'

'You were in the scouts, were you?' Alex quipped, nodding towards the twisted rope. She'd always been slightly envious of the local cub pack when she was a child; never saw the appeal of Guiding.

'Actually no.' Johnson broke through her thoughts. 'I'm a member of the Yacht Club at Sale Water Park. I'm studying to get my Skipper's Licence.' Clearly unused to any form of attention, the man's face was beetroot. 'I'm sure my instructor could help you with the knot, Sergeant,' he stammered. 'I could show him the prints if you like, see what he's got to say?'

Coupland looked at Alex, then nodded. They had nothing to lose, and since he knew bugger all about sailing knots, any advice gleaned from an expert would be gratefully received. They stood quietly looking at the rope. It was a medium weight, twisted twine. 'What did they use it for?' Coupland wondered aloud. The door closed quietly behind them and he realised guiltily that Johnson had gone. One of life's invisible men, he thought. Happier to spend his life behind the spotlight, rather than under it. Alex turned to leave too and Coupland suddenly remembered something that had troubled him since seeing her earlier that morning, when she'd been sat at her desk making calls.

'*Alex*.'

She paused at the door and turned, raising her eyebrows for him to continue.

'*Is* everything all right?'

Her mind whirred into action as she tried to work out what he was talking about. She thought they'd been through all this in the canteen, wondered if he was ever going to forgive her earlier criticism of the case. That was the problem when you let your guard down. She cursed her emotions that seemed to be all over the place recently.

'Yes…' she faltered, '…why?'

Coupland glanced around the CID room to make sure their conversation couldn't be overheard. 'When I walked in earlier you were on the phone, scribbling onto a pad.' He cleared his throat. 'What were you drawing?'

Perplexed, Alex cast a look towards her desk; saw the writing pad covered with cartoons she'd doodled whilst she'd been kept on hold. She could scarcely remember what she'd scribbled down absent-mindedly.

'Er… faces, trees, I can't remember, really.'

'But the last thing you drew,' he persisted, 'when I asked you to come over?'

For a moment her forehead creased in concentration, wondering if it really sodding mattered. 'Oh,' she said, as the image came back to her. 'Leaves,' she said, reddening, 'why?'

Now it was Coupland's turn to flush. 'I'm sorry,' he said awkwardly, mentally kicking himself. 'No reason.' It must have been the angle he'd seen them, or the mood she was in. The mood *he* was in for that matter. Perhaps the problems in his marriage were sending him off kilter. Either way when he'd seen the droplet shaped patterns on Alex's pad an entirely different image had come into his mind.

He'd thought they were tears.

CHAPTER 13

When Alex returned to her desk there were two scribbled Post-it notes left at the side of a coffee cup she'd long since forgotten about. The first one read: *Charlie Preston returned your call – no message.* The second: *The Kavanaghs have landed.* Dialling the number she'd called earlier – she recognised the code as a local number – she drummed her fingers on the top of her desk as she waited for the person on the other end to pick up. Charlie's name had not been entered into Tracey Kavanagh's Filofax, just scribbled on a post it-note and stuck on the inside cover, so Alex was none the wiser if this was a casual acquaintance or friend. She could've waited until she spoke to Angus again, she supposed, but she didn't want to bother him until she had something concrete to say, so she'd decided to press on.

If she was honest with herself there was another reason she was in no hurry to see Angus again, an altogether selfish one. Put simply, she couldn't bear to see him in so much pain. She'd felt the same with Roddy Lewisham, after his daughter's murder. Both men had suffered every parent's nightmare and whenever she looked at them all she could see was herself in their shoes, all she could imagine was how it would feel if it was Ben… Thinking like that scared her, as though in some superstitious way just imagining their misfortune could make it happen and then she'd feel guilty, for this wasn't about her but rather the loss suffered by two ordinary men who were fathers one day and the next… displaced, their identities wiped out in the blink of an eye.

After several rings the answer machine picked up – one of those automated American voices telling her to leave her message after the beep. At least Charlie checked his messages regularly, she thought, so she left him another one, suggesting they meet up. She looked at her watch, reckoned it would take her half an hour to drive to the airport, another half an hour to take Angus's parents to the Copthorne Hotel where they'd made an open-ended reservation. She calculated she'd be back in an hour and a half tops; spoke softly into the answer machine, suggesting Charlie come into the station just after five. Replacing the receiver she looked back at the Filofax bookmarked at T-Z, saw there were still several calls to be made. It looked like she'd be making another night of it.

Reaching for her car keys it occurred to her that she should ring Carl, let him know she'd probably be late home again. Last night had been tense. She'd returned home later than planned, missing Ben's bath time, which always put her in a bad mood. To top it all, she'd picked at the dinner Carl had eagerly cooked for them, listening to his reasons why The Time Was Right for Another Baby.

He'd cooked them a steak. Pushing the boat out in her view, but she'd had the sense to keep quiet, not air unasked-for views.

Isn't it great having Ben around? he'd asked her.

No question about that.

Hadn't he brought them closer together?

No argument there either.

A photo on the landing wall in Tracey Kavanagh's home materialised in her mind's eye: Kyle at Disney. She and Carl had taken Ben there the previous year; he'd been terrified of Captain Hook, refused point blank to go on the Peter Pan ride.

You're such a great mother.

Tracey's house had been warm and inviting. Kyle was clearly well-nourished. A pile of soft toys had lain scattered on his bed; a bookmark had been placed inside the latest Horrid Henry, an empty glass of milk beside it. His pyjamas had been folded neatly on his pillow.

He'd been well cared for.

Alex cut into her steak, stared in horror as the blood oozed around her plate, reminding her of the drain beneath Benson's post mortem table.

A child is a blessing.

She'd found herself visualising Kyle's hollow torso, his organs laid out for the pathologist to measure and weigh. The sound of cutting and slicing echoed around her head.

A baby would seal our happiness.

Tracey's fully formed infant with its face peeled back.

Alex didn't recall knocking over her wine glass. All she remembered was swallowing bile and the mist that descended when Carl played his final card.

Besides, you're not getting any younger…That night they'd slept in separate rooms.

Shrugging, Alex walked out of the office. Unable to face another scene, she decided she'd call him later.

*

Given the size of the detached houses along the stretch of road where the Kavanaghs lived, the neighbouring properties were some twenty yards either side of the executive-style home, separated by a bank of trees. Cherry blossoms added a pink sugary coating to the picture-postcard frontage. The blue and white police tape and uniformed officer on the Kavanaghs' doorstep was the only blight on the horizon, an ugly reminder that wealthy doesn't equal happy.

A couple of reporters were camped at the bottom of the drive; Coupland recognised two of them from the local paper. A news van had pulled up too – Look North TV. The driver hurried round to the back of the vehicle and began to unload AV equipment. The news reporter leaned against the side of the van, sipping from a bottle of water, a mobile phone stuck to his ear. Moving on quickly before the reporter glanced up and spotted him, Coupland pulled up outside the neighbour's house, keeping his face from view as he headed for the door.

The front of the house was similar to the Kavanaghs', only instead of red brick the first floor was finished with white facia boards with green panelling to give it a Tudor-style effect, and the garage was on the opposite side of the house. The cars on the driveway were just as big, German-built. He had time to tap the door once before it opened and a plump woman in her mid-fifties greeted him. Her hair was cut into a short style and devoid of any colour so that it was a shock of white – platinum almost – against her suntanned skin. She wore calf length trousers and a white linen shirt; a pair of gold coloured sandals revealed salon-painted toenails.

'Mrs White? I'm Detective Sergeant Coupland,' he offered up in greeting.

She smiled sadly at him. 'You're the one in charge then?' she asked. 'Your colleague said you would call – the woman detective?'

He nodded, held up his warrant card, which she didn't bother to look at.

'I expect you'll want to see Angus?' she asked, closing the door behind him, turning on her heel while he followed.

'Can I get you anything, Sergeant? Tea? Coffee?' She turned to him again, looked disappointed when he shook his head.

They were at the far end of the hall, about to enter a set of double doors leading into a sitting room similar to the Kavanaghs' in shape, although the taste in décor was that of an older couple: flowery walls and curtains, a large chintz three piece suite facing into a mahogany coffee table. A matching cabinet in the corner contained a display of crystal ornaments and framed graduation photographs of a young man and woman Coupland took to be the couple's offspring.

'I thought we could go through to the conservatory?' Mrs White asked.

Coupland nodded, following her through the sitting room to the patio doors and into a sunlit conservatory containing two cushioned sofas, a small table and several large tomato plants.

'Ripens them up nicely doesn't it?' she said to the man reading a newspaper on one of the sofas, eyes half closed as he scanned the business pages. The man nodded in agreement, although Coupland was certain he hadn't heard what his wife had just said. Anything for a quiet life.

'This is Detective Sergeant Coupland, Harry,' the woman informed him, 'Sergeant Coupland, this is my husband Harry.' The men looked at each other.

'Ooh,' the woman gushed, barely stopping for breath, 'I didn't introduce myself! I'm Diane.' She held out her hand formally; when Coupland shook it he noticed the top of her cheeks turn a deep shade of pink.

Harry folded his newspaper and lay it down on the wicker tabletop. 'You'll be wantin' to speak to Angus?' he asked, and Coupland feared they were about to repeat the whole conversation he'd just had with Diane. He looked from husband to wife but neither gave any indication of intending to move. He tried not to let his irritation show: 'If one of you wouldn't mind letting Angus know I'm here…'

Diane's hand flew to her mouth in a flurry of embarrassment. 'What must you think of us?' Flustered, she hurried out of the room leaving Coupland standing in the middle of the conservatory, still on his feet. He turned to look out onto the well-stocked garden, nodding towards the immaculate borders. His eyes slid over to Harry, noted that he wasn't quite retirement age.

'You have the same gardener as the Kavanaghs', Sir?' he asked.

Puzzled by his question, Harry gave Coupland an odd look before answering. 'It's possible,' he said. 'Diane would know.' Harry offered Coupland a seat but he refused, preferring the freedom of moving around. An awkward silence fell between them.

'Look, we're all in shock here,' Harry informed him. 'My wife's not been able to sleep for thinking about what's happened.'

A pause.

'It was the girls that were friendly,' he said by way of explanation. 'Diane had Tracey over for coffee once a week, brought the little kiddie along as well, before he started school. Our own children have flown the nest, not a grandchild in sight. I think Diane saw them as a surrogate family, though she'd kill me if she heard me say as much.'

His face drained of colour as he realised what he'd said. 'That was in bad taste,' he said. 'I wasn't thinking.'

'It's okay,' Coupland reassured him.

They lapsed back into an uneasy silence and Coupland wondered what it was that weighed heavy on the older man's shoulders. He didn't have to wait long to find out.

'Thing is,' Harry blurted out, 'we're still not clear… about what happened. Angus has said so little, 'cept that the house hadn't been broken into, and we didn't want to press him. The other detective… well, she didn't seem to be looking for anyone in connection with the murders. It's just that…' He looked away awkwardly, then levelled his gaze slowly on Coupland, lowering his voice. 'We're not harbouring a criminal, are we? I mean… has Angus done this?'

Just then there was a gasp, and they turned to see Diane standing in the doorway covering her mouth with a hand, beside her their neighbour, a look of incredulity etched onto his face.

Harry leapt to his feet. He made a move towards Angus but the look he received for his trouble left him rooted to the spot.

'Angus!' Red-faced he gestured for him – and again Coupland – to sit down.

'Angus, I didn't mean for you to hear it like tha—'

'You haven't told them?' Angus challenged Coupland, who wondered if Diane's habit of constant questioning had worn off on him, then chided himself for being uncharitable.

'I'll take it as a "No" then,' Angus quipped. It was the most he'd uttered in the past two days and all three of them looked at him in surprise.

'Angus,' Coupland began, 'we're still carrying out tests, obtaining medical reports—'

'For God's sake,' Angus interrupted angrily, 'why don't you just spit it out, man, put them out of their misery.' He glared over at Harry, who'd been wondering how much his neighbour had heard, before flinching when Angus uttered: 'I'm sure you'll all sleep much easier once you realise that I'm not the fucking culprit.'

Diane blanched at his use of coarse language, then looked back at Coupland as though expecting him to put them straight.

Coupland frowned, he was struggling to find the right words and knew he had to tread carefully. Diane saved him the trouble. She'd been watching Angus as he collapsed into a chair, burying his head in his hands. She spun round to Coupland and caught her breath as the horror of the situation began to dawn.

'No!'

Her hands flew back up to her mouth again as the truth she'd been avoiding loomed before her, larger than life.

'Are you saying Tracey did it?' she whispered, 'Tracey… killed that beautiful little boy… then herself?' Coupland cursed under his breath. He assumed Alex had been through all this with them, but then why would she, when she didn't believe Tracey was capable of this crime either.

'Mrs White,' he began, 'we're conducting a series of enquiries which I'm sure you understand I cannot comment on right now, but I can confirm that two days ago Mrs Kavanagh took her own life.'

Diane and Harry were shocked into silence. After taking a moment to contemplate Coupland's words, Harry was the first to speak. 'We did wonder, what with the police and everything, and the way the news bulletins have been worded, but with Angus so distraught it really wasn't our place to upset him further…'

A derisive snort from Angus echoed around the room.

'But…' Diane's voice had risen an octave; her palm was pressed flat against her chest, '…had there been some kind of accident?' she screwed up her eyes as though trying to see the truth of it. 'Is that why Tracey did it… because he'd been hurt?'

'Don't you get it, you silly cow?' Angus's head reared up, his eyes were dark and hate-filled. 'She was giving Kyle his bath.

She pushed him under the water, held him down...'

Diane raised her hands to cover her ears, collapsing into the chair behind her. Shaking her head from side to side as though rejecting what she'd been told. 'No… No… No…' she said simply, over and over, as though denying it would put it right; turn everything back to how it had been before, how it should have been. 'No.'

Coupland got to his feet, walked a couple of yards towards the end of the conservatory, looked out onto the well-kept borders. 'You all use the same gardener?' He inclined his head in the direction of the garden, expanded his hands to indicate the neighbouring houses. It was Diane who answered. Red-eyed and gulping back tears she looked out into the landscaped lawns and smiled. If she thought his question was odd, irrelevant to the case, she showed no sign of it.

'Yes,' she said. 'The houses aren't that old. When we moved in there were dozens of business cards and leaflets pushed through the letterbox from local contractors. We found our decorator, gardener and cleaner from them, and when Tracey and Angus moved next door Tracey asked if we could recommend anyone. I passed their numbers on…'

Coupland nodded, his mind elsewhere. 'Angus,' he said, turning round, 'I need to ask you a couple of questions.' He stopped, looked from Diane to Harry and slipped his hands into his pockets, waiting them out.

'Oh,' said Diane, flustered. She got to her feet, signalling to her husband to do the same. 'We'll be in the kitchen if you need us.' They slipped out of the room wordlessly, grateful for the respite from the icy atmosphere. Angus did not acknowledge them.

'The toxicology reports on Tracey's blood were clear, Angus,' Coupland began once he was sure they were out of earshot, 'so we can rule out that she was under the influence of drink or drugs.'

Angus's head jerked backwards, his eyes levelled coldly into Coupland's. 'And that's supposed to make me feel better is it? The fact that she was of sound mind when she murdered our son, that she knew what she was doing?'

'No.' Coupland shook his head. That wasn't what he'd meant at all. 'We have to rule every possibility out; part of the procedure I'm afraid.'

Angus said nothing, remained still while he digested the information. Suddenly, without looking up he began to speak. 'We were happy, you know? The business was going well; Kyle had settled into school; we were looking forward to…' His words petered out but Coupland guessed what he was referring to.

'Did you see the nursery?' Angus asked, and slowly before Coupland's eyes he sprang back to life again, as though someone had slipped new batteries into his back. His face brightened at the thought of his children, his mouth shaped itself into a grin. Only his eyes remained empty.

'I'd spent the last two weekends decorating it,' he said. 'Tracey wanted their rooms to have a theme. All that stuff's popular now, isn't it? Licence to print money if you ask me, but Tracey was really into it all. Guess it's a woman's thing…' He was animated now, and Coupland knew it was because he'd blocked it out, that right now he was just sitting in his neighbour's house, talking about his wife and son while they waited for him at home.

The power of delusion.

'Kyle's room's a racing circuit,' he enthused. 'I painted the track on the walls myself.' Angus's chest actually puffed up as he said it. 'Tracey wanted us to get a designer in but I wasn't having any of it. Dad's privilege, I told her.' When he spoke softly like this, his Edinburgh burr rolled gently from his tongue, and Coupland found himself wondering if Kyle had had a Scottish accent too, or whether he'd picked up the harsher Salford inflection.

'I mean,' Angus's face lit up, 'it's every dad's dream, isn't it? A chance to re-live your childhood.' He looked at Coupland for agreement. Coupland jerked his head slightly in what he hoped was a nod. His father had been an alcoholic. He never wanted to re-live his childhood ever again.

'The nursery was a railway,' Angus continued. 'I'd painted trains around the walls, big puffs of steam, large as clouds. "But what if it's a girl?" Tracey kept asking, and I said to her "Girls like trains too".'

He stopped then, and Coupland could tell from the droop in his shoulders that the make-believe walls of his world were crashing down around him. His facial muscles began to jerk in opposing directions as a multitude of emotions flashed across his face. A low growl erupted from deep within his body as he covered his face with his hands. His wedding band glinted in the afternoon sun.

'She was having another wee boy, after all.'

His words were bittersweet. A mixture of pride and despair in equal proportions.

A gentle breeze stirred the branches outside and Coupland found himself picturing Kyle as he played in his neighbour's garden while Tracey had coffee with Diane. A small boy wearing Wellington boots and a beanie hat, a smudge of jam around his mouth. Mucky fingers sticking to the glass like limpets as his mother chided him for making a mess, unable to conceal her smile as he rubbed his nose against the glass. An Eskimo kiss, Lynn called them, and the thought of her now made his insides ache.

He watched helplessly as Angus succumbed to his grief, his shoulders rising and falling in time with his sobs. Coupland lurched to his feet, hurried through to the kitchen, back to Diane and Harry, sitting numbly at a small round table.

'Are you done?' Harry asked him when he appeared in the doorway, as though Coupland alone was the cause of Angus's pain.

The detective nodded.

Diane slipped soundlessly through to the conservatory, placed a blanket around her neighbour's stooped shoulders, whispered that maybe he should get some sleep. Easing his head down onto a cushion, she lifted his feet until he was curled like a foetus on top of the sofa. Returning to the kitchen she rummaged in a cupboard until she found a chamois leather, ran it under the tap until it was damp, then let herself out through sliding patio doors.

'She likes to keep busy,' Harry explained, but Coupland was no longer listening. His chest thudded as he followed her round to the side of the conservatory; saw her dabbing at several sticky prints on a pane of glass. Finger-sized jammy smudges, the height of a small child.

CHAPTER 14

Hurrying in through the station doors Alex called out to the desk sergeant. She'd been delayed getting back, caught out by the volume of traffic leaving the airport. It had been busier than she'd anticipated – it didn't usually go berserk until the end of summer term, which was still a couple of weeks away. Added to that she'd been overwhelmed by the sheer bewilderment of Angus's parents, Donald and Morven. They were clearly devastated by the loss of their only grandchild but, like most people touched by the case, they weren't sure where to vent their anger. They sat in silence on the back seat of the squad car she'd taken to collect them.

Stunned silence.

Picking through every memory they had of their daughter-in-law and their grandson to see if any of them were real. Re-living every word and conversation to find the missing clue that would have tipped them off, warned them of the ticking time-bomb they'd taken into their family. Would they ever stop blaming themselves, Alex wondered, for not doing more?

Alex hated this part of the job. She could cope with the bodies, well, most of the time. What she couldn't handle was meeting the families, for the relatives humanised the loss, put it into its proper perspective. Linked by a heritage and a cacophony of cells each family member belonged to a certain place in the family line. Two days ago Donald and Morven were grandparents; did that mantle leave them now that Kyle was gone?

Donald, a consultant at the cancer hospital in Edinburgh, was a tall angular man, all elbows and knees with a head of thick white hair and large glasses. Morven was tall and slender with a boyish frame that suited the trouser-suit and plain v-neck t-shirt she wore. A simple scarf was arranged around her neck, held in place by an expensive looking brooch. A GP, she worked part-time at a surgery in Edinburgh's West End. Quietly spoken, with a slightly more pronounced Scottish accent than Angus, they'd wanted facts, asked for the name of the pathologist who'd carried out the post-mortems.

'Maybe if they'd come home after they married we'd have seen it coming, been able to head it off at the pass,' Donald articulated to Alex as she drove them to their hotel.

'That was never going to happen,' Morven responded with venom, confirming there was no love lost between Tracey and her mother-in-law. They'd bickered for a moment then, the way long-term married people do, informing her they'd be happy to answer any questions she had but first they had to see their son. Alex had nodded, turning the car round to take them over to where Angus was staying. Of course they would want to see him first. It was natural that they needed to be sure he was okay. On the way over Alex studied Morven in her rear-view mirror. Her face was pale, drawn. Eyes red-rimmed and bright, making her look startled. When she'd looked at her son as a child, what had she hoped for for his future, Alex wondered?

Not this.

Rushing into the station half an hour behind schedule Alex looked at her watch and cursed. Charlie Preston would have been and gone by now, she chided herself; it would probably take several days to set up another meeting. As she entered the main double-doors she brushed shoulders with an overweight woman dressed new-age style in a long dark skirt and crushed velvet top. Her dark curly hair had been pinned up, framing her chubby face with tightly wound tendrils that moved with a life of their own putting Alex in mind of an Octopus. The woman glanced at her and nodded, continued to make her way down the station steps.

The sergeant on duty looked up as Alex approached the main desk, began pointing back the way she came. 'Has a Charlie Preston called in to see me?' she asked, ignoring his pointing finger, leaning onto the counter top while she waited for a reply. 'Charlie Preston hasn't,' he replied dryly, 'but Charlotte Preston just passed you on the steps.'

Irritated that he hadn't said so sooner she thanked him tersely and raced back out of the building to the small parking area at the side of the station reserved for members of the public. Alex had underestimated the woman's bulk, which didn't impede her transit in any way. Before she had time to run down the steps the woman had climbed into an aging Citroen Saxo and sped off in the direction of the city centre. 'Shit,' muttered Alex, 'Shit, shit, shit.' She turned around and trudged back up the steps toward the station building, annoyed at herself for being late. They'd probably end up playing ping-pong phone calls for another couple of days and she wasn't even sure how useful the woman would be to the investigation anyway.

The desk sergeant called out her name as she passed the reception desk, held out a business card. 'Charlotte Preston left you a message,' he said smugly, 'said she doesn't live too far from here, could call back in to see you same time tomorrow.'

'Why the hell didn't you tell me?' Alex snapped as she snatched the card from him, her eyes falling onto a logo she recognised in the bottom right hand corner.

'I just did,' he retorted, but his reply fell on deaf ears. Alex had seen the woman's job title, was already intrigued as to what her significance could be to the investigation.

By the time she'd had returned to her desk following her brush with Charlie, or rather Charlotte, her head was spinning. Picking through the melee of messages taken in her absence she opened Tracey Kavanagh's file trying to fill in the missing gaps. She wondered briefly what it was they didn't know, what secrets Tracey had chosen to take with her…Sergeant Coupland passed her desk with Turnbull, touching base before they went their separate ways again. Coupland seemed more buoyant than he had been for a long time; Alex wondered if it was good news.

After sending Turnbull for drinks Coupland spoke quietly. 'Lynn's agreed to meet up after work, maybe I've not burnt all my bridges after all.'

Alex smiled approvingly.

'How'd you get on with Angus's parents?'

'Christ, they don't know what's hit them. They're a close family by the looks of it, though I don't think it extended to the daughter-in-law. Still, no one could've predicted this.' Or could they? Was there something ticking away in Tracey's past that was always going to lead to this? Was it possible that Kyle, and his unborn brother, could've been saved?

'Making headway with Tracey's contact book,' she added.

Coupland nodded. 'Anything specific?'

Alex was tired. She wanted to read through the file she'd put together on Tracey in peace, so she could get home on time to read Ben a bedtime story. She didn't want to run through it with Coupland just yet, wanted to let the ideas bounce around in her mind a little longer. She looked up at him and shrugged, played down the fact that she might have just made a breakthrough…

'Oh, just tracked down a contact from Tracey's past,' she replied carefully, looking at the logo on Charlotte's business card. 'Works with ex-offenders.'

Coupland shook his head. 'When *will* they learn, eh?' he sneered. 'These *agencies*.' He spat the word out like he'd tasted something foul. 'Full of do-gooders in comfortable shoes who believe in rehabilitation right up there with Santa Claus and the Easter bloody Bunny.' He shook his head, his jowls falling into his familiar hangdog expression.

'He's off…' someone called out. Turnbull smiled in readiness for the lecture.

'An *ex-offender*,' Coupland sneered, 'is just someone who hasn't committed his next fucking crime.' He parked his heavy backside on the edge of Alex's desk, ready to put the world to rights. Turnbull returned with their coffees, blowing across the top of his own before parking himself on a chair with wheels and manoeuvring it to Coupland's side. It was weird how, since Coupland's marriage had hit the skids, the DC seemed to have latched onto him, followed him around like a lap-dog. Turnbull had been through a devastating divorce the previous year, maybe he saw Coupland as a future comrade-in-arms. Whatever the reason, Coupland seemed to enjoy having his very own rent-a-crowd.

'Look,' he added, relishing the opportunity for a good old rant, 'what does an actor say he's doing between jobs?' Turnbull eagerly shrugged his reply, basking in Coupland's attention.

'He's resting, of course,' Coupland answered for him, 'they don't suddenly become ex-actors just because they're out of work. Stands to reason, doesn't it? It's the same with cons, only they're never going to bloody admit it, are they?' He raised his voice to catch the attention of a couple of DCs who'd just walked in, exaggerated his Salford accent, making a point of rolling his 'r's. 'Yeah, yer 'ono, ah used to be a pilferin' bastard but ah'm between scams right now.'

Alex stifled a smile. She could rely on Coupland, out of all of them, to sum it up just about right. To call a spade a spade.

Coupland turned his attention back to Alex. 'They're bloody restin', love, that's all they're soddin' well doing. Waiting for the next job that's worth their while… and these do-gooders that "work" with ex-offenders,' he made quotation marks with his fingers around the word work, 'what they're really doing is spending tax-payers' money playing silly beggars. The revolving door of rehabilitation, eh, don'tcha just love it? – The shuffling of tables, moving of cons from one list to another. Anything in fact, that hides the fact they're still breakin' the bleedin' law.'

Coupland looked at his watch, realised he needed to be somewhere else. He lifted his buttock off the desk, gave it a rub where his arse-cheek had gone numb. He made to go towards the CID room door, pausing for effect in case anyone had missed his point. 'Massaging the figures, that's all they do, so the unsuspecting public can sleep soundly in their beds.' He turned swiftly, headed down the corridor towards the entrance to the car park.

Alex shuffled papers on her desk, attention shot, thinking she might as well call it a day. She closed her eyes and rubbed the tension away in the back of her neck, snapping them open when Coupland's rugged voiced rumbled from the direction of the main reception area: 'Ex-bleedin'-offenders…. If it walks like a duck and quacks like a duck, it's a duck. Stands to bloody reason eh? Stands to bloody reason…'

Enough.

Alex closed the file on her desk, logged off her computer. Time to go home and see my little angel, she thought, then smiled. Well, he looked like an angel, and when she held him close he sure as hell smelt like an angel, it was hardly surprising he was the apple of her eye.

Stood to bloody reason…

Coupland sat in his car watching the officers coming off their shift, heads up, hands in pockets as they headed towards the car park or took a detour home via the Volunteer Arms. A couple of officers nodded in his direction, making the universal hand gesture for *fancy a swift one?* followed by under the thumb gestures when he shook his head. Although his shift was due to end he wanted to call at the hospital to check on Ricky Wilson, see if there was any progress.

He enjoyed the peace that being on his own brought, for it enabled him to think things through at a deeper level. He thought about Ricky Wilson and Tracey Kavanagh, the parallels between the two cases: two families – one sticking together despite the odds, the other imploding at the first hurdle. He thought of Roddy Lewisham and his dignity in the face of a living nightmare. He felt ashamed; his job brought him into contact with families cruelly blown apart yet instead of counting his blessings he'd as good as aimed a grenade at his own front door. He closed his eyes; hoped to Christ tonight would be the night he made inroads with Lynn.

The alternative was unthinkable.

*

Carl was in the kitchen designing a stencil of the planets he wanted to paint in Ben's room. Alex leaned over his shoulder as he sat at the table. 'Not bad,' she observed a little grudgingly; she didn't have a creative bone in her body. 'Is it Pluto?'

'That's not even a planet anymore,' he corrected. 'It was relegated.' He pointed to a book on the Solar System he'd borrowed from the library. He'd propped it open so that its centre pages fell open to display a range of rocks around the sun with names she could barely pronounce. It wasn't the solar system she remembered from school – had the earth moved into another galaxy when nobody was looking? 'It's life, Carl,' she conceded, 'but not as I remember it.'

Ben sat beside his father, 'helping'. He seemed to have inherited Alex's artistic style, his planets distinguishable by neither shape nor colour. The orange blobs resembled a field of pumpkins rather than anything astrological. 'That's lovely, Ben,' she encouraged automatically. 'We can put it up on the wall when it's dry.' She kissed the top of his head, revelling in his bubble-bath smell.

She put a pan of milk on the stove, spooned generous heaps of powdered chocolate into three mugs, her mind flitting back to something Sergeant Coupland had said about the Kavanaghs' home: the noticeable lack of Kyle's artwork on the walls. Maybe Angus and Tracey were more critical of Kyle's efforts than most parents, more discerning when it came to what their offspring produced. Either way, Alex wasn't sure that it signified anything, other than some parents praised their child's every action, others preferring to hold back. There was no right way or wrong way – most of the time.

She was brought back to the present by the sound of hissing, as though several snakes had slid into the room and were discussing what to do next. The milk had boiled over the pan, forming brown puddles around the gas ring.

'Shit,' she muttered, mouthing sorry to Carl as he shot her a filthy look over the propped-up planet book. Beside him Ben chuckled into his chest, his hand gripping onto his paintbrush like a Jedi Knight holding a lightsaber. 'Mummy said 'shit' again, Daddy.' He giggled.

'I know, son,' Carl said gravely, enjoying the view from the moral high ground for once.

*

Coupland ranked hospitals the top spot on his list of most hated places to be. Something about the smell of piss and cheap bleach that didn't do it for him, made him want to give them as wide a berth as possible. Even Amy had been born at home, though more through impatience on her part than any plan of Lynn's, so apart from a boil on his backside ten years earlier, when he'd been side-lined to a ward beside an insurance rep with polyps who'd tried for three days to sell him a funeral plan, he could honestly say he'd been successful in keeping away on a personal level.

Perhaps, if like Lynn, he worked on the Special Care Baby Unit, or SCIBU, he'd feel differently, seeing fear turn to joy in the faces of new parents who traipsed through the ward each day. As it was he was more acquainted with the discreet entrance at the back of the hospital, where the clientele were called cadavers and sirens no longer wailed to signal their arrival. Instead, ambulances took their time as they made their way into the parking bay, careful not to draw attention to the cargo they were carrying.

It was quiet too. Dead quiet, he often quipped. Footsteps were never hurried in a hospital mortuary; the urgency had gone, along with the deceased's last breath.

He could fill The Willows rugby ground with the number of grieving relatives he'd chauffeured back and forth over the years to identify the bodies of loved ones who'd found themselves in the wrong place at the worst possible time. He breathed out a long slow breath, just because he could. It was no surprise then, when he thought about it like that, why hospitals came way down on his list of places to visit. But this time he had a live one and, though Ricky Wilson still hadn't regained consciousness, there was hope. If he could just get the family talking, jog their memories a little more, he'd be able to put the bastards who'd put them through this away for a very long time. So far their descriptions of Ricky's attackers were hazy and there was still nothing solid as yet to link the incident to Brooks and Horrocks, but there was definitely something Ricky's family could clear up for him.

Lynn had agreed to meet him at the hospital's main entrance at the end of her shift. He'd promised to text her when he was finished in ICU, and from there they'd go for a drink then on for a meal depending how things progressed.

He walked down the wide corridor to the lift and pressed the button. The metal door slid open and a gaggle of nurses stepped out, shift over, going on somewhere, by the look of it. He recognised a couple of normally scrubbed faces, now sporting bronzing powder and glossy long hair. He stood to the side to let them pass before stepping in alongside a porter pushing a woman in a wheelchair, her patient file balancing on her lap. At the second floor he got out of the lift, following signs to the Intensive Care Unit along a grubby-looking corridor before entering a double set of doors which led to the small reception area.

Melanie was standing in the relatives' room with Ricky's consultant; a grave-looking nurse stood beside her, rubbing her back. The waiting area was airless and smelt of painted heating pipes. Coupland tugged at his tie, felt as though he was stepping into a vacuum. As he reached the threshold of the relatives' room he hovered momentarily, and all three faces turned towards him before Melanie's legs buckled from beneath her and, as he held out his arms to catch her, he was reminded once more why he hated hospitals so much.

CHAPTER 15

A girl in dirty jeans and with a bird's nest up-do played an old guitar badly and sang 'Tried to make me go to Rehab' in a dull monotone. Beside her on the pavement a blanket displayed a collection of euros and dimes, the odd twenty pence piece scattered among them. A couple of clouds were starting to form overhead causing passers-by to speculate on whether the freak hot weather was coming to an end.

Coupland was past caring. Ricky Wilson was dead. After a discussion with his consultant he'd spent ten minutes fending off Melanie's angry relatives demanding answers he couldn't provide. It seemed cruel to tell them that Ricky's death had now escalated the case into a murder investigation, automatically increasing the resources available. Instead he assured them, whilst backing out of the room, that his officers were doing everything they could to bring the perpetrators of the evil crime to justice.

With half an hour to kill before Lynn's shift ended he had chosen to take a drive around the city centre to clear his head, found himself listening to the Winehouse wannabe as he sat at a set of traffic lights waiting for them to turn green.

Lynn had been quiet that morning. It could have been a thick head from the night before but he doubted it. In truth the only one who was well-oiled by the time she'd come home had been him. The whisky had made him arsey, firing questions at her without listening or even waiting for her answers. This morning there'd been a quietness about her, a preoccupation that delayed her responses, made her oblivious to the round of toast he'd made for her, the pot of tea freshly brewed placed beside her favourite cup. Conversation had been sparse, limited to the barest of details surrounding their day: who was doing which shift, who had time to pick up a ready meal for Amy's dinner. In the absence of anything more to do or say he'd set off to work, wondering how in hell his marriage had disintegrated so quickly.

The text he'd sent her mid-morning had been brief, not wanting to get off on the wrong foot he'd asked simply:

Fancy a drink after work?

Meal if you're up for it…

He'd not had to wait long for a reply, within ten minutes his mobile vibrated, signalling Lynn's answer:

OK. Need to talk anyway.

Don't book anything, see how it goes…

He wasn't sure he liked the sound of them *needing* to talk, but the fact she'd been willing to meet him at all had made him feel that all was well with the world, right up until he'd had to peel Melanie Wilson from the floor of the ICU relatives' room where she'd thrown herself in sorrow, moaning for the man she'd spent her entire adult life with.

Coupland's shoulders sagged. He was such a fucking idiot; he'd come close to throwing away all that he held dear. He didn't deserve Lynn's forgiveness but he craved it anyway. The thought of her leaving him, of her starting a new life on her own, terrified him. He scowled at the slow-moving traffic. The last thing he could afford right now was to keep Lynn waiting on top of everything else.

A billboard outside a newsagents announced: WILLIAM AND KATE TO VISIT SALFORD. Poor sods, he thought.

Lynn was standing at the mouth of the hospital's main

entrance as Coupland pulled into one of the disabled parking spaces. She hadn't spotted him drive in, was too busy watching the cars approach from the other direction. Coupland climbed out of his car and flicked the doors locked with his key. Lynn had changed out of her uniform into jeans and a v-necked t-shirt, her long shiny hair spilling over her shoulders. She'd kept her figure trim over the years, and not for the first time Coupland found himself wondering what the hell she still saw in him. It was at that point, as he moved towards her, that he registered two things: firstly, that she'd applied eyeliner and refreshed her lipstick, which he took to be a good sign, and secondly, something altogether more worrying caught his attention.

She wasn't alone.

CHAPTER 16

In his dream he is drowning. The water is clear and warm like fresh urine. He swallows a mouthful as he panics and it tastes sour and salty at the same time. The water is high above his head and still rising; his hands thrash about for something to hold onto, to give him some leverage. An air bubble escapes from his lips, followed by several more.

He is sinking.

A shadowy figure comes into view, her silhouette dark against the backdrop of white tiled walls. An arm extends itself and plunges into the water and he raises his hand to touch it, to pull himself up. He feels a pressure on his shoulder, sharp and heavy, and he realises too late that she's not there to save him.

She's holding him under…

Coupland's eyes snapped open. Pushing himself into a sitting position he glanced around the room, his gaze lingering in the darkest corners, listening to the rhythm of his heartbeat as it returned to normal. He puffed out his cheeks and blew out a long, slow breath. At least his lungs – which moments ago felt heavy and full – were in perfect working order. He leaned over to the small table by his bed, lifted a cigarette out of the packet of Silk Cut he'd left there the night before and lit it, blowing smoke rings into the humid air. A glance at his watch told him it was five thirty am. Already the sky was bright with the promise of sunshine. Beside him Lynn's chest moved rhythmically, and he swallowed hard as a bubble threatened to rise in his throat. He slipped carefully out of bed, stepped into the suit trousers he'd worn the day before and lifted a freshly-pressed shirt out from his wardrobe. He felt light headed and his stomach rumbled, yet he couldn't believe he was hungry. They'd not bothered with dinner the previous night, turned out neither had had the stomach for it.

Unable to face Lynn, he slipped out of the house. He climbed into his car, started the engine before realising he didn't have the stomach for work either.

The Ship was a grubby, tired docker's bar left over from a time when Salford Docks had a shipyard and a purpose. Every morning at six it opened its doors, prompt, as though the national economy depended on it. The local economy certainly did, Coupland thought dryly, as he passed several punters making their way unsteadily towards it like toddlers towards an ice-cream van. It was a place for the burnt-out and the bewildered: street girls at the end of their shift; battle-scarred coppers at the start of theirs…

Coupland's hair was flat around the back of his crown – his earlier nightmare had put him off taking a shower, at least until the sound of water sloshing against tiles stopped making him shudder and the feeling of someone holding him down evaporated. He ran his fingers through his hair, though he suspected the regulars hadn't even registered him, let alone gave a shit how he looked.

The interior of the pub could be summed up in one word: dismal. The drab décor had been the same for as long as he could remember. Shabby walls, dark rings on the threadbare carpet, furniture chipped and unstable. Stepping across the grubby threshold he was hit with the stench of cheap air freshener, and something else entirely unpleasant. There was a sign over the door to the only toilet stating it was Out of Order; the smell of a backed-up drain radiated from it. The carpet was so sticky that Coupland's feet made a sound like Velcro strips ripping apart as he crossed the room to the bar. He attracted a couple of glances from the clientele but only briefly, not out of interest or even hostility, simply because he had crossed their line of vision.

There were about a dozen or so drinkers in the bar. In one corner, a woman with heavy blusher and a bee-stung mouth dragged on a cigarette. Between punters and her next fix by the look of her, eyes tired rather than vacant stared into the bottom of an empty glass. Her lipstick was wonky, as though painted on by a toddler, an epileptic one at that. Coupland wondered if she'd put it on hurriedly, in the dark, in the back of some executive's car after an expense account blowjob. She looked like she was smiling even when she wasn't. She caught him watching her and the red stain of her lips spread even wider across her face. She stuck out her chest and tugged her dirty v-neck an inch lower. Horrified, he averted his gaze, escaped to the other side of the bar.

'What can I get you, love?' the landlady asked without looking up, reading an article from a women's magazine. The magazine had been folded over, a photograph of two unhappy sisters emblazoned across the middle. The landlady tutted and shook her head a couple of times and Coupland hoped it was aimed at the article's cheating love rat who'd wronged the gullible siblings, rather than him.

The landlady finished her article and looked up from the magazine, stared at him impatiently as though he was keeping her from something pressing. She was short, five two at the most, with a large bust that made her head look curiously small. Several gold chains – heavy links, not hollow – hung from her crêpey neck. A gold watch was fastened securely on her flaccid wrist, several bangles and a lucky charm bracelet jangled loudly on the other. She was tanned too, a recently baked tan made all the more obvious when she frowned as white lines appeared around her eyes and mouth – she had obviously laughed a lot on her holiday. Probably laughed all the way to the bank, Coupland found himself thinking as he contrasted her complexion with the pallid, indoor skin of her regulars.

There was money to be made from the poor and the desperate and everyone was cashing in – from the money-lenders and drug dealers to the sharply dressed store staff who peddled TVs and stereos on credit, not giving a toss about how the repayments would be made, or whether they'd be made at all. Funny how the poorest towns were all the same: crap schools and shoddy housing, high streets full of bookies and off-licences; electrical shops and video stores; over-flowing pubs selling cheap booze and knock-off fags.

The segregation was subtle; banks were pulling out of inner city areas, setting up call-centres in far off places that only people with phones and telephone-banking accounts could access. Closed branches were converted into trendy bars – more places for the neglected to drink themselves silly when their benefit came through. The only professional services the high streets round here offered were defence lawyers and ambulance chasers, and naive women who climbed into strangers' cars to score crack for their men.

The landlady stared at Coupland. The lines round her eyes and mouth resembled ancient tribal markings.

'I'm looking for Flemish Joe,' he informed her.

Her mouth tightened. The rumble of a smoker's cough nearby distracted him. He waited for the dislodged phlegm to be either ejected or swallowed; he didn't much care to turn and discover which.

'He's not welcome in 'ere any more love,' the woman replied. 'Stank the bloody place out.'

The words had been spoken without a shred of irony and Coupland stifled a smile, his eyes flitting over to the sign on the toilet door and back again. The last vestiges of courtesy disappeared from her face now she knew the company he kept. She folded her heavy tanned arms.

'Anything else?'

She barked the question as though he was keeping her from something vital and he looked back at the magazine she'd discarded on the counter for confirmation – the TV crossword, perhaps? His eyes were drawn back to the optics as though under the power of some magnetic force and he wondered if for one magical moment they could truly drown his sorrows.

'A scotch please. Make it a large one.'

A cruel smile played on her lips; she'd met his type before – many times he didn't wonder – saw him for what he was, rather than the man he wanted to be. He took his drink and threw the money onto the bar before striding over to the hooker with the clown-like lips. He placed the glass down in front of her. Before his brain registered what the hell he was doing he gave her a nod then slammed out into the warm morning air in search of his friend.

The first time Coupland had set eyes on Joe he'd been sitting in the doorway of the Flemish Weaver, a concrete pub looking onto Salford Crescent station, a suburban railway line providing links to Manchester City Centre in one direction, and Blackpool in the other. The previous night had been a bitter one, with temperatures dropping below zero and no let-up in sight. It had been during the week-long bender he'd embarked upon following the murder of Siobhan Lewisham. A week of serious drinking punctuated by short bursts of sleep and a craving for fried food. It was a time when each morning came as a bitter-sweet shock to him, proof that he'd made it through another night. He'd not long been promoted to Sergeant, and already he'd come to the attention of the powers-that-be – though for all the wrong reasons. A period of extended leave had been the official recommendation, a reminder that he couldn't kick the shit out of suspects anymore; the days of the ends justifying the means were long gone.

It was during this particular fall from grace that Lynn had taken Amy and moved back to her mother's. It was only ever intended as a short sharp shock, she admitted later; a wakeup call that his recklessness was impacting their marriage. The house had run to ruin, the cupboards bare, the kitchen bin overflowing with take-out cartons and chip shop wrappers. One particular morning he'd set off in his car driving slowly – careful not to draw attention from the boys on traffic – towards an all-night café on a side road just off from Salford Crescent. The thought of hot food had drawn him like a magnet, so when he first spotted what appeared to be a pile of rags in the pub doorway he'd tried to ignore it – even when it moved. It wasn't like this was an unusual sight – far from it. With an increasing number of towns being hit by unemployment many hard-working men began their short journey to homelessness through addiction to drink or drugs. Rejected by their families, they relied on soup vans for hot food and shelters for the occasional place to bed down.

When he thought about it later, two things had drawn Coupland to Joe that day: Firstly, when he'd passed him at the side of the road he'd continued to watch in his rear view mirror as Joe clambered to his feet standing ram-rod straight and meticulously brushed down his overcoat, inspecting it for dirt. Secondly, he'd pulled a rag out of his pocket and spat on it before carefully polishing his boots. Before the drink took over, Coupland's father had held great store by how smartly a man kept himself, a barometer that Coupland found himself using more and more. *The poor sod might be down*, he'd muttered to himself, *but he's certainly not out.*

Doubling the car back round in a u-turn Coupland had pulled up his car on the opposite side of the road and walked towards the vagrant who was shuffling along the pavement like a psychiatric patient. He was as tall as Coupland but broader too, although it was hard to tell if it was the several layers of clothes he wore that made him look stocky. Matted brown hair framed a gaunt face hidden by stubble. He had the haggard cheeks of someone malnourished or dependent on drugs yet his eyes were sharp and focussed. He stopped his shuffling as Coupland approached and surveyed him warily, his heavy breath hanging before him like rolling mist.

'I don't know about you but I'm starving,' Coupland had said to him. 'Will you let me buy you something to eat?'

He'd kept the driver's window open to keep a fresh blast of air circulating around the car, and offered his companion a smoke. His name was Joe, he'd informed him, reluctantly at first, but he began to relax when Coupland made it clear that he wasn't after a hand-job, that there was no expectation of sexual favours in exchange for feeding him. Turned out he was an ex-naval officer, which was no surprise. The number of homeless had swelled with ex-servicemen medically discharged from Iraq and Afghanistan; considered sick in the head they were dispatched quietly, denied a hero's return.

After their introductions they'd lapsed into silence, an easy one, given the time of day and their respective blood-alcohol levels. The all-night café was just off the crescent and a sign outside stated: *All Day Brekfasts surved here.* Apart from a hostile glare the owner sent in Joe's direction when they'd first walked in – quickly remedied by a flash of Coupland's warrant card – their meal was a pleasant one, and they quietly devoured two full greasy fry-ups and several mugs of all-you can-drink, bitter-as-tar coffee.

Joe was quietly spoken, polite. He took his time answering Coupland's questions, as though he felt they deserved a well-thought out answer. He was a thinker, a dweller, a man who pondered on life's possibilities far more than was good for him. Nonetheless Coupland, himself a man of few words, found that he was drawn to Joe.

Joe had served in the Royal Navy during the Falkands conflict. A petty officer on HMS Plymouth, in charge of sonar equipment. 'We were hit on the eighth of June,' he informed Coupland, piling a large knob of butter onto slightly overdone toast. 'Just before the bloody war ended, can you believe that?' Coupland had nodded, he knew all about the vagaries of fate. 'Aircraft attack,' Joe continued, receding gums displaying tar-stained canine-length teeth. His breath was foul but, like with most unpleasant things after a period of exposure, Coupland had become immune to the stench, focussing instead on what his companion had to say.

'I remember bouncing up into the air, looking down on my fellow officers, all of them grown men, crawling into the smallest spaces for cover. I thought I had died, that that was why I was up in the air while everyone else remained on the ground, shouting.'

He took a bite of his toast, wiped his chin with the paper serviette where the butter had melted, leaving a patch of clean skin.

'I saw the bodies of our Chief Mechanic and Stoker burn to nothing, could hear their screams, but I was powerless. It was as though I was stuck in some sort of limbo… By the time I came to I was in a makeshift military hospital, was told I'd been suffering from shock.'

He said the words dismissively, as though ashamed he'd survived the attack while others had perished.

'The problem with fighting a war 8000 miles away,' he'd added, 'is that for many it just wasn't real. People back at home carried on with their day-to-day lives, the war to them meant nothing other than a ten-minute bulletin on the evening news. Unless you had a father, a brother, a husband or a son caught up in it, it passed you by.'

Coupland had dropped his gaze, conscious of the truth in Joe's words. He'd been a youngster at the time, preoccupied with his own problems and weaknesses. He remembered the sinking of the Belgrano, and the Welsh guardsman who'd been horrifically burned on the Sir Galahad, but little else. He hadn't given a thought to the servicemen, hadn't concerned himself with their families and what they'd been going through.

'It's okay,' Joe had reassured him, 'why should you be any different? Life goes on.' They'd met regularly for breakfast after that, and each time Joe had offered up a little bit more of himself. He'd had a wife, Marie, and a daughter, Sophie. Six weeks old when he'd gone off to war. Both killed in a hit and run while he'd been recuperating in a mental hospital following the first of his many breakdowns. 'Like I told you, Kevin, the war didn't change anyone's lives over here. Criminals carried on committing their crimes, and gutless bastards carried on ploughing into pedestrians and driving off without a second thought.' He was poised as he said this. Measured. But his watery blue eyes told a different story. 'I talk to her sometimes,' he'd said unexpectedly once, on another of their meetings. 'My Marie… I know that sounds stupid.' Coupland knew better than to think that. He'd had a number of conversations with the dead himself, over the years.

Joe hadn't got over the death of his wife and daughter. They'd been his anchor in a country that largely only gave a damn about its servicemen when there was a war. During peacetime, the armed forces were an extravagance to be pared down, kept out of view like a battered wife. Joe's decline had been swift, terrifying. There'd been no military support for his ailing mental health; instead he'd had to wait his turn beside the binge-drinkers and drug addicts, waiting in line to get his referral for psychiatric help. It would be many years before his post-traumatic stress was treated seriously.

Driving through the streets in search of Joe now, Coupland knew enough about his friend's routine to know he wouldn't be far away, that if he hadn't been able to bed down in a city centre hostel he might have spent the night under the railway arches at Chapel Street, a couple of hundred yards further along. A couple of the arches were boarded up, had been converted into workshops and a garage. The remaining arches were open. They provided shelter from the rain but not the biting wind, and so they were used mainly during the summer months, as a protection from frequent showers. *You get used to the discomfort*, Joe had told him once, *but you never get used to the dishonesty. You have to sleep with your boots on, Kevin, if you want to see them again next morning.* He'd come across dozens of ex-servicemen over the years, men paid to serve their country who'd suffered a sense of loss the day they'd handed in their ID card. Institutionalised, the only people they'd ever known were other servicemen. It was a sad fact that for many, being sectioned was the best thing to happen to them since being discharged. Out of the thousands who went to the Falklands to fight, more had committed suicide since coming home than had actually died out there.

Did joining up make you weak-willed, Joe had asked Coupland once, *because everything was done for you?*

Coupland hadn't known what to say to that.

He'd read somewhere that three months of homelessness took three years to get out of the system. He thought of Joe and did the maths, wondered if there was any hope for his friend. After scanning the pavements for several minutes for signs of Joe he came into view, his proud frame heading into Salford from the direction of Chapel Street's railway arches, his cardboard box port-a-bed folded neatly under one arm. Joe always looked ahead when he walked, never glanced around or stopped to study his surroundings: workers beginning their early shift; cars speeding towards Manchester's city centre. He moved forward with a purpose. His direction never wavered, yet in a sense all he ever did was look back. It wasn't just his memories that were frozen in time; in a way Joe himself was trapped, unable to slough off his military identity and feel at ease in civilian skin.

Recognising Coupland's car Joe raised his hand in salute, a smile breaking out across his face at the prospect of a full stomach.

Half an hour later they were sat at their usual table in the café, Joe listening without interrupting as Coupland told him about Tracey Kavanagh. Not one for passing judgement, he studied Coupland's face as he talked him through the case and understood far more by the set of his friend's jaw and the downturn in his voice than any of the words he was using.

'And you say there was no prior warning?' he asked when Coupland had finished.

The detective shook his head. 'By all accounts, no. The usual medical and social reports have been carried out, pretty unremarkable so far.'

Joe attracted little attention these days. Over the past year he had swallowed his pride and accepted Coupland's hardly worn clothes and shoes and, depending on whether he'd been lucky enough to get a night in the shelter and a shower, the stale smell of unwashed sweat was kept to a minimum – though it always helped, of course, if you sat downwind of him. Occasionally Coupland had tried to do more, to fix him up with work, to find him somewhere to stay, but each time he was met with polite refusal.

'Don't you see it's my penance, Kevin,' Joe had explained once, 'for not doing anything to save the men that perished on my ship? For not being around to protect my Marie and Sophie?'

He'd dismissed the detective's logical reasoning, that he'd been suffering from shock during the aircraft attack, that he'd not been in a fit state to help anyone. And again, when he'd been committed to hospital following his breakdown, the events that led to the hit and run had been beyond his control.

'Doesn't make it any easier to bear though, eh?' he'd said simply.

Coupland had merely shaken his head. He knew how slowly time passed for the grieving.

'You know, I'm not convinced,' Joe began evenly, once their breakfast plates had been cleared away and he'd wrapped up the left-over toast in his paper serviette for later, sliding it into the pocket of his hand me down jacket. Even on summer days he wore it, wouldn't take it off his back. *True meaning of the capsule wardrobe,* he'd said with a laugh, and Coupland knew in that moment that Joe would never return to a *normal* life, that he was intent on serving his penance.

'Just how reliable is the information you have regarding this woman's state of mind?'

'Well, like I said,' Coupland replied, 'the reports we've had back don't flag up any areas for concern.'

'Maybe not,' Joe countered, 'but I'm telling you, the clues will be there… This young mother was deeply troubled by something she felt she needed to protect her son from. Something big enough to justify her actions – to herself anyway. Something she felt unable to share with anyone else.'

He paused, his eyes shutting down as though he was looking inside himself for the answer.

'Do you think she was mad?' Coupland asked.

Joe rolled his eyes towards the ceiling, shaking his head. 'How the hell would I know?' he reasoned. 'I'm a walking talking Looney Toon, but I recognise the actions of a desperate person, someone afraid to unburden their fears in case they are judged. It's a typically British trait, stiff upper lip and all that… Realising you suffer from a mental illness is terrifying,' he said purposefully, 'it's not just a condition, it's a definition. It becomes who you are, or at least who the outside world thinks you are. From then on in, every action or reaction you have is put down to your illness and there is nothing you can do about it.'

He paused; spread his calloused hands flat on the surface of the table. There was dirt under his fingernails and they were broken. Tell-tale nicotine stains on the index finger of his right hand. On his left hand, scratched and battered out of shape, was a wedding ring.

'I tried so hard to stay well for my Marie. She was struggling to cope with the little one *and* me. I'm sure there were days when she thought her life would have been easier if I hadn't been discharged, or better still, if I'd been killed on that ship. The burden of caring for me was tearing her apart.' He paused. 'The nightmares I had about the ship being hit and the burning bodies didn't stop.' He looked across the table at Coupland.

'The nightmares have *never* stopped, Kevin, I just learned to stop talking about them…'

'Didn't medication help?'

'I don't want a life of numbness!' Joe spat. 'I want to grasp life by the thorns until my hands bleed – isn't that what I deserve?'

He looked down at his wedding ring, traced the edges of it with the index finger on his right hand. His voice shook when he spoke next. 'It's a fragile cord that binds us to sanity, Kevin, and wouldn't we do everything in our power to cling onto *that*?'

Coupland said nothing. It was as though the life-force that had propelled him to the café that morning had finally deserted him. His shoulders looked a good couple of inches lower than when he'd first sat down.

Joe leaned back on his plastic chair, studying Coupland as though he were an exhibit in a zoo. 'What's wrong?' Joe asked quietly.

'What do you mean?'

'You've been on edge since we got here, like the past twenty minutes have been a warm up to something else, something bigger. I thought maybe you were building yourself up to it. Are Complaints on your back again?'

'No.'

'Then what? You've listened to me drone on enough about my problems in the past, if there's something bothering you,' Joe opened his arms expansively, 'I've got all day.'

'Lynn's got cancer.'

Even as he said the words aloud he didn't quite believe them. His mouth filled with bile and his eyes felt as though a thousand needles were pressing into them. He swallowed the sour tasting liquid, blinking his eyes several times in succession. 'And all the time I was worried that she was upset with me over something *I'd* done.' He slammed his fist down hard on the table, his action barely drawing a glance from the guy behind the counter.

'I was too far up my own backside to realise something serious was troubling her. I took her moodiness to be her way of punishing me. I never gave a moment's thought that she might be ill.'

When he'd drawn level with her the evening before at the hospital's main entrance, she'd introduced him to a consultant whose name for the life of him he still couldn't remember, all he could think of was *bastard*. She was leaving him for a colleague and for some reason that was beyond him she thought it was helpful he meet the man who would replace him in their bed. Strangely, Dr Bastard didn't look very smug at bagging himself a stunner. In fact he looked pained, as though he'd rather be anywhere but here with his new girlfriend and her fat husband. They'd both looked at him then, as though he'd spoken aloud.

'Kevin?' Lynn whispered. She had that look in her eye when she wanted him to do something he was dead set against. 'Nick has just asked if he can have a word, his consulting room is on the ground floor, just past the lifts.'

Good for him.

'It's more private there,' Dr Bastard added.

They turned in unison as though they'd been practising and walked back into the hospital leaving Coupland with little option but to follow. He remembered he'd left the car in a disabled parking spot and the wardens round here were like Nazis. He shrugged.

Bring it on.

The corridor was longer than Lynn had implied. Coupland found himself taking a left past the café and WH Smith then a right along a row of closed doors before slowing in a department signposted Oncology. Dr Bastard removed a bunch of keys from his pocket and unlocked his office, ushering Coupland and Lynn in ahead of him before asking them to take a seat on the two chairs in front of his desk. Funny how Lynn chose to sit beside Coupland rather than stand beside her new fella, Coupland observed, old habits die hard, he supposed. The consultant took his seat and began talking once more, only Coupland found himself having to concentrate really hard to keep up.

'I've known Lynn for a number of years, worked with her back in the early days before we both moved into our specialisms…' So what? Was he trying to justify their attraction for one another, rationalise it as something inevitable between good friends? Coupland glanced at Lynn suspiciously; she dropped her gaze but leaned towards him to take hold of his hand. He knew at that moment that something was badly wrong, he just didn't know what. He felt like he wanted to empty his bowels. Now it was Lynn's turn to speak.'I wanted to be sure before I said anything, wanted to be done with the tests so I could tell you facts, not suspicions.' Christ, you could tell she was a copper's wife. 'But even then I couldn't bring myself to do it. You'd think being in the trade I'd know how to handle breaking bad news but that just isn't true. For two nights on the run I've sat at my mum's with a bottle of wine but by the time I got home I took one look at you and couldn't bring myself to say the words.'

'What words?' Coupland asked slowly, already fearing the worst.

'Lynn has breast cancer,' Dr Bastard said, as gently as he could, following it with a barrage of facts about survival rates and treatments, but all Coupland could hear was the sentence no one had spoken out loud yet.

Lynn was going to die.

When Coupland looked up Joe was standing beside him, his hand gripping his shoulder as though they were on the edge of a cliff and Joe was trying to prevent him from jumping.

'I'm so sorry,' Joe said softly.

Coupland's throat was sore, as though he'd swallowed a bag of razor blades. He merely nodded, pushing himself to his feet so that the two men were standing eye to eye. 'How the hell will I cope without her?'

'She's not gone yet,' Joe said sharply, 'You need to be strong. For Lynn, for Amy but, most importantly, for yourself.'

'What if I can't cope?'

'You won't have a choice,' Joe said simply.

CHAPTER 17

Salford was a city of extreme contradictions, Coupland observed as he drove to the station following a quick shower after his breakfast with Joe. It was still early morning and the sun was beginning its slow ascent above the tower blocks of Ordsall, the air still cool but pleasantly so. He'd taken the longer route to work, relishing the joy of chain smoking without judgement. The rhythmic tones of Bob Marley rose up from the car radio, reassuring him that every little thing was going to be all right.

Lynn had insisted on business as usual. She'd dressed for work, was hanging washing out in the garden by the time he'd returned home. Her operation was scheduled for the following week, it would be good if he could give her a lift, she'd said, but she knew it might be tricky with his job and what have you. They'd tell Amy at the weekend, give her time to get used to the idea before Lynn was admitted. Coupland marvelled at her calm, as though now he'd been told she could get on with the practicalities.

Prepare for her exit.

Pedestrians strolled in short-sleeved t-shirts, taking their time, making the most of the freak Mediterranean-style weather. Canal-side cafes spilled illegally out onto the pavements to tempt passers-by into taking a pit stop. Even the junkies were enjoying their methadone al-fresco, sprawled out on benches outside the local chemist, a day of stupor-filled inactivity spanned out before them. There was culture too, from the local artists who set up their easels close to where the canal boats moored, to the exhibition of work by local rent collector turned artist L.S. Lowry that hung proudly in the Lowry Museum. As Coupland drove through Pendleton he studied the graffiti sprayed carelessly onto boarded-up shops and wondered if in fifty years' time this urban *art* would be put on display in some contemporary museum and folk singers would write songs about the anonymous artists' work.

He sure as hell hoped not.

The city was a combination of neglected, poor places with uneasy pockets of wealth: a sports car garage; rows of executive-style homes; and the flagship apartments at the Quays. A few yards along from a Frankie and Johnny's diner a working-men's club stood empty. Behind it a row of derelict houses awaited demolition, already stripped of their boilers and copper piping; stolen by boys from the neighbouring estate and sold for scrap. Not all the money went on drugs, Coupland knew that much; some of it was handed over to their mothers for keep.

The mobile library had broken down once outside Tattersall, a sprawling estate separating Salford from Manchester by a ring road. By the time the librarian had returned to the vehicle it had been stripped. What depressed Coupland about that was not the theft – for the boys on the estate thieving was the only gainful employment they knew – but the fact that so many of the books would have been sold on unread – not because the kids weren't interested – but because they were unable to read.

As he pulled into one of the bays in the station car park he closed his eyes for a moment to gather his thoughts, to try to inject some enthusiasm when all he wanted to do was howl at the heavens.

'You okay, Sarge?'

Alex's voice startled him. She leaned into the open driver's window, her face creased with concern. Coupland followed her line of vision to where his knuckles were gripping the steering wheel so tightly his hands looked welded on.

'Everything's peachy,' he said flippantly, 'apart from the fact that Wilson didn't make it. Bastard 'ad us goin' for a while, thought he was gonna pull through at one point, his missus 'ad sent their young lad home for some rest.'

'Christ, what a way to lose your partner.'

A wave of fear rose up inside Coupland. So powerful he could only wait for the moment to pass. 'I'll see you back inside, Alex,' he said, dismissing her.

As his eyes followed Alex into the station building it occurred to him that even the people he came across in his line of work were full of contradictions: Ricky Wilson had put up a desperate fight, clung on by the tips of his fingers as he tried in vain to stay with the family who meant so much to him; Tracey Kavanagh on the other hand, couldn't wait to leave hers.

*

A telephone message on Coupland's desk had been written in red biro. Forensics had given the all-clear for Angus to return to the family home. Coupland screwed the note into a ball, aimed it at the wastepaper basket beside his desk. People were complicated. What you saw wasn't necessarily what you got. He tried to second-guess what part of Tracey's life had made her so dissatisfied.

Had Angus been unfaithful?

Did he abuse his son?

If only he could turn back the clock and ask Tracey herself.

If only she'd spoken to someone about how she felt, someone who could have helped her.

If only…

He needed to know more about the family, about the couple – what made them tick. It would do no harm to go back to the Kavanaghs' place, look it over with fresh eyes. The news that Angus could move back into the family home couldn't have come at a better time. He decided to deliver this information in person.

Coupland declined an invitation to sit in the conservatory; instead he remained standing while Angus perched on a kitchen stool, Harry and Diane relegated to their sitting room. There was a hint of colour in his cheeks, and Angus explained that he'd been for a run – a habit he'd picked up since working from home – got him out of the house, he explained – the blast of air in his lungs set him up for the day.

'Do you find it oppressive then, working from home?' Coupland asked him.

'Far from it. It's the most liberating experience – especially with a youngster. Instead of lunch in a tired staff canteen Tracey would make up a picnic and we'd take Kyle off to the park for an hour, or we'd head off to McDonalds if it was cold.'

Whatever medication had been prescribed it was certainly helping him function – and think – rationally. Coupland decided to take advantage of Angus's good spirits. 'Can you tell me a little bit more about your work?'

Angus rested his elbows on the kitchen counter and rubbed his chin. 'Well, what do you need to know? I'm a Management Consultant; I work for myself, I've built up quite a loyal band of clients…'

'Where do you find your clients, Angus?' Coupland interrupted. 'Word of mouth? Do you advertise?' Not an unreasonable question, he thought. At least Angus had had the grace to redden.

'Many were from the client list I account-managed at the firm I worked for before going self-employed…' He tailed off. Coupland smiled to himself. What different worlds we live in, he concurred. What copper in his right mind would contemplate taking *his* client list with him when he left the force? All Coupland's notable clients were behind bars.

'How did you manage to poach them?' he asked. 'Weren't they taking a risk, moving to a one-man band?'

'I offered them more for their money, Sergeant,' Angus said simply. There had been a time when this kind of questioning might have made him defensive but the tranquillisers softened all the edges. No frayed tempers in his world. 'They were paying over the odds for attending appointments in fancy offices with ornate cornices and oak-panelled walls, for three members of staff to handle every transaction. When I showed them how I could do more for their business at no extra charge it was a no brainer. No one, no matter how wealthy they are, likes to throw money away.'

'Are all your clients wealthy, then?'

'Several are, but I've started to move into business development. Some of my newer clients are small business owners who want to grow their company but don't know how. And before you ask what's in it for me – if I advise them successfully today they'll be tomorrow's wealthy clients, needing even more of my services.'

It seemed logical. Coupland moved on. 'Did Tracey keep in touch with her family?'

'Tracey's parents are dead,' Angus volleyed. 'Your assistant's already asked me that question.' Coupland smiled at Angus's reference to Alex.

'I was referring to other members of the family – or was she an only child?'

'There's a brother she never talks about. Look, I've been over this—'

'No aunts and uncles, old neighbours, friends from school?'

'Tracey wasn't particularly outgoing,' Angus replied, pausing as though something had just occurred to him. 'It wasn't that she was antisocial, just wasn't one of those insecure types who collect acquaintances. Tracey kept most people at arm's length; the most important people in her life were at home.'

Or in the hospital mortuary, depending how you looked at it. Coupland kept this thought to himself.

'Is this part of the process,' Angus accused Coupland, 'you asking me the same questions as your colleague, acting as though you've not read any of the notes in an attempt to trip me up?

'Is there anything to trip up?' Coupland asked, calmly.

Angus sighed as he shook his head. 'You'll say and do whatever you want to anyway,' he said as he raised himself from his chair. 'I'm as well to let you get on with your job.'

Coupland waited while Angus went back up the stairs to pack the items of clothing he'd brought over from his house, all neatly laundered and pressed by Diane.

He watched Angus hesitate as he descended the stairway, as realization dawned that he was returning to an empty home, a home that days before had lived and breathed his family. Coupland offered to take his bag but Angus declined, as though he needed to show he could do this small thing for himself. And so they walked the short distance between the two houses, each lost in their own thoughts. Coupland took a deep breath before asking the next question. 'Was it a happy marriage, Angus?' He slid his gaze over to the widower to gauge his reaction.

'Christ!' railed Angus, taken aback. 'What kind of a question is that?'

'A pretty straight-forward one, I'd have thought.'

'Of course we were happy – very *happy*.' Coupland pictured the PC's notebook, the number of times he'd underlined the word. Had he been influenced by his surroundings, he wondered, mistaking the trappings of wealth for security?

'Did Tracey have any reason to feel insecure,' Coupland ventured, 'competing with another woman perhaps?'

'Are you asking me if I was having an affair?'

'Were you?'

'Jesus Christ!' Angus shook his head as though the idea was pathetic. It was Coupland's job to ask awkward questions. He didn't enjoy it. Didn't get any sadistic thrill out of twisting the knife. Sometimes, like right about now, he felt like a hypocrite. Late last night while they'd lain in bed staring into the dark Lynn had asked Coupland if he wanted to leave. She'd understand, she whispered, if he wanted to start a new life with this other woman. *'Will you get it into your head there is no fucking other woman?'* he'd yelled, *'She was a mistake, a five-minute grope that led to fuck all! There's never been anyone else for me, Lynn, and there never bloody will be!'* His temper had scared both of them; Lynn had flinched when he reached out for her, trembling into him as he whispered over and over into her hair that he loved her. Was he a good enough husband? He sure as hell hoped so.

Coupland waited while Angus fumbled in his pocket for his house key, saw the slight quiver in his hand as he inserted it into the lock. He wondered if Tracey could see what she'd done, the life she'd resigned him to. Time to change tack again. 'Would you describe yourself as a good father, Angus?'

Angus stopped in his tracks. Turning to Coupland he shook his head from side to side. Not in answer to the question, but through sheer helplessness.

'I thought I was.' He replied so quietly Coupland had to

lean forward to hear him. 'Only not good enough though, eh?'

Angus closed his eyes as though imagining Kyle's face when he realised too late what his mother was doing. His eyes snapped open as though under a hypnotic spell. They were standing in the hallway and Angus looked around him as though seeing his home for the very first time. He turned back to Coupland. 'What did I do?' His question was simple enough. 'I ask myself over and over. Was it something I did, or didn't do, that convinced her they'd be better off without me?' He looked Coupland straight in the eye.

'Be sure to let me know, Sergeant, if you find the answer to *that*.'

CHAPTER 18

As he eased his car onto the East Lancs Road Coupland rifled one-handed through a selection of new tapes on the passenger seat, inserted one he'd picked up cheap on Pendleton Market. An Oasis tribute band assaulted his favourite track and he cursed inwardly for allowing himself to be ripped-off. Turning the volume to *low* he lit a cigarette, not for the first time wondering about the purpose of his life. The fucking point of it. The news about Lynn had tilted his world, made him maudlin. He thought back over his career, at his paltry attempt to repair lives torn apart by circumstance. What he did never brought peace, only closure. He thought of Tracey Kavanagh hunched forward on a makeshift noose, of Kyle, just yards from her, lying in his watery grave.

Their lifeless bodies waiting to be discovered.

Maybe his DC's guilt was understandable, he conceded, but for a very different reason.

They *had* been too late.

They were detectives, but they didn't *detect* anything. They merely picked up the pieces, *after* the tragedy, time after time after time.

Despite the fact that it kept him in work Coupland hated that bad things would always keep on happening. He'd once asked Joe, who had suffered enough hardship to last a lifetime, why this was so. It was the only time he recalled his friend stalling; it seemed that for once he didn't have an answer, yet it was surely something he'd thought about, a dark voice that counselled him in moments of doubt.

They'd been sitting on a bench at Light Oaks Park, working their way through Joe's roll-ups and watching a group of small boys play football, the air thick with concentration. They'd trudged along a well-worn path over lawns displaying signs to keep off the grass. Joe's face was covered in a sheen of sweat, but from exertion, not anxiety. It was hard to imagine he'd been up three nights in a row, unable to cope with the recurring nightmares of his last moments on ship, of the last time he'd seen Marie and Sophie.

He'd blown smoke rings into the air, the corners of his eyes crinkling at a passing toddler who ambled John Wayne style beside her mother. The child slowed by the bench and pointed at the exhaled smoke, mesmerised by the cloudy patterns, her rosebud lips shaped into a perfect 'O'. Joe pulled the edge of his mouth into a smile, turned to Coupland just as a cheer broke out and someone shouted *Goal!*

Maybe bad things occur, he'd answered slowly, *because it's the only way we can recognise good when it happens.*

By the time the tribute band had finished murdering the best of the Gallagher brothers, Coupland was pulling into the car park of the Evening News, his mouth down-turned in distaste. If there was one thing he hated with a vengeance it was the press. Bloodsucking leeches, earning their money through trading in others' misery. He remembered one time turning up to tell a young woman she'd been made a widow, only to find a reporter had got there first. The hack had also managed to mention that her husband hadn't been alone when his car had driven off the road – did she want to make a comment? Coupland had almost burst a blood vessel; the insensitive bastard was already working the street by the time he'd arrived, asking the neighbours if they'd been aware of any trouble in the couple's marriage. Keying the twat's car hadn't been enough, gave him no satisfaction at all. Only later, when his fist had made contact with the tosser's jaw, did his temper begin to subside. Coupland remembered standing over him as he spat out broken teeth and stringy blood, made a point of asking if *he* wanted to make a comment. The reporter had cautiously shaken his head in reply, making a mental note not to cross paths with the narky copper again.

Coupland made his way to the archive room, intent on finding an article that had gone to press six months before. A reporter from the paper had called to give him a heads up that he'd written an article on the growing crime wave among young girls. Girls as young as twelve and thirteen were resorting to handbag snatching, selling on credit cards in return for a fix, or a wrap, or a bundle – whatever it was that floated their pubescent boat. He was sure the girls who'd been arrested for taking Melanie Wilson's bag had been interviewed anonymously in his article – maybe if Coupland found something useful he'd give him an exclusive? Coupland had grunted his agreement into his chin, scribbled the word *knob* into his notebook.

An hour later and, ignoring the stony looks from the bloke on the archive desk, Coupland ploughed through the micro-fiche records relentlessly until he found the article and printed it out. What shocked him most wasn't the blatant cockiness of the girls whose pixelated photos protected their criminal identities, nor was it their casual attitude towards taking other people's property. In a way he could understand their bravado, for he had a damned good idea who was providing them with local protection, *and* probably selling the goods on for them as well. And it *was* the girls he and Turnbull had collared, the tracksuits were the same, newer, the same fake Uggs finished the look. What shocked him most was something else entirely.

'I need to speak to one of your reporters,' he barked at the surly archivist, without bothering to look up.

CHAPTER 19

It was with some degree of trepidation that Alex pulled into the car park close to the main entrance of Salford University. She'd not been back since the end of her first term, when she'd left in the knowledge that she'd never return – as a student anyway. An academic career hadn't been for her. It wasn't so much that she didn't enjoy the Psychology course – far from it – even now she was fascinated by the vagaries of human behaviour; what made two people react differently to the same set of circumstances. It was just that the timing had been wrong. She'd just split up with Carl, felt driven to start afresh in every aspect of her life.

Although the topics she'd begun to study were fascinating, she'd been impatient to embark on a new career. Conducting research into the conditions of the human mind might well improve the way modern mental health patients were diagnosed and treated, but it wasn't for her. Instead she'd been drawn to the way the mind – especially the conscience – affected people at a fundamental level. She'd wanted to work with people at close range, where her actions made a difference. Policing had seemed the obvious answer, and for the most part she'd had no cause to regret her decision. Yet this current investigation troubled her. Ate away at her insecurities and affected her work, her judgement, her family life even. Tracey Kavanagh's actions disturbed her on every level: as a wife – the ultimate betrayal of Angus's trust, and then as a mother, a symbol of nurture and love.

The case had unsettled her, and something Coupland had said – about her needing help – struck a chord more loudly than she'd cared to admit. All it had taken was a couple of phone calls to track down an old lecturer she'd particularly admired and a meeting had been arranged for today. When they'd spoken on the phone he'd sounded pleased to hear from her, interested in her choice of career.

Would he feel the same, she wondered, as she locked her Fiesta and made her way to the main reception in the Psychology Faculty, once he saw the thinly veiled mass of contradiction and uncertainty she'd become?

The Peel Building was the oldest on campus. The Gothic style red brick structure sprawled over four floors, its imposing design mocking the tower blocks behind it, not yet thirty years old but already earmarked for demolition. Walking up the stone steps towards the entrance she felt for a moment like she'd travelled back in time and was a student once more, hurrying to her next lecture. Just for a nanosecond she wondered if she'd made the right choice after all, wondered how her life would have turned out if she'd finished her degree. She pushed those possibilities out of her mind as she made her way to the receptionist to confirm her presence.

'While an unthinkable crime, Alex, filicide, or the murder of one's children, is seen in many countries around the world and in every social class. Although child murder is not common, it is a leading cause of death in developed countries and, when it occurs, the perpetrators are most likely to be the child's parents.'

They were seated in Professor Robert Ansell's office, a hodge-podge of a room lined floor to ceiling with shelves laden with textbooks, research papers, and periodicals. A cardboard box containing test papers balanced precariously on the top of his desk, a stack of leather-bound dissertations beside it were slightly off-kilter and were leaning into the box, nudging it nearer the edge. A computer and monitor occupied the only other remaining space. Family photos and academic awards were displayed on the wall by the window. The professor's wife and a number of offspring smiled down at Alex as she sipped at her tea, balancing the cup and saucer on her knee through lack of any other available space. The professor had presented a paper on filicide at a Symposium in Milan the year before and, like most academics, was only too pleased to demonstrate his level of expertise in his chosen field.

In the eight years since she'd last seen him time had been kind to him. He was much the same build as she remembered – tall, wiry – and his passion for all things sweet still hadn't added anything around his middle. His taste in clothing was as appalling as ever, garments worn for comfort and warmth with little care for passing trends in fashion. One of his daughters had called onto the campus once, when Alex was an undergraduate – an attractive girl in her late teens, dressed up to the nines – and Alex'd realised then that the professor probably got as much ribbing for his poor taste in clothes at home as he did in the faculty – and he clearly couldn't have cared any less.

Looking at him now Alex was grateful he hadn't changed; the familiarity comforted her, the knowledge that in a world that seemed to be spinning out of control, some things remained the same. 'Society is reluctant to accept the concept of murderous mothers, Alex. The relationship between a mother and her child is an especially tricky one to fathom where filicide is concerned,' he went on. 'This relationship is, after all, the most pivotal one in life. Primordial, one could say. A mother brings us into the world, suckles us, nurtures us in the most critical early stages of our existence. For this reason and this reason alone the law is most reluctant to disturb, let alone rupture, this relationship – unless the trust which society places upon her has been profoundly breached.'

'You mean society will side with the mother every time – until she does something to prove otherwise?'

Ansell nodded.

'But by then it could be too late,' Alex challenged.

A shrug. 'Nothing's ever simple, Alex. There have been a number of large-scale studies into society's "unthinkable crime", and a profile of offenders has identified several distinct groups with their own characteristics and motivations for committing this crime. A look at this study may help your investigation.'

Alex nodded, keen to hear anything that could help her understand *why*.

'Well, this is where it gets interesting,' said the professor as he got up from his chair. Ansell was a bundle of nervous energy; his larger than life eyes blinked behind thick glasses. He opened his desk drawer and she heard the rustling of paper. With a sinking feeling she watched him pull out a report which, if its thickness was anything to go by, spanned several hundred pages. He offered it to her but she shook her head.

'Perhaps you could summarise, Professor?'

Ansell smiled. Walking round to the front of his desk, he straightened the pile of dissertations before plonking himself down beside them. 'One of the most prominent systems to classify the different types of filicide was created by Resnick back in the late sixties, based on 131 case reports from world literature on child murder by both mothers and fathers, from the end of the eighteenth century to the middle of the twentieth century. The five categories in this system relate to motive, and they are: altruistic, acutely psychotic, unwanted child, accidental and spouse revenge.'

He glanced at her to check she was still with him and, for the second time that day, she was transported into the past, this time inside the lecture theatre, taking notes in a shorthand she never mastered. She nodded to him to show he hadn't lost her. Yet.

'Resnick describes altruistic filicide as murders committed out of love. In acutely psychotic filicide, the parent is suffering from a severe mental illness or psychotic episode, whereas an unwanted child filicide occurs where a child is illegitimate, or his or her paternity is uncertain. *Accidental,* is rather self-explanatory as is spouse revenge – when one parent seeks to get back at the other, following infidelity, for example.'

Alex remembered the news headlines surrounding the trial of John Hogan who, convinced his wife had been having an affair, threw his six-year-old son Liam off the balcony of his holiday apartment in Crete in 2006 before jumping 50ft with his two year old daughter Mia under his arm. She was about to ask a question when Ansell, reading her mind, held up his hand to silence her:

'But wait – it gets more complicated. Data suggests that most non-violent murders of children under twelve years old are committed by mothers.'

'So what is it,' Alex asked, 'that tips them over the edge?'

Ansell leaned towards his desk and prised open the lid of a tin of travel sweets with one hand, placing one into his mouth and crunching loudly. He held out the tin to offer her one. She shook her head politely, waiting for him to acknowledge her question.

'I think we're dealing here with something more primitive, an innate desire to protect, or remove, their offspring from a harmful situation – taken in the extreme.' He paused to let his words sink in. 'Think of the mercy killing of a sick or suffering child—'

'How does this differ from battering mothers – mothers who beat their children senseless – doesn't it amount to the same result?' Alex butted in. She could feel herself getting wound up just thinking about it. Ansell shook his head impatiently, as though dealing with a difficult student. 'Not at all,' he reassured her. 'A mother who raises her hand in frustration and anger has reached the end of her tether. She feels unsupported, unable to cope either financially or emotionally. They've usually suffered a turbulent time: relationship problems; worries about money or housing—'

'—My heart bleeds,' Alex cut in contemptuously. In the year Ben was born she'd had problems with all three yet hadn't felt the need to resort to violence. Nor did most other women for that matter.

'And if you'd let me finish,' he said slowly, causing Alex to flush, 'they strike out in temper, with an intention to punish. They have no clear impulse to kill. You know, Alex, I'd happily go through the mental, social and economic reasons that make a mother raise her hand, or even allow others to do it for her,' Ansell interjected, 'but we're veering off track. From what you're saying this investigation isn't concerning the case of an angry mother gone berserk. This is something else entirely. Done with careful planning and rational thought.'

'Was she mentally ill?'

Ansell paused long enough to unwrap another sweet. He held it poised between his forefinger and thumb.

'Were there any instances of impaired reality?' he asked.

Alex shook her head, then stopped. 'I think I know what you're about to say.'

Ansell smiled, popped the sweet into his mouth. Using his

tongue to push it behind his teeth he regarded her with his bulging eyes. 'I sincerely hope you do… otherwise your term here would have been wasted.'

The silence hung between them, interrupted by the sound of crunching and the drumming of his fingers on the side of his desk. He stood up, paced around the room as though he was giving a lecture to a packed auditorium. After a minute or two the crunching subsided.

'Everything is relative, Alex. What may seem incomprehensible to you will seem perfectly rational to a person suffering delusions. Their feeling of suffering – or that of their child – is so extreme that yes, filicide is rational to them. You have to stop looking at the world from your point of view.'

'But this was a woman betraying her flesh and blood in the most primitive way,' Alex persisted.

A look of irritation flitted across his face.

'Perhaps we should end this discussion,' he said.

'No!' she retorted. 'If you're implying I'm not capable of understanding—'

'Ha!' he batted her words away. 'Far from it! Despite your obvious – and quite understandable in the circumstances – prejudices to this case, you seem prepared to at least try and open your mind.' She remained silent. He didn't need to know that paying him a visit was a three-line whip from above.

'Let's stick to what is known about this mother, okay?'

Alex nodded.

Ansell had stopped pacing, sat himself abruptly on a low, imitation-wood table by her side, sweeping a pile of undergraduate prospectuses to the floor. His knees jack-knifed out at ninety-degree angles. He looked spectacularly uncomfortable, Alex thought, but remembered enough about him to know that when he got his teeth into something, he was oblivious to his surroundings.

'If she was suffering from a mental illness – and remember this is an *if* – then it is unlikely this would be an isolated act out of the blue. I don't mean there was a way to predict this – sadly, we're no nearer that, I'm afraid. What I mean is that usually there is a history of contact with psychiatric services, or social work, due to schizophrenia or a postpartum illness.'

'You mean the baby blues?'

'Yes, but the term baby blues is putting it mildly. The fluctuation in mood and delusional thoughts that affect some women in the first year of their baby's life – even during pregnancy – can be a sign that there is a significantly increased risk of harm to the infant,' he explained.

'We checked with Tracey's GP,' Alex informed him. 'She never presented any symptoms of depression. She and Kyle appeared to be well-nourished and content.'

Ansell nodded.

'Okay. Let's look at the facts. She was… how old?'

'Late twenties.'

'Okay, so she's not a slip of a girl who thinks she's tied herself down too early with kids. She's married, with no relationship problems and a supportive husband. The children were a conscious decision?' He looked at Alex for confirmation.

She nodded. 'According to the father.'

'All well and good.'

He consulted the file Alex had brought along, his finger moving slowly along the page as he read her hastily typed notes.

'Husband's business is doing well,' he read aloud, 'so there were no financial worries.' His finger paused, 'Now, it says here she kept herself to herself, but so what? There *is* a high incidence of filicidal women who have been socially isolated except for a relationship with their child's father. And it's true that if this is the only major social interaction she had, then any factors threatening that scenario may make her feel particularly vulnerable, enough to tip her over the edge, so to speak.'

Another pause as he read some more.

'She was pleasant by all accounts, cared enough about her community to join the local PTA. Reliable enough, by the sound of it,' he said, nodding vigorously. 'Responsible. Any of that sound odd to you?' He looked over the top of his glasses at her.

Reluctantly Alex shook her head.

'She didn't abuse her child, nor take any risks during her pregnancy. According to her husband and local midwife she ate well, didn't put her unborn child in harm's way at any time. She was considered by those who knew her to be a good mother, indeed spent most of her time focussing on her son and his needs.'

He placed the file down on the floor between them, returning his attention to Alex.

'Out of the blue she commits this unthinkable crime, but in the context of her delusional mind it is a rational act, carried out to save her son from some awful fate, or even from being motherless after her suicide. Look at the way she ended his life. Not with a gun or a knife, nor was she drunk. Maternal filicide is usually committed in a way that entails close physical contact between mother and child.'

Alex straightened herself. 'She held him under the water till he drowned.'

The words were still no easier to utter. She could feel pinpricks stabbing behind her eyes.

'Deconstruct your sentence, Alex.' Ansell said gently, reaching out for her hand.

'She. Held. Him.'

The tears fell freely down her face as she considered his words. She swiped angrily at her eyes to stem the flow. He studied her gently as he spoke, noticing the lines around the corners of her eyes and mouth.

'Whatever stresses were praying on her, her tipping point kicked in and she reacted in a way that seemed almost altruistic to her.'

Letting go of her hand he picked up the case file again, flicking through the pages of her notes as though looking for something, then paused, pointing to a line on the second page with his finger.

'Your notes record that witnesses say she was devoted to her child. *That's* my point, you see – devotion itself doesn't form a protection. In fact, high levels of emotional attachment can put a child at risk.'

Footsteps stopped outside Ansell's room, followed by muffled voices deciding whether or not to knock. A slim plastic folder slid under the door. 'Late again, Jones!' Ansell bellowed loudly, before turning his attention back to Alex. He smiled sadly; balancing his elbows on the top of his knees, he made his hands into a steeple, resting his chin on his out-turned thumbs.

His next words would haunt her; pray on her mind in the darkest hours. Make her analyse and agonise over and over her strengths – and failings – as a mother.

'I'd say if she was guilty of anything Alex, she was guilty of loving her son too much.'

CHAPTER 20

Coupland had no sooner sat down at his desk when a hesitant knock on the goldfish-bowl door found him staring at Johnson, the red-faced photographer, together with a man Coupland assumed to be the instructor from Johnson's sailing club.

Sergeant Coupland?' Johnson began, 'This is Tony Jeffreys. I mentioned to you that he might be able to help…' His sentence petered out and Johnson looked at him helplessly, waiting to be invited in. His companion had no such social insecurities, stepping forward confidently and offering his hand.

'Pleased to meet you,' he said, pulling over a seat and settling himself into it before looking over at Johnson, who shifted uncomfortably on his feet until Coupland motioned for him to do the same. Coupland regarded Tony for a moment, decided it'd do no harm to hear him out.

'I'm sure Johnson has explained to you the sensitive nature of the case,' Coupland began, 'so…' He tailed off, hoping the other man would pick up where he was heading.

'I've helped on a number of confidential cases for the police over the years,' Tony assured him. 'Rivers and canals have been the keepers of secrets since time began.' What he said was true; no one knew how many bodies had been dumped into the Bridgewater Canal over the years, it was a secret that only time itself would reveal.

Coupland nodded as he looked Tony over, deciding to take him at his word. He was a stocky man, late fifties. Grey hair worn long, in the same style, Coupland suspected, that he'd sported as a younger man. His face was weather-beaten, craggy, the result of years on deck come hail or shine. His cheeks were riddled with broken veins, giving him the look of a drinker. Casually dressed in jeans and a chunky-knit crew-neck sweater he folded his arms and leaned back into his chair with the confidence of someone used to giving out orders – and having them followed.

Johnson, who'd been superfluous until now, handed the photographs he'd shown Tony back to Coupland. They were the close-up shots of the knot securing the rope to Tracey's bed, and one taken from the back of her head. Coupland grunted his approval at Johnson's choice. They were anonymous shots, taken without the backdrop of the beautiful home or the heavily pregnant mother. It kept the discussion objective – at least for now.

'So,' Coupland began, 'Can you tell us anything about the knot? Anything that might be useful.'

'Well,' Tony began, 'Johnson was right about it being a bow-line knot, which in itself doesn't tell us a great deal, I'm more interested in the rope itself, and the *way* it was tied.'

Coupland reached over to his desk drawer and unlocked it. He shook the rope free from its protective wallet and watched it fall onto the desk. Keen not to touch it, he gestured for Tony to take it. The memory of the feelings it evoked when he'd held it two nights ago was still very fresh in his mind. He didn't want to touch the ligature ever again, if he could help it.

Tony held the rope across the palm of his hand as though weighing it, before turning it over in his hands, much the same as Coupland had done.

'Rope is constructed in two basic ways,' the older man said, 'twisted, and braided, although there are variations on the theme. The twisted variety is usually made up of three strands coiled around each other. You'll see it everywhere – from the rope on a child's swing to towing lines. This rope has been braided which makes it stronger, less likely to stretch – works better in a pulley than the twisted variety.'

He ran his fingers over the fibres. 'It's made from polypropylene, a synthetic material which floats well in water.'

'So you're familiar with this type of rope then?'

'Absolutely, although most seamen hope they never need to use it.'

'What do you mean?'

'It's most commonly used in rescues.'

'Any idea why the deceased would have it?'

'I suppose she could have had a passing interest in sailing, perhaps. One she grew out of, anyway.'

'What makes you say that?'

Tony pointed to the time-worn, discoloured edges of the rope. 'It's starting to degrade.' Then, 'Can I see the video of you untying the knots?' he asked Coupland. 'I understand you had Johnson record you untying them.' Tony looked from Coupland to Johnson, who waited for his cue from Coupland before setting up the AV equipment.

Coupland nodded, lapsing into silence while Johnson moved the trolley containing the TV and video player towards his desk. It struck Coupland that Tony's self-assurance came from his meticulous eye for detail. It was hard not to feel anything but complete confidence in the man; a safe pair of hands in an emergency.

If Coupland ever decided to step off terra-firma and venture out to sea he'd have absolute faith in him as a skipper, which was more than could be said for Johnson who seemed to be taking an inordinate amount of time to rewind the tape and set it to 'play' again. Finally, after a couple of protracted sighs the young man sat back in his chair, pointing the remote control at the blank screen which was immediately replaced by a close-up of the ligature in Coupland's hands.

Tony watched intently as the video replayed Coupland loosening the knot and the moves he made to untie the loops. When the video ended he reached into his pocket and pulled out a coiled length of thin rope – similar to the one Tracey had used – and replicated the knot.

'Can you show me?' Coupland asked eagerly.

Tony unfastened the knot and tied it a second time, showing Coupland each hand movement before undoing it again and handing it to him to try.

'We can see from the chivality – that's the direction of movement of the knot - that you're right handed, Sergeant Coupland, in the same way it is clear the deceased was left handed. We can also compare your hesitant knots, which are small and pulled far too tight, with the skilfully proportioned knots made by a confident hand. At either end of the loops you can see she used slip knots that held perfectly when she applied her weight but, if tugged gently in the opposite direction, would have released the entire tangle.' Tony paused, 'We see these knots fairly often in ships rigging, but how many people use – correctly – sailing knots?' His question hung in the air as Coupland mulled it over.

Tony continued, 'To be certain this was done by the deceased's hand you could look around for evidence of other knots in the house. Most people have at least one pair of shoes that they leave already laced up which they can lazily slip their feet into.'

Coupland felt the familiar tingle down the back of his neck he got when a case began to come together. A simple search of

Tracey's wardrobe would hopefully provide the evidence needed to close the investigation and submit his report to the coroner. He conjured up a smile as he shook Tony's hand warmly, patting Johnson on the back as he guided them both towards the door of his office. 'I appreciate your help Mr Jeffreys – and yours,' he said to Johnson, who suppressed a smile and puffed up his chest before turning proudly to Tony, offering to give him a tour of the station.

*

Ten minutes later Coupland paced the corridors looking for Alex. Unable to find her, he asked a passing DC for her whereabouts and was informed she'd gone out for the afternoon, had an appointment over at the university. Deflated, Coupland returned to the CID room. Turnbull was at his desk, putting the world to rights with a couple of DCs.

'Have you got a minute?' Coupland asked. 'This isn't something I thought I'd ever say to you, but I'd like to tie you up.'

The room burst into a sea of cat-calls and wolf whistles as Turnbull sashayed across the office, comic grin firmly in place. 'Why Sergeant, shouldn't you buy me dinner first?'

Coupland rolled his eyes, indicating they use Curtis's office. 'He's out at some equality workshop,' he added, stoking the humour, 'so we'll not be disturbed.'

After half an hour of replicating the noose-style loop that Tracey had made and tying it to the handle on Curtis's desk drawer for leverage, Coupland was able to demonstrate to Turnbull how easy it would have been for Tracey to tie the knot behind her head, and, chillingly, that a simple tug on the knot would have released her at any time. Once he was convinced it was safe, Turnbull allowed Coupland to put him into a noose identical to the one Tracey had concocted, before

Turnbull pulled the slipknot to release himself.

'I feel like a Norfolk turkey at Christmas,' Turnbull grumbled as he straightened himself. 'What I don't understand though,' he said, not unreasonably, 'is why she would build in a safety device she had no intention of using?'

Coupland shrugged his shoulders in reply.

'Tracey might have *sought* death, but still have a fear of it,' he suggested, 'Maybe she'd built in the release knot as a get-out safety mechanism in case she changed her mind, decided she wanted to live after all.' Maybe it had been a way of demonstrating strength in her resolve – she could've backed out – *literally* – at any moment but didn't want to. Any thought of her son lying cold and still at the bottom of the bath would have been enough to focus her mind, remind her that life as she knew it had already ceased to exist.

Coupland wondered if he'd ever be closer to understanding Tracey's actions. The morbid thoughts that had seeped into her mind the day she'd drawn her last breath seemed to have infected him, too. He pictured Lynn as she'd waited for him anxiously at the hospital's main entrance, her life – *their* lives – taking an unexpected twist. *What will become of us?* he wondered.

There were so many uncertainties in this investigation, in his life right now; uncertainties that he knew would rob him of sleep for a long time to come. The truth was that the only way anyone could ever gain a real insight into the way Tracey's mind had twisted and imploded *in extremis* would be to plumb those depths themselves. Coupland shuddered. He had enough on his plate right now to even think about contemplating that. All he could be sure about was that when evening came and the sky grew thick and dark around him, both Tracey and son would haunt his dreams, and in the solitude of the night he would hear sobbing, the sound of water splashing, and the underwater echo of heels as they pushed against the side of the bath.

Over and over again.

CHAPTER 21

Swinton precinct was a place best avoided after midnight. Coupland was reminded of this when he returned to the scene of Ricky Wilson's stabbing with DC Turnbull and a local news team to film a reconstruction that would be broadcast the following evening, in an attempt to jog memories and loosen nervous tongues. Ricky's widow Melanie was sitting in a patrol car with her kids, a WPC sat solemnly in the driver's seat, talking them through what they'd be expected to do over the next couple of hours. Several actors had been drafted in to play Ricky and his family, and Melanie was expected to advise where everyone had been standing – and their subsequent actions – when the attack, or rather the *murder*, had taken place.

'They've got to re-live the whole bloody thing again,' Coupland muttered to Turnbull, whose role was to scan the crowd that was beginning to form and suss out the bystanders from those with a more sinister reason for watching the proceedings.

To come and fucking gloat.

A wooden sign nailed to the wall of nearby flats warned pet owners they would be fined for letting their dogs foul the square. Coupland baulked, wondered where the notice was that warned parents not to let their drink-soaked offspring puke in the stairwells and along the concrete walkway. He stared at the puddles of pastel-coloured vomit, the range of shades it came in thanks to the fruit flavoured alchopops that had become so popular. Extortionate prices for designer drinks kids threw up within minutes of gulping? He shook his head, wondered what the hell the world was coming to.

A couple of youngsters were shouting the odds on the balcony of the flats above the shops that bordered the precinct, calling Coupland a *Fat Wanker.* Older ones had plucked up courage to throw missiles at the police car; empty bottles of Vodka and Bacardi Breezers shattered as they hit the pavement along Chorley Road. A quick call to uniformed back-up had the older ones rounded up and given a bed for the night, a message that sent the younger chancers fleeing to the safety of their homes, not daring to venture out for the remainder of the evening.

After what seemed like an age the patrol car door swung open and Melanie teetered across to where a slightly better dressed look-a-like Melanie stood with a man who looked uncannily like Ricky. This was the second time she'd seen him; the first time had been earlier in the evening and the shock of his likeness had sent her reeling, staggering back to the car and the sympathetic female officer.

The reconstruction had initially been arranged for a couple of days earlier when the crime was one of assault, but when Ricky passed away there'd been talk of postponing it. Coupland had cornered Melanie, told her there was more chance of finding Ricky's killers if the reconstruction went on air now, rather than in a month's time when the horror of the attack had died down and the public's attention had moved on to someone else's misfortune. Melanie had agreed and, with the aid of a couple of tranquillisers and a nip of gin, she had overcome her fears of returning to the scene of the attack. Two of her nieces and a nephew had volunteered to play the part of her children. Her own daughters, Nicola and Sharon, were huddled in the back of the patrol car watching the proceedings in silence. Unable to hear what their mother was saying they stared at her mouth as they tried to lip-read her instructions.

A couple of well-built men dressed in black hovered by the pub's entrance. One lit a cigarette and inhaled on it greedily, the other shooed the smoke away as he waited for the cameras to roll. The Melanie look-a-like nodded at something Melanie said, then laid her hand reassuringly on the woman's arm.

'I wonder if she does a lot of this kind o' work,' Sharon asked her sister. They were huddled together on the back seat of the patrol car, trying not to lean on their brother Paul who was still smarting over not being at his father's bedside when Ricky had passed away.

'Maybe that's the only kind of work she can get,' Nicola replied.

'She's a copper, luv,' the WPC sitting in the driver's seat informed them. 'So are the men playing the bouncers and... your dad.' She paused, wondering whether she should part with the next piece of information. 'Keeps the costs down,' she said gently.

Paul tutted in disgust and slammed out of the car, crossing the pavement to stand close to the cash machines on the corner, hands thrust deep into his pockets as he balled them into fists. Someone out of sight shouted Action and suddenly he was transported to four nights ago, watching his family leave the pub and walk quickly past the empty taxi rank before making the fatal decision to cross the square and head towards the stop for the all-night bus.

'Come on,' Ricky called out to Melanie who was struggling in her heels. 'The bus is at the bloody lights already.'

Sensing someone approaching them Melanie turned to see two men pass her quickly, their faces obscured by hooded sweatshirts pulled low over dark baseball caps. She called a warning to Ricky, yelled at him to watch out, but no sooner had he turned than he was set upon, one of the men drawing back his arm as though readying himself to jar Ricky hard below the ribs. There was a glint of steel in the lamplight and then the men went silently on their way, running this time.

Ricky was standing with a look of surprise on his face; his eyebrows arched high on his forehead. Melanie ran towards him, asked what was wrong but he didn't speak. He'd been holding his stomach, and when she pulled his hand away black liquid pumped out of him and he collapsed onto the ground. Cradling her husband she rounded on their children who were standing nearby.

'He's bleeding,' she roared, 'get some help.'

The girls froze at the sight of their old man's injury, began to sob in unison. Back in the patrol car Nicola and Sharon avoided each other's eyes.

The nephew who was playing Melanie's son jolted into action shouting 'Bastards!' He bolted after the retreating figures before running back around the corner in response to his mother's screams. He pushed past the bouncers as he ran into the pub, yelling that his old man had been stabbed.

'Stop!' the real Paul yelled. He ran in front of the camera crew waving his hands, angry tears streaming down his ashen face. Coupland hurried over to where the boy stood pointing at the policemen-dressed-as-doormen in front of the pub's entrance.

'What is it?' Coupland demanded, gripping the youngster's shoulders firmly in an attempt to calm him down.

'That's not fucking right!' Paul shouted over and over, until one by one everyone stopped what they were doing and turned to stare. Spit flew from his mouth as he shouted, gesturing at the two bouncers.

Something was wrong.

Needled, Coupland looked from the boy to the small crowd that had gathered around the edge of the square. Bystanders, rubber-neckers, gawpers. He felt a sensation; not fear but something like it. Apprehension? If so, it was the sort of apprehension that could be felt in a crowded place.

'When I ran into the pub I had to ask the barman to call an ambulance.' Paul spat.

He was rabid with fury, his eyes staring wildly at Coupland as though it were his duty to second-guess his anguish. When Paul spoke next his voice was low, deadly. His words dripped like acid from his tongue. He pointed to the pretend bouncers standing at the pub's door, gave them a look as though he'd found them under his shoe.

'Them two,' he spat, 'weren't even fucking there.'

Half turning, Coupland scanned the blackened doorway of the building behind him. Two men were lurking in the shadows. When they saw him look in their direction they withdrew so quickly he wondered if he'd seen anyone at all.

*

Amnesia was overrated. Angus came to this conclusion after a shrink his parents had organised came to see him at home and attempted to explain why he could no longer remember anything relating to the discovery of Tracey and Kyle's bodies. When the first officer on the scene had sat with him, scribbling notes into a pad, he'd been able to answer general questions: How long had he and Tracey been married? What age was Kyle? But he'd been unable to recall the name of the client he'd been to see, or even the purpose of his appointment.

All he could remember was that he'd gone to a business meeting, which hadn't lasted long… and suddenly his life went into free-fall, splitting into two distinct parts, his life before, and his mere existence afterwards. The events that followed once he'd let himself into his home were a blur. All he'd been able to tell the policeman was that they'd been happy, over and over, until he stopped asking questions and put his notepad back in his breast pocket.

It was perfectly normal, according to the psychiatrist, for the mind to protect itself from re-living something that was distressing, something that could otherwise tear you apart. The doctor had made it sound like a good thing, as though he was lucky that the scene he'd stumbled upon had vanished from his mind. But he was wrong, because Angus had been left with all of the pain, all of the emptiness, but none of the comprehension. None of the memory, just an unfathomable loss. Part of him was missing, he just couldn't piece together why.

This shouldn't be happening, he kept saying to anyone who'd listen.

But it already had.

CHAPTER 22

Nothing was straightforward when it came to the skewed landscape of depression. It was two in the morning when Coupland took an apologetic call from a male nurse on duty in Hope Hospital's Casualty Department. He'd barked his name and rank into the bedside phone automatically, throwing the nurse off track.

'Sorry to disturb you, Sergeant, but we've been given your details as next of kin.'

Coupland's blood ran cold. Lynn, had something happened to her? A feeling of panic washed over him. Why had she insisted on working as normal when their lives were now anything but? He held his breath as he waited for the nurse to continue.

'We have a…' There was a pause while the caller cleared his throat, tried to put his words in order. 'We have a homeless gentleman here.' Coupland's first thought was one of relief, that Lynn was okay – at least for now. But then it occurred to him that it meant Joe was with them and he sat bolt upright, swung his legs over the edge of his bed as readied himself to spring into action.

'What is it?' he demanded, his mind running into overdrive.

'Severe trauma to his face and neck, sir, I'm afraid. He's in surgery now.'

Bastards, Coupland thought. Someone had had a pop at him, overpowered him in a doorway. Probably one of the local wasters who saw picking on the vulnerable as a leisure activity.

Up there with dog fighting and beating up the missus.

'I'm on my way,' he said, imagining Joe's quiet dignity in the face of mindless violence. He sneered at the term, for what other kind of violence was there? His blood pumped faster through his veins as rage gripped him.

'How the hell did it happen?'

The nurse cleared his throat again, and Coupland was just about to shout for Christ's sake get on with it when the man replied hesitantly, as though, because he was the messenger, he feared he'd somehow get the blame.

'He put his head through a shop window.'

'Bollocks.'

'There are witnesses. According to the police who brought him in, he'd been seen staggering through the Arndale Centre in the city centre, drunk as a lord, swearing. Then he just seemed to… snap.'

One of the more intriguing aspects of being on medication, Joe had once observed, was the way that it whittled away life's rough edges, all potential sharp emotional corners, left you feeling placid about the shit life threw at you.

'*I don't want a life of numbness*,' he'd insisted when Coupland broached the subject of taking something for his depression. '*I want to grasp life by the thorns until my fingers bleed – isn't that what I deserve?*'

Thirty minutes later and Coupland found himself back in the emergency department of Salford's Hope Hospital, barking Joe's name to the same pissed-off-looking receptionist who'd been on duty the night Wilson had been admitted. She pointed half-heartedly to the triage area, to a middle-aged man with shaved hair and a tired smile. The male nurse recognised Coupland's name from his warrant card, held out his hand. 'He's still in theatre, I'm afraid. Made a right mess of his face.

One ear was hanging on by a thread.'

Coupland clenched his jaw. He felt as though he'd been struck dumb, couldn't think of a single sensible question to ask. 'Will he be all right?' was about as much as he could muster.

'Well, put it this way,' the nurse continued, 'he won't be needing a mask come Halloween.' At that moment Coupland's own face resembled a mask, a mask of anger that silenced the other man's attempt at further humour.

'Look,' the nurse said, keeping his bald head low as though ashamed at his tactless remark, 'I'll take you through to the ward; you can wait for him there. Poor old bugger.'

'Old?' Coupland repeated. 'Old?' He was still pissed off with the nurse's attitude, wanted to put the little upstart in his place. He looked at the paunch beneath his tunic, the balding scalp disguised by the barber's razor. 'He's younger than *you*.' That seemed to shut him up. The nurse led the rest of the way in silence, walking briskly so that there was no possibility of a further conversation between them. He pointed to a room with a television and uncomfortable looking chairs, told Coupland to wait there, that the ward sister would come for him soon. He then walked over to the nurses' station, shared a joke with a weary-looking woman at the desk before looking back and pointing Coupland out to her. He raised a hand and waved before disappearing through a set of double doors. Coupland ignored him.

He rubbed his eyes and looked around the drab room that cried out for a lick of paint and the flick of a cloth. He wondered what had happened to the men and women who used to push floor polishers up and down the corridors all day and night. Hospital floors never seemed to shine any more. Another cost-cutting exercise by the men in suits, he supposed. A cheap Formica table displayed out of date grubby magazines with curled up edges. The television was mounted so high on the wall that only the top five per cent of the population had a say in the programmes that were aired since there was no remote control. A woman with large breasts gyrated on screen in front of a gleaming American car. A group of black men in bandanas postured for the camera and sang, white teeth and gold chains gleaming in the Los Angeles sun. The sound was turned down. Coupland thanked God for small mercies.

He folded then unfolded his arms. Wished he'd brought a paper, a coffee, anything to relieve the monotony of just sitting there. He'd radioed the station on his way over to the hospital, left a message for the uniforms who'd brought Joe in to have a report on his desk first thing. Somewhere right now some copper was cursing him, unable to clock off until he'd finished his paperwork, probably wishing he'd left the pissed-up wino well alone, waited for someone else to call it in. Coupland shrugged, didn't give a toss where he stood in the division's popularity stakes. His head was in turmoil. Given his state of mind and his hatred of hospitals he wasn't even sure what use he'd be, but being useful was way down on his priorities right now.

Right now, all he was bothered about was staying awake, keeping alert long enough to see his friend wheeled safely onto the ward.

CHAPTER 23

Alex couldn't sleep. She'd been distracted all evening and even Carl had had the sense to keep out of her way, taking himself off to the spare room to work on his computer once Ben had gone to bed. She tiptoed downstairs to the kitchen so as not to disturb them, poured herself a glass of milk before perching on a stool at the breakfast bar.

She'd expected her visit to Professor Ansell to allay her fears, to reassure her that only a certain type of person acted the way Tracey had. Instead she'd come away with the worrying knowledge that everyone had a tipping point, and when that point of no return was crossed, anything was possible. The lesson she'd learnt was that there were no lessons; the relentless point of trying to understand Tracey's actions was futile.

Any action could be rationalised.

She wondered if she and Carl should count their blessings, quit while they were ahead. They had a family and it worked. Why tempt fate?

Tracey Kavanagh's Filofax lay open before her on the kitchen counter. Alex had called a couple of the contacts in the address book after she'd read Ben his bedtime story, most of them distant acquaintances from Tracey's ante-natal group who'd read about the tragedy in the evening news but hadn't really kept in touch with the young mother and her son. They asked Alex to pass on their condolences to Angus. There were only a couple more pages to go, and she flicked through them idly wishing it were morning so she could complete her calls and hand it back. Carrying the address book around had become an unwelcome reminder of the investigation and she chastised herself for bringing it into her home. No wonder she had trouble sleeping.

Outside the kitchen window the sky was at its darkest giving the illusion that black card had been placed against every pane of glass, obscuring any decent view. Alex stared into the gloom and sighed. What kind of a life had she chosen for herself? It was the middle of the night and her husband and son were sleeping soundly upstairs while she read through the address book of a dead woman.

She flicked through the remaining pages, comforting herself that at least there weren't many names left for her to call: there were no entries on the Z page, a solitary Young, George, on the page before, and only three listed under W. She dragged her finger down the list of names: Watts, Paul; White, Sandy… but it was the final entry that caught her off-guard, making her sit up and try to second-guess its significance.

CHAPTER 24

Coupland stayed on the ward long enough to see a sheepish Joe come round from the anaesthetic. He'd only had time to utter a relieved 'we'll talk later,' when the ward sister ushered him out. He put up no resistance, following the exit signs as though searching for the Holy Grail. Rather than return to the car park, he headed towards the Maternity wing, to the smaller entrance at the side of the building that led directly to the Neo-natal Unit, its entry system the most secure in the hospital. He pressed the buzzer, glaring at the CCTV camera while staff went in search of his wife. After a couple of minutes Lynn let herself out of the building, giving him a look that told him she thought he'd lost the plot. He probably had. Bathed in light from the illuminated sign behind him he resembled an avenging urban angel.

'What are you doing here, silly?' she chastised him. 'I'm going to have to take this as my break now, you realise that, don't you? Got to practice what I preach.' She was smiling as she said it, so no real harm done.

'Come here,' Coupland pleaded, folding her into an embrace, nuzzling the top of her head with his lips. His eyes were shiny, his mind alert, processing thoughts that for the moment were better left unsaid. 'You know that I love you, right?' he whispered into her hair, 'and that everything else is just bollocks.'

Lynn nodded into his chest, her hands moving greedily over his shoulders.

After all these years he was still like a caged animal, one liable to turn wild at the slightest threat. 'I feel so fucking helpless,' he confessed, 'it doesn't seem right that there's scum out there—'

'Shh…you can't talk like that,' Lynn chastised him. 'No one deserves cancer.' Coupland wasn't so sure. They stood like that for several minutes, holding onto one another, each afraid to let the other out of their sight for very different reasons.

*

Coupland had been back on the road five minutes when his radio crackled to life. A disturbance had been reported at an address on the west side of town, close enough to where he was now for him to respond. He recognised the address immediately as Angus Kavanagh's place. He'd radioed back that he'd take the call, that he was nearest to the location and that he knew the family.

Correction – he knew the sole survivor.

As he pulled into the cul-de-sac his eardrums were assaulted by the boom of a stereo on full blast, blaring from the windows of Angus's home. Every window was open for maximum effect. Angus's neighbours, Diane and Harry White, were standing on the shared expanse of lawn between both their homes, looking up at the master bedroom window, towelling dressing gowns wrapped tightly around them. They hurried towards Coupland as he climbed out of his car.

'It's not that we wanted to complain, did we Harry?' Diane informed him, looking to her husband for corroboration. 'You know, about the noise?' She pointed to Angus who was precariously leaning out of the open upstairs window. 'We were worried about what he might do…'

Coupland ignored them and shouted up to the lone figure

in the window: 'I'm coming in Angus, now you can either open the door or I'll get some ham-fisted copper keen to clock off his shift to knock it down, it's up to you!'

Seconds ticked by as Angus digested the information.

Despite the adjacent properties being spaced widely apart, the commotion had alerted most of the neighbouring homes to Angus's distress. The cul-de-sac was too upmarket to twitch curtains; instead the man of each house had been dispatched outdoors to glean what they could. And so, with wax jackets thrown hastily over ironed pyjamas, they began to seep noiselessly out of their homes and huddle in a small group at a safe enough distance from the exploding scene. Chatting nervously amongst themselves they half listened to each other as they craned their necks to watch their neighbour rail against the world.

One clean-cut city type asked Coupland if he needed any help. Coupland's mouth twitched. There was a time when he would've taken the piss, asked if maybe he could extend his overdraft for there was little else the nosy bastard was built for. Wiry glasses and smug, he looked like someone who crunched numbers for a living.

'You could maybe arrange for rent-a-crowd to go back indoors,' Coupland answered instead. The man was as good as his word, dispatching embarrassed onlookers back to their pushy wives, excitement at the troubled house over for one more night.

At that moment the music blaring from Angus's stereo stopped. Seconds later the front door opened just wide enough for Coupland to squeeze through. He caught a glimpse of Diane and Harry as they looked over helplessly, motioned for them to leave him to it. As the front door closed behind him Coupland's eyes adjusted to the darkness, took in the state of the hallway. Where previously there had been order, now there was disarray, milk bottles had been taken in but left on top of the hall table to turn sour. Dirty footprints criss-crossed the floor tiles like a mad aunt's embroidery. Letters and junk mail lay scattered across the floor. The sitting room was no better. Each chair contained a combination of discarded clothing and blankets. A bottle of scotch stood atop the square coffee table, beside it a brochure from the local funeral home and a blister pack of paracetamol.

Was this what Coupland had to look forward to?

Framed photographs clustered every surface: Tracey, Kyle and Angus in every combination: a younger, happy Angus with an older couple Coupland took to be his parents; Angus in his graduation gown; on a climbing expedition; on his twenty-first birthday, surrounded by helium balloons and homemade banners. Angus cleared a space for Coupland to sit on the armchair nearest the fireplace.

'Didn't expect you to be making night calls, Sergeant,' he said as he swiped a pair of running shoes from the chair opposite. His words slurred into one another and Coupland reckoned there were more bottles than the one on the coffee table lurking about.

He turned in his seat so the scotch was out of his line of vision. 'I was passing,' he replied, 'Thought I'd drop in.'

Angus had only just lowered himself into his chair when he jumped back to his feet. 'Need a drink,' he said, then raised a hand as if to halt the protest Coupland had no intention of giving, adding: 'Not the alcoholic type,' before staggering from the room. He was wired, edgy. His edginess seemed to permeate Coupland's skin. The detective looked around the room for something to focus on.

A framed wedding photo stood upon the mantelpiece.

Taken after the service, the picture captured the newly married couple before they left for the reception. Sitting in the back of a white limousine, a beaming Tracey held out her hand to her new husband. Dark hair framed pretty eyes, a heavy smattering of freckles across her nose. A sun worshiper once, before it got added to the list of contraband pastimes up there with smoking and unprotected sex. Coupland couldn't remember the last time he and Lynn had taken a holiday. In the photo Angus was gazing at Tracey's wedding ring, trying to suppress a grin that suggested he felt like the cat that got the cream.

It was probably the happiest day of his life.

No prizes for guessing which was his worst, Coupland thought, as he turned to face the young widower zig-zagging into the room carrying two mugs of strong coffee. 'The sedatives leave me groggy,' Angus explained, 'and the booze leaves me numb.' He spilt a little of the contents of the over-full mugs onto the light-coloured carpet as he handed one to Coupland. Angus didn't blink. *Not like I'm going to get a row for the mess,* he seemed to shrug.

Now wasn't the time to point out that coffee would make his edginess worse, that soon enough he'd need the pills again to calm himself down, swilling them down with drink to soften the edges while he waited for the drugs to kick in. He was on a downward spiral that Coupland had seen many times before, although this time he understood the temptation. He'd be doing neither of them any favours if he stayed too long. He put his untouched coffee on the table.

'Tell me about Tracey's pregnancy,' he began.

This seemed to throw Angus, and he jerked his head up sharply as though he'd been asked a trick question. It took several seconds for him to compute Coupland's words. He leaned back into his armchair, swung his polished black shoes onto the coffee table. The soles were barely worn, insteps yellow and unmarked.

'We did all the things expectant parents enjoy doing,' Angus told him. 'Making preparations for the baby. Talking about the future, making plans. Everything was coming together.'

'How did Tracey cope?'

'Tracey? She just got on with it. Didn't like to make a fuss. Didn't even go to all her ante-natal appointments because she felt fine. Said the doctors were trying to turn something that came naturally into a science.'

Angus's head bounced as he spoke, as though someone was pulling his strings. It gave the impression that he was emphasising certain words, as though making a point: *fuss* and *science*. Perhaps Tracey didn't like people looking into her private business.

'And Kyle's birth?'

Angus shrugged. 'You're asking the wrong person, aren't you?... It was a long labour, I remember that. She'd wanted a home birth but we learned the baby was breech. She didn't want to go into hospital, waited until the very last minute before she let me take her in.'

Coupland found himself wondering if Angus had cried in the hospital's car park after Kyle had been born, decided that he probably had. He looked at him now, wondered how it must feel to bear such loss.

'Tracey used to be a sound sleeper,' Angus continued, 'but after the birth she would wake up instantly as soon as Kyle cried out, and feed him on demand, which meant she was getting up every two to three hours. She'd sit with him in a chair in the nursery in semi-darkness, feeding and burping him until he fell asleep. Sometimes when she put him down she didn't return to bed, just stayed in his room by the cot – less disruptive that way, she said.' He nodded at the words *she* and *said*. They featured a lot in Angus's playback of their life together. Another man who did as he was told for a quiet life, Coupland pondered. Or a man so besotted with his wife he overlooked the things she didn't want him to see.

'I saw an easel in the mud room, Angus. Did Kyle like to paint?'

'Och, he loved it,' Angus gushed. 'His teachers commented on how good he was from the day he started school.'

Coupland nodded. 'Funny, then,' he said, 'that there aren't any pictures around the place.'

Angus seemed to sober in an instant. He looked around his surroundings with fresh eyes, surveying the walls. 'I suppose you're right.'

'Any reason why that is?' Coupland prompted.

Angus shook his head from side to side. He looked confused, or as though he was trying his hardest to remember something.

'Tracey liked to keep everything Kyle drew. Said his pictures were too good to stick on the wall with Blu-tak, fading over time. Told me she was going to frame them.'

'Do you know where she kept them?'

A shrug. Angus raked his fingers through his hair. 'No.'

Without warning Coupland got to his feet. The earlier uneasiness had got the better of him and he knew why. He wanted a drink. Something to quell his panic at the thought of losing Lynn. He needed to leave now while he still had power over his actions. He walked out into the hallway, blinking several times in succession. Standing in a row beside the front door were two pairs of trainers – a woman's and a small child's. The smaller shoes were unfastened but he recognised the loosened knot already tied onto the larger pair – tied the same way as the noose had been around Tracey's neck. He picked one of the trainers up, found himself disappointed rather than relieved that he now had the evidence which proved Tracey's fatal knot had been tied by her own hand.

Angus's voice startled him.

'Do you need them for the investigation?'

Coupland nodded.

'Take them.' Angus instructed. He sighed for so long Coupland wondered whether he ever intended to draw breath again. He looked at Angus's unshaven face and crumpled clothes; signs screaming out that trouble lay ahead. He needed to get out of there, away from the whiff of boozy breath, back to his own home. While it still felt like one.

CHAPTER 25

Coupland flicked through the TV channels, tutting at the number of stations devoted to selling cheap jewellery and useless cleaning products to the infirm and the inebriated, for who else would be watching TV at this time? The rest of the country was asleep, or trying hard to be. Lynn's shift wouldn't end until 7am and the thought of climbing into an empty bed depressed him. He flicked off the TV, finishing the dregs of his coffee before heading back into the kitchen for a top up. Sleep was overrated anyway. His mind flitted to Roddy Lewisham, then Angus, alone in their picture-book homes; to Joe, homeless, jobless, two different ends of the social spectrum yet the road they travelled was the same. Three damaged men, connected to him by a common fate. He shivered. What kind of a friend was he, what kind of a *person,* if all he could do was offer platitudes?

Tracey Kavanagh's trainers, placed carefully in an evidence bag, stood guard in the hallway. They were plain, white. Expensive but non-descript. A bit like the life she'd tried to carve out for herself. The coffee machine was empty bar a tarry mess at the base of the glass jug. He rinsed it through, refilled the tank with water, taking comfort in the familiar sounds: the grinding of beans into powder, the pumping of water and the hissing of steam.

Everyone had a past. A relationship with friends or family that defined them, spanning locations and generations intertwining and meshing together until it was hard to tell where one ended and the other began. If Coupland closed his eyes he could see his father lurching into the cramped flat of his childhood, sense the chaos that his presence brought. He'd been in the Job too, retired on ill-health, couldn't cut it as a civilian. He'd never meant Coupland any harm, probably loved him in his own particular way, but his bouts of anger, his unpredictability, had left their toll. *We are the sum of our parts,* Coupland spoke into the silence, *whether we own up to it or not.*

Yet something about Tracey Kavanagh baffled him. She was self-sufficient, capable, had no need for close friends, yet that only explained the here and now – or rather her life leading up to her suicide. Kyle's birth had brought a certain routine into her marriage, a comforting predictability that most families fell into, and on this topic Angus was well versed. Yet anything concerning Tracey's past was a blur.

What had she done with her life before she'd had Kyle? Before she'd met Angus for that matter? There was rumour of a brother but no contact details, no other family to speak of, but did that really equal no history? When Coupland had accompanied Angus back to the family home he'd scanned every wall and surface yet found no photographs of Kyle's maternal grandparents or uncle. In contrast, photos of Angus's family could be found in several rooms.

Neither could Angus recall any anecdotes that Tracey had told him about where she'd grown up, no snippets that spoke of a happy childhood or even a crap one for that matter. For all intents and purposes it was as though the day he'd met her she'd been plucked from thin air.

Coupland racked his brains to think what circumstances could make someone appear as if by magic, entering people's lives without leaving a ripple – and he could think of only one. The realisation when it came felt like something cold inside him had shifted; raised questions he knew he wouldn't like the answers to. But first, he'd need to make several calls, cash in a few favours if he wanted to confirm his suspicions.

Morning wouldn't come fast enough.

CHAPTER 26

Alex could tell it was a fee-paying school by the gleaming spires and sweeping drive that shouted *money* and lots of it; a convoy of Chelsea tractors slowed at the turning circle allowing immaculate mothers to drop off their offspring without having to step one foot out of the car. A group of girls dressed in identikit navy skirts and white blouses beneath navy and red blazers hurried towards the entrance. Their expensive uniforms brought to mind Alex's own school ensemble: grey acrylic jumper over a nylon skirt which she either rolled up at the waistband to make it shorter or wore down around her hips to add length, depending on the fashion at the time.

She'd attended the local secondary modern; a sixties-built building standing several storeys high, as though the local education authority equated height with prestige. The building had been demolished several years ago to make way for the erection of a *community school*, whatever that was.

An uncomfortable feeling settled on Alex's shoulders yet she wasn't sure why she felt so ill at ease, she just knew she'd be glad when her visit was over. There was something unpalatable about places like this; places that excluded the masses in favour of the privileged few that didn't sit well. It was the implicit superiority of the place, from the grand design of the building to the impeccable uniform, ways that claimed *we're better* without ever having to prove it. In a nutshell she resented the way that not paying for Ben's education made her feel inferior, implying that what she was able to offer him was second best.

She shrugged her shoulders, rationalising she shouldn't beat herself up over circumstances she was unable to change.

She'd approached several mothers dropping off children similar in age to Kyle but had found it nigh on impossible to get them to wind down their car windows let alone step out from their warm leather seats. A closer inspection revealed why – most of the women wore pyjamas beneath their Barbour jackets – almost a uniform in itself. Alex stifled a smile.

Not so immaculate after all.

She had better luck indoors, where a young female teacher in formal attire offered to take her through to Kyle's classroom while the rest of the school attended morning assembly. The woman smiled at Alex kindly.

'I only wear this first thing in the morning when the little darlings are dropped off and again at home time.' she said conspiratorially, referring to the knee-length black gown she wore over a mid-calf skirt and white blouse. 'Makes the parents feel as though they're getting their pound of flesh.' The tone in her voice hinted that she thought the whole idea was ridiculous. Alex liked her immediately.

The woman, who turned out to be Kyle's form mistress, introduced herself as Miss Caplan. Olive-skinned with frizzy hair, she displayed dazzling teeth when she smiled, although the smile was short-lived when she remembered the purpose of Alex's visit.

'I was so sorry to hear…' she began, casting around for the right words, deciding there weren't any, '…we all were.' She raised her arms helplessly, as though addressing a Gospel choir. 'If only we'd known…' A life summed up in four tragic words. That was half the problem, Alex supposed, there was nothing anybody *could* know, no danger signals they could have responded to. She tried to find something anyway. 'What was your impression of Mrs Kavanagh… of both Kyle's parents for that matter?'

A pause.

'They were a nice couple,' Kyle's form teacher began. 'Thought the world of Kyle. Both looking forward to the birth of his little brother or sister.' Alex blinked away an image of Benson cutting into the foetus, focussed instead on the tight curls spiralling out of the teacher's scalp. She'd picked up on the woman's hesitation, wondered if she'd misread it. She decided to backtrack.

'How would you have described Kyle's mother, Miss Caplan?'

'Please, call me Adele,' she insisted. 'She liked to keep her own company, hadn't fallen in with any of the cliques that quickly emerge in any school.' Her arms had dropped back to her sides and she folded one across her stomach forming a barrier between them, placed her other hand under her chin as though her head had suddenly become too heavy for her neck to support.

'She was quiet, but I wouldn't say shy, just choosy about the company she kept, I suppose. She got involved with school life – helped out on trips, that kind of thing. Joined the PTA, typed up the minutes of the meetings, manned the stalls at the Christmas Fair – she was always willing to help out. Everything she did she based around little Kyle; it was clear she doted on him.'

Alex's heart seemed to jar at the words, but she wasn't about to let her feelings get in the way of her professional responsibilities. She let the moment pass.

'Had she been acting strangely recently, anything strike you as odd?'

Adele pursed her lips in concentration. 'Not really… I suppose if I had to pick something then she was perhaps a little quieter over the last week or two – I'd put it down to tiredness during her last trimester. I didn't ask, she wasn't someone you felt comfortable enquiring after.'

Another pause.

'What is it, Adele?' Alex persisted. She didn't have the time to tiptoe around but it was obvious Kyle's teacher was troubled about something. She decided to appeal to her on a personal level, in the hope that it might loosen her tongue.

'Look Adele, if you do know something, *anything* that can help me piece together this horrendous puzzle I'd appreciate it. I've never come across anything like this.' She paused, checking Adele was really listening to what she had to say.

'How does a doting parent turn into a killer overnight?' she pleaded. 'I *have* to find out why. I have a young son, I need to point to a reason that explains why this happened, to reassure myself I won't one day wake up and be a danger to my *own* child.' *Christ,* she had no idea where *that* came from, but somehow, baring her soul to a stranger seemed to calm nerve endings that had been jingling ever since she'd taken on the case.

And better still Adele began to nod. 'Well, one thing struck me as odd, I suppose,' the teacher informed her, unfolding her arms and letting her neck do some of the work again. She leaned back against the cool wall of the corridor. 'Most parents think they've given birth to the next Messiah, right?' She turned to face Alex, looking for corroboration. 'You mentioned you've got a son, so you'll know what I mean?'

Alex inclined her head. She tried not to picture Ben's face when she was discussing Kyle, fearful that tragedy was contagious.

Adele nodded, satisfied. 'I only have to compliment one

of my pupils on the slightest achievement and suddenly his parents think they've a child genius on their hands. If he wins the egg and spoon race, the following week he'll be despatched to school with running spikes and a personal coach in tow wielding a stopwatch. If they do well in a maths test mummy hires a tutor to coach them towards exams they're nowhere *near* mature enough to sit.'

Adele studied Alex's reaction, saw her cheeks flush at the description of precocious parenting.

'Sounds familiar?' she asked, smiling.

'Ye-es,' Alex acknowledged. 'Only I hope to God I'm not as bad as that.' She remembered a conversation she'd had with Carl about booking piano lessons for Ben because he'd been thrilled with a toy organ they'd bought him the Christmas before. Carl had laughed, hadn't realised she had been serious.

'So it was all the more surprising really,' Adele continued, forcing Alex to snap her attention back to their conversation, 'that when I made a point of speaking to Mrs Kavanagh about her son's quite obvious gift, I got a cool reception. She was so disinterested in his emerging talent that I thought *Sod it, if she's not wanting to nurture it then I bloody well will.'* Her voice caught, and she turned away for a moment, began walking towards the Infants' wing. 'You know, I saw Kyle run over to his mother on Monday.' She swallowed hard, as though admitting a difficult truth. 'I'd let him keep a piece of work he'd completed in class. He wanted to show it to her and, to be honest, I thought that if that didn't melt her heart then nothing would.'

She shook her head slowly, as though trying to fathom the unfathomable. 'She had a talented son yet she seemed to treat his gift with shame.'

Another pause.

'He ran over to her so pleased with himself, holding up his

work, showing her what he'd done.' A single tear rolled down Adele's check leaving a track in her make-up.

'What did Tracey do?' Alex asked softly.

Adele dabbed at the corner of her eye with a tissue she kept folded inside the sleeve of her blouse. She blew her nose, leaving a trail of stringy snot above her lip. Alex glanced away while Adele wiped it off with her index finger and thumb.

'She just seemed to freeze… and then…'

'Go on.'

'Well, she gave him this weird look… as though he was a stranger she was trying to place, like she was studying him for the first time… I was called away at that point, another parent wanted to speak to me, and by the time I returned they had gone.'

They had travelled the length of the school along a central corridor lined with senior school artwork and photographs of different year groups, the only constant on the changing roll call was the row of staff seated in front of each photo, older and fatter as the years went by. At five years' service Miss Caplan was still considered a newcomer, she explained with a wry smile, and Alex had been about to say something similar, that the police force probably wasn't so different in that respect, when Adele led her into Kyle's classroom and pointed out a drawing that sent every one of Alex's senses reeling.

CHAPTER 27

'I reckon he was abandoned when he was a kid, there's a whole load of pent up anger going on down there.'

'I'd heard he wanted to be a butcher but that wasn't upmarket enough for his Cheshire set family.'

'Maybe it's attention seeking.'

They watched the first incision as the blade sliced through flesh from chest to navel.

He had their attention now. Coupland stood beside Turnbull in the observation gallery in the hospital mortuary. The room overlooked the operating table where several feet below them Harry Benson was conducting the post mortem on Ricky Wilson. It was a fairly routine procedure; the cause of death was peritonitis, which had set in following the knife wound that had ruptured Wilson's bowel. Benson was searching for evidence that might help identify the weapon used, or the assailant.

The advantage of the observation gallery was that it gave them a bird's eye view of the procedure without the background ambiance of sloshing sounds and the smell, which Benson had warned would be particularly ripe given the infection that had set in. He communicated with them via a microphone positioned above his head. The officers watched as he stood back to allow a technician to take photographs of the damage to the bowel and repaired entry wound, which would be used for evidence if the case went to trial.

Coupland was aware that most people thought pathologists

were macabre, harbouring a zest for the dead that bordered on ghoulish; that they'd chosen this path because of their inability to connect with living patients, yet he knew that was far from the truth. If anything, Benson's bedside manner was better than most of his peers whose patients still had a pulse. He could be sanctimonious at times, but he was respectful of the dead and the part that they'd played in the lives of others and, importantly, Coupland trusted his judgement.

Benson smiled at the banter wafting down from the gallery above, the gentle mickey-taking the detectives used to distract themselves from the bloodthirsty procedure. He understood it was a coping mechanism, nothing more. 'You plods are all the bloody same,' he observed good naturedly, 'full of wise-cracks to mask the sound of your bowels twitching.' What he said was true, Coupland conceded. He could handle the violence; it was the aftermath he found disturbing: the blood splatters and clots; the punctures and leaks; the brain fluid and shit.

A murder was like a relay race, Coupland reasoned as he watched Benson take measurements of Wilson's knife wound before placing his finger into the bowel to feel where the surgeon had carried out his futile repair. A few minutes more and he'd be able to inform them as to the *how*; it was up to them to take that information and establish the *who*.

Benson leaned into the microphone and addressed his audience: 'A single sharp-edged blade caused the penetrating wound.' Coupland nodded impatiently, this much he knew. The pathologist held up a bloody mass of guts as though he was about to make a pagan sacrifice. 'I can tell you that the weapon penetrated Wilson's abdomen at an upward angle with such force that it sliced open his bowel.'

The organ was tubular without beginning or end; Coupland thought it looked like a bloodied eel. Benson pointed to an area that to the untrained eye looked no different from the rest.

'As I said, the weapon sliced open his bowel, stopping only when the knife hilt came into contact with the surface of his skin.' Benson smiled smugly; *that* had shut the buggers up.

'From the measurements I've taken,' he spoke directly to Turnbull, 'I *can* tell you that the blade used matches the length and width of your standard kitchen chopping knife.' He dropped the organs back into the body's cavity, nodded to his assistant that he could begin stitching Wilson back together.

'From the angle that the knife entered the body, I can also advise that the attacker was shorter than his victim. Given that the victim was five foot nine, I hope this helps narrow down your suspects.'

Turnbull whooped and punched the air before flashing Coupland a grin. 'The Sportsman serves food prepared on the premises, Sarge, and Jimmy Brooks and Charlie Horrocks are a pair of short-arsed little fuckers.'

Coupland nodded, his eyes twinkling at the prospect of nailing Wilson's killers. 'About bloody time.'

He'd been about to follow Turnbull when Benson signalled that he wanted a word. He assumed it wasn't about Wilson – technically it was Turnbull's case and he wouldn't thank Benson for going over his head.

'Can it wait?' he said to Benson. He still had to brief DCI Curtis on his suspicions about Tracey Kavanagh and there was no way he was missing bringing Brooks and Horrocks in – every job had its perks and he'd especially relish this one.

'Give us five,' he called reluctantly to Turnbull, who was already on his radio requesting back up to meet them at the wine bar where Wilson's wife had had her bag stolen.

Coupland walked the short distance along the corridor towards the pathologist's office, waited for him to emerge from the lift's double doors.

'I was going to call you,' Benson said briskly as he led the way to his large book-lined sanctuary behind a glass-panelled door. Inside the immaculate room there was a wide metal desk on top of which sat two wire trays containing several files. A laptop sat between them, its power cable unplugged at the wall.

'I keep forgetting to re-charge the bloody battery,' Benson explained ruefully, and Coupland wondered if these lapses in memory had any bearing on why he preferred working on the dead.

'After a while it seemed like too much trouble to start up the stupid thing.' Benson confessed. 'So it's lucky for you I still make notes by hand otherwise you'd be waiting forever for me to power this damn thing up.'

He regarded the computer as though it was some alien object that had landed on his desk. 'Management dictated it would improve efficiency,' he muttered scornfully, 'if we typed up our own sodding records. You can see where it'll end: clerical staff being laid off in a cost-cutting exercise, then in a year's time the NHS'll recruit hundreds more consultants to free up the time the current consultants spend doing bloody admin.'

He looked over at Coupland, 'Sorry,' he said sheepishly, 'rant over.'

Coupland thought of the refurbished canteen at the station, manned by fully trained catering staff, only for the accountants to advise that there wasn't enough money in the budget for the kitchen to prepare fresh meals. It was not surprising the surly assistants thought themselves overqualified to spend most of their time defrosting and reheating trays of ready-made meals – specially prepared trays of food that had been made *off* the premises. All in the name of progress.

'You wanted a word?' he prompted Benson.

'Yes, sorry.' Benson was a couple of years younger than Coupland, dark-skinned, with a swathe of unruly black hair and dark eyes. Would look more at home on an archaeological dig, Coupland mused, then reminded himself pathology was just another form of excavation – into the recesses of the human body. He watched Benson methodically work his way through the pile of files on the left and right of his desk, frowning.

'Ah,' he said moments later, 'here it is.' He waved the manila file in his hand, and Coupland could see – written in thick black marker pen – the name *Kavanagh, K.*

Benson motioned for Coupland to take a seat on one of two plastic chairs on the other side of his desk, before taking a seat in his own comfortable leather chair. He opened the manila file.

'As you know Kevin, most people can be classified by their blood type.' He paused, waited for Coupland to nod before continuing.

'While there are extremely rare or exotic blood types, most of us can be classified in to the A, B, O or AB blood types.' A pause for Coupland to nod again.

'The fact that AB type exists at all told early investigators that every individual actually carries two alleles, or traits that determine blood type – one inherited from each parent. You with me so far?'

Coupland wondered how many times he'd have to nod. He'd tell him when he needed a diagram. 'Further studies proved that if each parent contributed an O allele, the child would be type O, but if one parent contributed an A and the other an O, then the O dominated.'

Coupland's nod was slower this time, but he was still with him.

'A and B do not dominate each other though, so if one parent contributes an A and the other a B, the child displays both traits and is AB. Obviously having no A or B factors, two O parents can only have O children. Two AB parents can never have an O child, as neither of them has an O allele to pass along. Two parents of types AO and BO could combine their O's to produce an O child, their A and B to produce an AB child, their A and O to produce an AO child, or their B and O to produce a BO child.'

Letters of the alphabet swam across Coupland's line of vision. His patience, which had been wearing thin, finally snapped:

'Christ, man, what the hell are you trying to tell me?'

The pathologist smiled smugly. 'Angus Kavanagh's blood group is O, and Tracey's is A. This means that Kyle's blood group should be O. Only it isn't. His blood group is AB. Assuming he got the A from his mother….'

'Yes?'

'Then Angus couldn't be his father.'

CHAPTER 28

What was it about the little man syndrome, Coupland thought as he and Turnbull returned to the pedestrianised square that was the scene of Ricky Wilson's murder. It seemed to him that what vertically-challenged crooks lacked in height they made up for in cruelty, and Brooks and Horrocks were no exception. Their criminal records were littered with violent assaults – gang fights with crowbars and broken paving stones, car doors rammed against victim's skulls. There had been rumours that they'd been involved in an attack on a city centre chip shop – pushing the owner's hand into the deep fat fryer – but no charges had ever been brought, their victim insisting he'd been clumsy; such was the fear of getting on the wrong side of the evil pair. Once, Brooks had drilled a hole through a rival's hand for a bet.

They were the failures of rehabilitation; the detention centres they went to weren't the sort of places to make them think about what they'd done, just provided them with a new stomping ground, a new set of dodgy contacts. Now they'd found work as doormen they were being paid to torment punters legitimately – *the management has the right to refuse admittance* – they must have thought they'd died and entered bullyboy heaven.

'Nice to see they're performing a useful function in society,' Coupland growled as he and Turnbull walked through the entrance to the wine bar. It was lunch-time and already half full. A group of bank clerks giggled in the corner as they handed a pimply youth in a polyester suit a parcel and a greeting card with *Happy Birthday* emblazoned across the top. Behind Turnbull several over-made-up girls from the local beauty college entered the bar; matching white tunics and off-white trousers strained to reveal ill-fitting bras and dimpled buttocks. It was hard not to notice their ankles were an alarming shade of orange. Feet encased in white wooden clogs clip-clopped as they passed a group of track-suited youths swigging greedily from bottles of imported beer, nudging and jostling each other now that totty had arrived.

'Ignorant bastards,' Coupland muttered to Turnbull. Wilson wasn't even cold, yet the staff and regulars carried on as though a stabbing outside their premises was no big deal.

Brooks and Horrocks were standing at the far end of the bar. Their shift wasn't due to start for another twenty minutes, the wine bar manager had informed Turnbull when he'd telephoned ahead. The pair were dressed in civvies but looked just as menacing. The place reeked of market-bought aftershave and attitude. They stood with two carbon-copy mates Turnbull recognised as witnesses who, when questioned earlier, had confirmed both bouncers hadn't left the doorway when the attack took place, providing them with an alibi. They all wore the identikit uniform of shaven heads and pierced or razored eyebrows. They were dressed in cropped-sleeved t-shirts that emphasized thick-set muscular frames, but it was a superficial bulk, one that would turn to flab before any of them hit thirty. Coupland should know.

Occasionally the job could be a pain in the arse but he never stopped getting pleasure seeing toe-rags' smiles slip whenever he got too close for comfort, and today was no exception. As he locked eyes with the younger of the two suspects he saw a moment of panic flit across Horrocks's dumpy face before bravado set in.

'Shouldn't you be out catchin' bad guys?' Horrocks called out mockingly before looking to his mates for approval. Several pairs of eyes bore into the two policemen. Coupland could tell what they were thinking:

Wankers.

'You've already taken our statements, this wouldn't be harassment, would it?' Horrocks challenged, and Coupland didn't need to guess which of the old biddies he'd questioned the other day had pushed this gob-shite into the world.

'I need you to clear something up for me,' Coupland replied as patiently as he was able.

'Not tellin' you owt without a lawyer,' Horrocks spat back, to group-wide approval. Coupland could feel himself rising to the bait. He wasn't surprised the runt was getting under his skin, all he knew was that he wanted him to shut the fuck up and preferably *soon,* before he started his shift with his knob for a necktie.

'Ignore 'im, officer,' Brooks replied as easy as anything. 'Always happy to help the police with their enquiries.'

Brooks shot Horrocks a sly grin, the gesture indicating that he was taking the piss, showing himself for the moron he was; that he didn't give a shit about the investigation, about the fact a man's life had been wiped out because of something he and his pathetic mates had done. Coupland was tempted then, sorely tempted to lash out quickly, break the smug fucker's nose. He glared angrily at Turnbull, narrowing his eyes. He'd sailed close enough to the wind on a couple of occasions over the years; couldn't afford to give Complaints any more ammunition. One thing was certain: he couldn't afford to screw up now Lynn was ill. Turnbull's demeanour defused his anger, his docile features telling him he was counting down the days to his thirty years, his eyes signalling he should get a grip. Coupland nodded, willing his anger to drain away.

Let the prick think he'd got the better of him.

'I want you to remind me, again,' he asked, 'what did you do when Ricky Wilson's son ran into the bar shouting that his dad had been stabbed?'

'How could we do anything?' the young gob-shite asked. 'By the time we heard about it the ambulance had already been called.'

'Funny that,' Coupland replied as innocently as he could, 'a slip of a lad running past you on the door.' He turned to Turnbull. 'Imagine finding yourself in Wilson Jnr's predicament and you need help urgently. You are right outside the friendly local wine bar, with two strapping bouncers in the doorway. What would you do?'

'I'd call for *them* to get help,' obliged Turnbull. 'No point trying to barge past them if it meant I could stay with me old man.'

Coupland had a glint in his eye as he listened, a look that told them they'd tripped up and he'd heard it, and his face creased into the smuggest smile he could muster. He couldn't resist smirking at the look that passed between the group – not just Horrocks and Brooks but rent-a-crowd too, for the youths standing with them had supported their claim that they they'd not moved from the bar's entrance; the mouthy little gob-shite had just made them all out to be liars.

'Well, gentlemen,' Coupland informed them, enjoying the moment, 'I'm loving your company so much I'm going to bring you back to the station so I can sit on your faces a while longer.'

He turned to Turnbull. 'Transport on its way?'

Turnbull nodded. 'Yup. The full shebang.'

While the waiting police vans took the youths over to the

station at Salford, Turnbull stayed with Coupland while the DS instructed uniformed back-up to conduct a further search of the premises – including the neighbouring retail outlets and banks. Back at the station's control room DS Robinson would coordinate the search of Brooks' and Horrocks' homes – once a warrant had been secured.

On the way back to Coupland's car Turnbull paused on the pavement, shook his head as though he'd heard something unbelievable. His face looked pained, as though he'd sucked on a lemon or was trying not to pass wind. He eyed each passer-by with suspicion.

'I know I should be past disappointment by now,' he said aloud to Coupland as though practising a speech, 'but it riles me when I see how communities have changed. People don't seem to give a shit anymore.'

What he said was true, Coupland conceded. There might well be a great deal of prosperity in Salford – you only had to look at the development along the quays to see that – but there was no longer the same sense of *We're all in it together* that there'd been when he was a lad. It used to be that living in a neighbourhood gave you an identity, a sense of who you were and where you belonged. Even the DCI, Coupland conceded, with his fancy education and university degree, was a Salford boy through to the core – why else would he have stayed when brighter lights beckoned? Now, following the dismantling of the shipyard and the subsequent redevelopment of the quayside into waterfront apartments, a new breed of wealthy incomers had been attracted to the city who had no understanding of – or gave a shit about – the local population. Over time this had fostered a resentment amongst those left behind – both financially and socially - that bred an *every man for himself* culture.

Coupland could feel it, the general shift in consciousness that despised the old virtues of solidarity, of people coming together to make things better. Instead, a new breed of people was emerging, a breed that screwed everyone to get the best deal they could. Greed was good, apparently.

'What can you expect these days?' was all Coupland said. He had neither Alex Moreton's passion nor his DCI's vocabulary to get into a political debate, especially at this time of day without the whiff of the barmaid's apron to bolster him.

CHAPTER 29

By the time Coupland got the chance to brief DCI Curtis it was mid-afternoon. The meeting had lasted all of five minutes: suspects for Ricky Wilson's murder had been brought in for questioning; the news about Kyle Kavanagh's paternity and his suspicions regarding Tracey Kavanagh's past. Curtis had held up his hand, like the Pope performing benediction. 'Anything to corroborate this?' Curtis asked irritably, as though he was being kept from something more important.

'A mate who started the same time as me but kept his nose clean,' Coupland countered, 'transferred to police intelligence… Let's put it this way: he confirmed my suspicions, wasn't willing to add anything else, and absolutely refused to let me quote him.'

'Shit,' Curtis had simply responded, using his hand to shoo Coupland out of the door before making the first in a series of calls.

Coupland's head was spinning with the news about Kyle's paternity, though he still wasn't sure of its relevance. A clerk from the coroner's office had been on the phone checking whether there were any extraneous considerations that he needed to declare that would extend his investigation into Tracey Kavanagh's filicide – a polite but firm way of telling him to pull his finger out. Surely, the information he'd just gleaned wasn't material to the case? All that was required of him was to confirm there'd been no foul play and, in the grandest scheme of things, there hadn't been. Before he had an opportunity to decide what to do next the phone rang, its shrill ring breaking into his thoughts. He barked his rank and surname into the mouthpiece. The male voice was nasal and ever so slightly condescending. Coupland raised his eyebrows, gave a couple of grunts into the receiver before replacing it. 'And why have I suddenly become so bloody popular?' he muttered, before hauling himself to his feet.

*

John Doyle, Acting Deputy Chief Constable of Greater Manchester Police, was waiting for Coupland and DCI Curtis in his office, on the third floor of Chester House HQ, a twenty-minute drive away from Salford. The journey there seemed to take forever, both men taking it in turns to second-guess the intention of the summons.

'We're being warned off.' Coupland spoke quietly, as if already resigned to the fact. There was a time when the prospect would have pissed him off but he was learning to accept there were things he had no power over.

'Does it matter?' Curtis asked aloud, 'I mean, to the investigation. Whatever's gone on has no bearing on what Tracey did to her son. We know it's a murder-suicide, whatever they tell us won't change the outcome.'

'Mebbe.' Coupland agreed. Privately he thought differently. Alex had accused him of trying to find a rationale for Tracey's crime but what was wrong with that? People justified their actions all the time – whether they were entitled to or not. The only difference was that Tracey had chosen to keep her reasons to herself.

They managed to find a parking space that wasn't designated to the senior ranks and, upon presenting their ID to the civilian on the desk, they were ushered through to the corridor outside the DCC's office.

John Doyle was considered one of the good guys; he'd served as a PC in Manchester City Centre before climbing the ranks to uniform Chief Inspector at Bootle Street, and was the senior officer on the ground when the IRA bomb decimated the Arndale Centre in 1996. He moved on to head up the Murder Review Department before taking over responsibility for the Serious Crimes Division, Force Intelligence and Liaison.

Coupland had met Doyle a couple of times before, once when he'd addressed a hastily-arranged press conference following a spate of drive-by shootings in Moss Side and a delegation of officers had been swiftly drafted in to provide an impenetrable united front during Doyle's whistle-stop attendance. He'd caught Doyle's eye for a couple of seconds, received nothing more than a curt nod. Coupland wondered what it was that suddenly made Doyle want to acquaint himself better.

'In you come,' Doyle barked, having opened his door just wide enough to stick his head around. By the time Coupland and Curtis had risen from the corridor's moulded plastic chairs and pushed the door all the way open, Doyle was back behind his impossibly tidy desk. There was a man seated across from him. He was wiry with a narrow face, every feature elongated – from his droopy eyes to his frown. He stood just long enough to shake both men's hands, introducing himself as Detective Superintendent Paul Randall, responsible for the Serious Crimes Operational Team.

'Thanks for coming in at such short notice, Kevin, John,' the DCC began. Coupland clocked the use of their first names, an attempt at intimacy he didn't feel. He decided to go along with it, see where it led. He knew Doyle's remit, understood enough about Randall's team at SCOT to know this wasn't a social call…

Randall spoke next, his smile not quite making it to his eyes. 'Can you tell me exactly what your interest is in Tracey Kavanagh?'

CHAPTER 30

Alex answered her phone on the second ring. It was an internal call, the duty sergeant informing her that somebody by the name of Charlie— 'I know the name,' she interrupted, 'tell her I'll be right down.'

The size of the woman waiting in reception came as a shock. She was larger than the person Alex remembered passing in reception the previous day, not that she'd paid much attention. As wide as she was tall, the thought *larger than life* came into mind.

'Charlotte?' Alex asked her, just to be sure.

'You're the detective who's been leaving messages on my answer phone then?' The woman replied in a friendly manner, extending her hand. 'Please, call me Charlie.' Her face was broad and flat with rosy cheeks and eyes that came alive when she spoke. She had a strong Irish accent, Northern Ireland, Alex thought. She found herself wondering if she'd grown up there at the height of the troubles. Wondered if that was why she'd moved over here.

'Look,' said Alex, suddenly feeling hungry, 'there's a café round the corner, can I buy you a coffee? Might even be a teacake in it, if we get a wriggle on.'

The woman smiled, nodding, and as she moved beside her almost rhythmically Alex was enveloped in a heady perfume: poison, if she wasn't mistaken. Charlie obviously liked her jewellery; both wrists displayed a collection of silver bangles that jingled as she walked, making her sound like a human wind chime. They passed Charlie's white Citroen Saxo in the public car park, an old car that had seen much better days. The woman glanced to see Alex taking in the dented bodywork and pulled a face.

'Had my car stolen a couple of weeks ago in Boothstown. Turned up the following day in Little Hulton. Buggers couldn't even do a proper job of stealing it.' She nodded towards the dented rear door. 'If I claim for the damage I'll lose my no claims bonus.' Alex smiled sympathetically.

The café was a short walk away from the car park and Alex was relieved to see that the interior lights were still on and the chairs hadn't been stacked upside down on the tables yet. A businessman sat at a table in the window, tapping keys on a laptop. Alex asked if Charlie had heard the news report concerning Tracey's death and the woman nodded solemnly, her ample face falling into a frown.

'A terrible tragedy, so it is,' she said, moving her head from side to side, oblivious to a falling tendril of hair that had worked its way loose.

'What was your connection to the family?' Alex asked her as she opened the cafe door and stood back to let Charlie pass.

'I work for the prison service,' Charlie replied, not really answering the question. Alex waited for her to continue as they hovered by the counter waiting to attract the attention of the café assistant. 'I'm a counsellor,' Charlie continued. 'It's my job to help high security offenders come to terms with their actions. Throwing them behind bars isn't enough—'

'—Well,' Alex interrupted good naturedly, 'I've a few victims' families who'd testify to that.'

Charlie tried to return her smile but it was clear she was irked that Alex had deliberately misinterpreted something she felt so strongly about. She tried a different tack. 'Sometimes,' she continued, 'part of the process is for them to talk to their victims, to face up to what they've done. Show their remorse.'

Alex thought of Siobhan Lewisham's hard-faced killer, wondered how he was supposed to talk to his victims. 'You're a clairvoyant then?' she joked, kicking herself immediately when she saw the set of Charlie's jaw.

'Sorry?' but it was obvious to both of them she'd heard. She was either challenging Alex to step up to the plate and say it again, or offering them both a way out. Alex hoped it was the latter.

'Doesn't matter,' was all she could muster.

'Many serious offenders carry a great deal of guilt,' Charlie continued, 'and one of the first steps of the healing process is to learn to forgive themselves. It's only when they're able to do that, that they can truly express remorse to their victims or their families.

Alex wasn't entirely sure of that, had her own strongly held opinions on exposing victims to their aggressors a second time, but now wasn't the time to get into semantics. The waitress came over and pointed to a table close to the counter, flicked a cloth over the top of it before going back to the counter for her notepad. Alex sat down opposite Charlie, grateful for the pause in conversation. The waitress took their order, told them she'd run out of teacakes but had a couple of left over Eccles Cakes she could throw in at no charge.

Alex waited until they were alone again, mulling over what Charlie had told her. Her brain stepped up a notch as she tried to make sense of what she'd just heard, of its relevance to Tracey Kavanagh, but it had been a long day and there were still too many dots to join up.

'I'm sorry,' she said, as she watched the waitress prepare their order. The businessman had long since packed up his laptop and gone, leaving two shiny pound coins at the side of his coffee cup. They were alone. The waitress, although within earshot, was busy singing the words to a top ten hit.

'I don't under—'

'Tracey's father was so sorry for what he'd put her through,' Charlie interrupted, leaning forward slightly as she looked Alex directly in the eye. 'All he wanted was to make amends.'

CHAPTER 31

Room temperature spiralled throughout the station. Air conditioning hadn't featured in the building design; it was Salford not San Diego, no one expected heat like this. Within hours the interview rooms stank of stale body odour. Coupland peeled off his jacket and tie and undid as many buttons on his shirt he thought he could get away with before someone in HR screamed harassment. As it was his shirt exposed more chest hair than both male and female staff were comfortable with and the sweat rings under his arms had turned several shades of yellow.

He didn't give a toss.

It wasn't a beauty parade, and with streetwise smart-arses like the one sat in front of him now he needed all the weapons he could lay his hands on. He looked through the file in front of him; saw that Turnbull was bringing out his notebook.

'Now then Danny,' Coupland began, 'want to tell us what was really going on the night Ricky Wilson was stabbed?'

'What?' Horrocks's mouth stayed open long after the word had left it.

'The night Ricky Wilson was stabbed,' Coupland repeated slowly, 'Your little Fagin's den of thieves had been doing you proud, eh?' He made a point of consulting his file. 'Only the victim's husband wouldn't give up, would he? Started to make a show of himself.'

'Why, what have people been saying?' The voice had taken on a harder edge.

'That the girls are well known in the area for shoplifting and petty theft. Something of a regular pastime for them. Seems that you and your mate take a share of their haul, using your old contacts to distribute house keys and credit cards so they go to the right people – brings a whole new meaning to recycling, eh?' Coupland taunted.

'That's bollocks.' Eyes reduced to mean little slits.

The female duty solicitor sitting beside Horrocks wrinkled her nose. 'You've been questioning my client for twenty minutes, Sergeant. I suggest you charge him or call it a day.'

Coupland forced his mouth into a smile, wondering for the thousandth time what made a nice young woman want to defend balloon heads for a living. He'd spotted her straight off when she'd entered the station. Slim. Fresh-faced, not overly made-up. A decent enough girl. He thought of his Amy, how he'd feel if she said she wanted to follow in his footsteps, or worse still, *defend* the little fuckers. He shook his head as though denying the thought the chance to take root. Amy was too clean for this game. Too pure. Oh, she led him a dance from time to time and he knew it, he wasn't stupid, but even her small acts of rebellion never amounted to the thoughtless actions that brought even decent members of society under his radar. Add to the mix the thieves and junkies, the insane and the downright evil that crossed his path and it was no surprise he was a cynical bastard. Every day he thanked God for Amy and Lynn, for balancing out his world. A lump formed in his throat that he couldn't seem to shift.

'Sergeant Coupland?' The lawyer regarded him closely, trying not to stare at the greying curls beneath the deep V of his shirt.

Coupland grunted as he cleared his throat. The uniformed officers searching the refuse bins belonging to the businesses along Chorley Road had been instructed to dig the street up if they had to. He needed to buy time. He flashed her his best compliant smile.

'Anyone for coffee?' he asked genially.

*

Alex had planned to go home. She'd intended to put Ben to bed herself then sit Carl down and share her fears about having another child. She wanted their discussion to be rational, an exchange of views rather than the tired slanging match that took place whenever she came home late and hungry, frustrated by some aspect or other of the case she was working on.

Feeling rational was becoming an alien concept these days. As each day wore on she became aware of a constant nagging in the pit of her stomach, a simmering unease like a pressure cooker at boiling point. One false move and she felt ready to explode. Her eyes were heavy, one blink away from tears. Maybe she was expecting too much of herself. Maybe right now she just couldn't do rational. She'd asked Coupland once if he ever felt the same, if coming into contact with badness each day had changed him as a parent. It was the one time he'd been serious with her, showed her a vulnerable side to his personality she hadn't previously known existed.

Being a parent means being paranoid, he'd counselled, *it went with the territory. But being a cop meant they saw things on a daily basis most parents didn't see. They* saw *the murdered children and the accident victims and the physical damage that one person could inflict upon another. Close up in graphic detail at the scene of crime, during the post mortem, in the photographs pinned on the incident room wall.*

Alex sighed; she thought she'd come to terms with all that. She'd learned to separate Alex the detective from Alex the wife and mother. They were two separate people that she tried to keep apart, like exes at a wedding.

Yet Tracey Kavanagh had made those two worlds collide. For how could she delve into Tracey's life and not make comparisons with her own? Here was a mother who idolised her child, loved him above everyone else, yet still caused him harm. Alex thought of Ben and the ferocity of her love – a love that would make her lay down her life for him – or kill others who got in her way.

Sometimes she'd catch herself looking at her son and her chest would fill so much she was overcome with a mixture of joy and dread; joy at the future and what it might bring, and dread, for exactly the same reason. She'd always been a capable person, but what if she stopped being able to cope, what if the constant worry became too much? The fact that she would die for Ben was etched through her veins, but this case had made her question herself. Could she ever become so desperate that she'd contemplate taking him with her? She needed to work out the answer to *that* – and soon, for until she did, another child was out of the question.

She'd intended to share these thoughts with Carl tonight. Carl, the free spirit who travelled through life by the seat of his pants and by God she envied that. It was partly the reason she loved him; if she'd hooked up with someone too much like herself they'd have worried themselves into the grave by now.

As it was, her plan for them to talk had gone up in smoke. Her meeting with Charlie Preston had been more than fruitful; it had been like walking through an over-ripe orchard. Sergeant Coupland would need to hear the information she'd become privy to as soon as possible, so after walking Charlie back to her car Alex had scanned the staff car park to check his car was still there before turning around and heading back towards the station steps.

*

Coupland looked as though he had taken root in his chair. He sat perfectly still, holding the telephone receiver mid-air with a perplexed look upon his face. His meeting with Doyle and Randall in the DCC's office had been a series of revelations, each one more shocking than the other. It just went to show, he thought to himself, that it was possible to love someone, share a life with them, yet not really know them at all.

People, and the lies they told, never failed to surprise him.

And disappoint.

He looked at his watch; Horrocks's solicitor had agreed to a twenty-minute break; the evidence his team uncovered during that timeframe would be crucial. They had motive, but nothing concrete to back it up. He'd made a call to Robinson, no luck so far. He slammed his fist down hard onto his desk in frustration. Surely these two head cases weren't cleverer than they looked?

He'd been intending to call Benson, clear up the final piece in the jigsaw that was Tracey Kavanagh's life. Bad news came in threes, didn't it? He might as well go for the full house. He was hunched over his desk cradling the phone with his shoulder when Alex walked purposefully into the CID Room. 'Sarge—' she began, but he held up his hand to silence her.

He nodded into the phone, said a series of 'uh-huhs' before letting out a long slow whistle. When he replaced the receiver he had the look of someone saddened by what they'd been told even though they'd been expecting it, like the death of a terminally ill relative. He stared into the corner of the room so hard Alex turned to see if someone was there but the space beside her was empty. She moved sideways a little so she entered Coupland's line of vision.

'Sarge!' she said impatiently, 'Tracey Kavanagh was on the

Witness Protection Scheme.' Coupland's eyes locked onto hers in an instant. He nodded his head gravely, wondering what else she'd discovered. Alex was a grafter, all right; she'd overtake him on the career ladder in the not too distant future, no question.

'I know' he replied evenly, reluctantly bursting her bubble. 'And I've just discovered the identity of Kyle's father.'

CHAPTER 32

Alex dragged her own chair to beside Coupland's desk and sat down. She was put out he'd uncovered Tracey's secret the same time she had, but her natural curiosity got the better of her. 'Charlie could only give me the bare bones. She'd been brought in to deal with Tracey's father after he was sentenced, her main role is coordinating restorative justice.'

'No kidding, eh?' Coupland skitted, 'Well I wish her well with *that*.'

Alex nodded impatiently. 'Go on. *Give*.'

Neither Coupland nor Curtis had been allowed to keep the confidential file Paul Riddell had slid along the desk to them but that was no hardship. What Coupland had read in the quiet of the DCC's office would stay with him for a lifetime.

The file provided a detailed back-story:

Number 17 Langley Road was an unassuming house in a quiet terraced street in the north west of England. The owner, Harold Sweetmore, was cheerful and hardworking. His wife Margaret was a busy, lively mother. They were generally liked by the neighbours either side of them, harmless enough by all accounts, although there had been gossip about the to-ing and fro-ing that took place most nights. Some felt they disciplined their children too harshly, although there was nothing specific enough to warrant a call to Social Services.

Harold was a trawlerman by trade, the photo on his file depicting the broken veined skin of a man exposed to harsh weather. A wide face topped with dark wiry hair. He skippered fishing boats in the North Sea, which took him away from home for weeks at a time. He'd tried to find local work but wasn't built for staying indoors, his frame too bulky to sit behind a desk, his shovel-like hands too big for work on a production line. Fishing was in his blood, was all he'd ever known as man and boy.

His father had been a trawlerman, like his father before him and during his childhood he'd never once ventured beyond the tight-knit Hebridean community where he'd been born. Fishing was a way of life, put food on the table, clothes on the islanders' backs and when the sea went against them every man on the island would join in the rescue without a second thought, continuing their search until all were accounted for – alive or dead. Life was a series of unforgiving storms punctuated by loss. The trade suited Harold; he thrived on the constant battle against the elements, the surge of power he felt when he'd ridden out another storm. He began to live for the rush of adrenaline that ran through him every time he was in complete control.

He met Margaret, the woman who would later became his wife, during her only visit to the island when she and her widowed mother came to visit an elderly aunt. A plain woman, with a body intended for heavy work, Margaret was flattered by Harold's attention. The romance blossomed quickly and when she returned home he accompanied her, moving her mother into a smaller bedroom at the back of the house, installing himself and Margaret into the master bedroom. Unwilling to learn a new trade he returned to his trawler on the North Sea, coming back to the family home every couple of weeks.

Riddell had then picked up the story: 'To help supplement the family income Margaret took in lodgers, young girls who'd had problems at home, most were runaways, many had grown up in care. Misfits.'

'Easy to spot if you know the places to look for them,' Coupland acknowledged. 'Bus stations, railway stations, burger bars.'

'The neighbours sniggered that it was always young girls,' Riddell continued, 'but their laughter turned to horror when the extent of what had been going on began to unravel in front of them. It was during a particularly hot summer that neighbours complained of a foul smell emanating from the back of the terraced row of houses. It was only when the drains were inspected, and the source of the smell pinpointed to be coming from the Sweetman property, that police were alerted.'

The Acting DCC John Dawson's input reminded them he was still in the room: 'Background checks into the couple revealed that following a complaint by an ex-lodger several years earlier they had been charged with a number of offences, including rape and buggery, but the case against them was dropped when the prosecution witness failed to testify. The Senior Investigating Officer…' He paused, scanning the case notes in front of him, '...a DI Janet Reid, who had also investigated the initial allegation, began to suspect that something terrible was going on at the house and obtained a search warrant enabling her to gain access to the property. The following day police started to dig up the garden.'

Coupland and Curtis read the remaining notes in silence; seemingly neither senior officer wanted to provide a voiceover for what happened next. A mechanical digger was brought in to remove the topsoil, followed by a team of thirty officers, working in relays, sifting shovelfuls of earth through a sieve. This was the start of an excavation so gruelling all officers involved would receive stress counselling. On the second day a trowel hit something hard and the loose soil was scraped away to reveal a human skull. Over the next five days the decomposing bodies of six women were unearthed in the grounds of the house. The victims had been sexually assaulted then strangled, their bodies trussed up with rope.

During the trial the lodger who'd escaped the Sweetmans' clutches gave evidence against the couple. A runaway herself, they'd offered her board and lodgings in return for looking after their two young children. What she hadn't bargained on was the couple's bizarre open marriage and their desire to include her in their sex games. After a couple of nights she took off but felt guilty about leaving the couple's little girl and her brother, who were no strangers to their parents' bed. Occasionally, to spice things up, or to keep them going while they were in between victims, they turned on their own son and daughter, raping them for entertainment. The children, both teenagers by the time of the couple's arrest, gave evidence against their parents in court.

Convicted for six murders, the couple were sentenced to life in prison. Weeks later Margaret was found hanged in her prison cell. She had made a noose by plaiting strips of sheet together. Standing on a chair she had tied the home-made ligature to a ventilator shaft, looped it around her neck and kicked the chair away.

Coupland kept the summary he gave Alex as succinct as possible, not pausing for questions but maintaining the pace of an oncoming train. Now he was coming to the part that had connotations for everything that came after; it had the potential to be a very long night.

He continued: 'Apart from the bodies, one of the most startling discoveries inside the house were the hundreds of pictures adorning the walls. Lifelike drawings and pen and ink sketches of family members posing with each unsuspecting victim were displayed in every room. This evidence played a crucial role for the prosecution in proving that the victims had been on the premises, at least long enough to have their portrait taken. The signature at the bottom of each drawing was D. Sweetman; the couple's eighteen-year-old son, David.'

The file notes contained reports from experts commenting on David's drawings of his sister. The teenager had managed to capture a range of emotions from fear to anger to sheer helplessness, the mental trauma she'd witnessed evident in every shadow in her young face, in every brushstroke planted on the canvas. These portraits would later secure him a place at Art College.

'However, such was the animosity towards the family as a whole that his gift became a curse. When drawings of the victims fell into the hands of local hacks they became front-page news, fuelling the public's belief that the brother and sister were somehow implicated in their parents' crime. Outraged families of the victims refused to believe that the couple's children had been completely unaware of the murders. They simply did not understand enough about fear, and the survival instinct, to accept that they'd merely been trying to make the best of a terrible situation.

For the teenagers' safety they were put onto the Witness Protection Scheme. Social Work reports stated that the brother and sister remained unhealthily close despite having recommended that since their parents' sexual deviances were their only example, the siblings should be separated. David was transferred to Scotland but after dropping out of Glasgow School of Art with depression he moved to Aberdeen, began work for an oil company.

The girl, born Tania Sweetman, became known as Tracey Harding. She set up home in a one-bedroomed flat in Salford, working in the refectory at the local university where she met a third-year accountancy student from Edinburgh and set about building the family life she thought she deserved. When she discovered she was pregnant a hastily arranged marriage was arranged much to the disapproval of her fiancé's parents. 'I doubt they even knew the half of it,' Coupland muttered sadly.

Alex was still trying to make sense of what Coupland was saying. She vaguely remembered the case. It had been front-page news for several weeks during the summer the bodies were discovered, and again throughout the trial. Reporters had camped outside the court to be assured a ring-side seat. But several years had elapsed and, like most tragedies that involve other people, she'd relegated it to the back of her mind. Coupland got up out of his chair and walked around to the front of the desk, perched a buttock onto a corner and folded his arms. There was an aspect of the job that challenged him the most; the constant second guessing of other people's reactions in order to explain why they took one particular course of action over another. He'd tried to put himself in Tracey's mindset, tried to understand which of the secrets that were beginning to emerge about her life would have put the most pressure on her marriage. It had been the drawing Alex had brought back from her visit to St. Margaret's that had done it. The startling charcoal sketch Kyle had drawn of his mother that normally resided on the classroom wall. Coupland had placed it beside a copy of a front-page newspaper article from the time of Sweetman's trial which he'd slipped into his pocket while Curtis blew smoke up the senior officers' backsides, thanking them profusely for their willingness to share. The article displayed one of David's most striking pieces of work: an ink drawing of a young Tracey, found at Langley Drive.

They were almost identical.

Despite the obvious time lapse between when the sketches had been drawn, it was clear that they were of the same person; even more striking was the similarity in styles. All Coupland had needed to do was ask Benson to make a couple of calls to the maternity unit where Margaret Sweetmore had given birth and within an hour he'd had his worst fears confirmed.

'You said something about Angus's parents not knowing the half of it,' Alex prompted him, trying to read the time upside down on his watch, wondering what Ben was doing right now.

Coupland seemed to sink into himself, as though he felt saddened even saying the words out loud: 'The baby Tracey was carrying when she walked up the aisle wasn't her husband's,' he informed her, 'but her brother's.'

CHAPTER 33

'You mean they kept on seeing each other?' Alex asked, 'even after the Witness Protection mob had gone to such lengths to separate them?'

Coupland nodded. 'It seems it was the brother who was reluctant to let go. Kept turning up at the university like nothing had changed.'

'Tracey must have encouraged him,' Alex challenged, 'or are you saying he forced himself on her?' Coupland gritted his teeth in order to bite back a rebuke. Alex seemed Hell-bent on seeing the worst side of Tracey's character, no matter what. He shook his head. 'No,' he said evenly, 'Psychiatric reports confirm she consented to their relationship, but then she met Angus.'

'So, having suffered rejection, David hightailed it back up to Scotland?'

'Pretty much,' Coupland acknowledged, 'and in theory, that should have been the end of it.' Now it was Alex's turn to fill in the blanks. 'Seems daddy had a guilty conscience,' she began. 'Wanted to make amends for what he'd done to Tracey, Tania, or whatever her name was back then. He contacted the offenders' agency Charlotte Preston works for in a bid to help him rebuild bridges with his children. She'd already been in touch with David—'

'Jesus.'

Alex nodded. 'Can you imagine what that little family reunion would have looked like?' They both sat grim-faced while they contemplated the devastation that meeting could have wreaked on Tracey's happy family.

'Did David know?'

'About Kyle?'

Alex shook her head. The agency Charlotte Preston worked for did not disclose personal details about victims to their clients without the victim's express permission, but the lines were so blurred in this case it would be impossible to be sure protocol had been followed with any degree of certainty.

'Kyle was the one good thing she'd salvaged out of her life before Angus, a secret she was willing to carry to the grave. How could she see her father without Angus finding out about her past and the infamous family she'd been born into? And if her father discovered she had a son – a son whose artistic heritage was undeniable, where would that lead? He would have been bound to pass this information onto her brother and what then? Would David want to claim a part of his son's life?'

Alex summed it up: 'A ticking time bomb.'

Coupland nodded. 'But how in God's name did this woman – Charlie – track David and Tracey down?' Coupland asked, perplexed.

'It seems David has written to his father in prison on and off over the years via a post office box number set up by the protection squad, so getting him to agree to a meeting was easy.' This seemed plausible. 'And Tracey?' Coupland persisted, 'How did this woman locate Tracey so effortlessly when I've had to put my crown jewels on the line with the powers that be just to *look* at the Witness Protection file?' And then it dawned on him.

CHAPTER 34

Before Coupland could articulate his suspicions to Alex the call he'd been waiting for came through; the knife thought to have been used to murder Ricky Wilson had been found. Coupland let out a long slow breath of relief. He sucked it back in again when he discovered it had been located in one of the large industrial bins belonging to the Italian restaurant wedged between the wine bar and a bank. The butcher-style knife – identical to the one used in the wine bar's kitchen - had been wiped, although specks of blood could still be seen around the base of the handle. It would be a couple more days before they'd know for sure if it had been the knife used in the attack, and whether the assailant's prints could be lifted. Reluctantly Coupland had had to let Brooks and Horrocks go, though he couldn't help staring Horrocks's lawyer down when she smiled just a little too smugly.

'Feel you've achieved something, do you love?' Coupland rounded on her when they crossed paths at the station's front desk. She shook her head as though *he* was the crazy person before sweeping through reception to meet her next client. *Hard-faced bitch,* he found himself thinking in an uncharitable moment.

'Don't take it personally,' a voice behind him sympathised. He swung round to give whoever it was a mouthful, to remind them it was easy being objective when it wasn't your fucking case, *your* knackers on the line. He found himself looking into Alex's concerned face and he swallowed his reproach.

'Their prints'll be all over it,' she reassured him. 'You just need to chill out, play the long game. You didn't expect the knife to be hidden under Brooks' pillow marked *here I am* alongside a note to the Tooth Fairy did you? Even so, you're hardly dealing with Einstein here. They're banged to rights, we just need to make sure that due process is followed so the bastards are put away for a long time.'

She leaned towards him, placing her hand reassuringly on his arm, 'You've got 'em, you're just waiting for the red tape to catch up.' Coupland nodded. All it had taken was a few well-chosen words and he felt his insides stop twisting. At least for the moment. Alex hesitated. 'Is everything okay, Kevin?' she asked, tentatively, 'only, you seem—'

'—What?'

'Uptight.' She stepped into his orbit so their voices wouldn't carry along the corridor. 'Things any better with Lynn?'

He felt as though he was choking, his throat constricted so that he was incapable of making any sound or even drawing a breath. He remained still, fearful any action might give him away. He counted to three. 'Just leave it, eh?' was all he could muster. Alex shrugged her shoulders as she backed away; there were some people you just couldn't help. Crestfallen, Coupland tried desperately to think of something to say that would make amends. 'Any news yet?' he blurted, referring to the result of the sergeant's exam. Alex was touched he'd remembered, none of the others had bothered to ask.

'Nope,' she said, dejectedly.

'No news is good news,' he said, smiling sheepishly.

She looked at him as though he'd left his fly open, responding in a way that told him she'd spent far too long in his company. 'What kind of bullshit is that? How can anyone say not knowing something is good?'

'Christ Almighty, I don't know!' Coupland grumbled, 'I was trying to be nice. Wish I hadn't bloody bothered.'

Alex adjusted the strap of her shoulder bag and laughed, although it came out like a witch's cackle. She shook her car keys at him. 'I'll be off then, before you come out with any other pearls of wisdom.' She'd almost reached the station's exit when Coupland remembered the newspaper clip about Tracey Kavanagh, he'd been about to tell Alex about it when the call had come through telling him Ricky Wilson's murder weapon had been located.

'Hang on a minute Alex,' he called after her, springing to life. 'I meant to tell you this earlier…'

Coupland dug out the article he printed out from the Evening News archive, the one the journalist who'd contacted him had written about the rise in crimes committed by teenage girl gangs. As well as the photograph of Dawson and Healey there'd been another photo; a picture of a woman who had fallen victim to their scam. Her bag had been stolen from under her seat at the local cinema; she'd lost car keys, bank cards, the lot. Her face blinked out warily at the camera's lens, as though she'd been caught in the act of stealing something herself, but there was no mistaking who she was, her face had stared out at him from the incident room wall each morning and night.

Tracey Kavanagh had once been a victim of this gang.

*

When Dawson and Healey, the two girls charged with stealing Melanie Wilson's bag, had been brought in and shown the newspaper article that had given them fifteen minutes of fame six months before, they'd nudged each other, sniggering like the schoolgirls they were; proud, rather than ashamed of their notoriety. Coupland had pointed Tracey's photograph out to them. Asked if either of them remembered knobbling her bag several months ago. The older, wider girl had sneered as though he'd made an ill-advised pass.

'We don't bother lookin' at their faces,' she'd informed him as though he was some kind of moron, 'but I *kind* of remember her. She kicked up a fuss when her bag went missing and I remember thinking she looked like she could handle herself, that she probably wasn't as stuck up as she looked. I think the only reason she didn't kick off big time was because she 'ad 'er kid with 'er.' She shrugged. 'It was a designer bag – we don't pinch crap,' she informed him proudly, 'but I remember thinking that underneath her fancy clothes, she was no better than me.'

Coupland's eyes narrowed, but he didn't respond. What was the point? The girls were robbing people on their own doorstep; ordinary people going about their daily business or enjoying what little leisure time they had.

A mother spending time with her son.

A builder taking time out to be with his family.

Yeah, maybe they did have a few extra bob in their pocket but it had come from hard bloody graft. They were Salford people, not the Sheriff of fucking Nottingham. Hardworking, honest, entitled to enjoy the fruits of their labour without hassle from stupid little girls with a habit to feed.

When he handed the article to Alex she went quiet, just for a moment, as though gathering her thoughts.

'So this was the catalyst?' she asked him.

'If it hadn't been for those girls Tracey's picture wouldn't have been in the paper. And if her picture hadn't gone in the paper her father wouldn't have been alerted to her whereabouts and asked Charlie Preston to get in touch.'

She'd shaken her head as though wishing it weren't that simple. Tracey's death, and Kyle's, for that matter, might have occurred by Tracey's own hand, but the blame rippled out to a series of incidents that had made a young mother's life that much harder to bear.

Was it reasonable to expect these stupid girls to be aware of such drastic consequences to their actions? Alex asked. Coupland muttered into his chest, managed to avoid giving her a direct answer. He preferred an altogether different version. The one that said if the twat of a journalist hadn't taken Tracey's picture nothing that followed would have happened. If the tosser hadn't been so desperate for a story that he'd circled round a retail park interviewing young women until he had enough quotes he could spin a few bloody lines, enough to pay his mortgage, or his bar tab for another month.

Coupland felt his anger return, rising in the pit of his stomach, spiralling outwards, but he felt helpless. He didn't want to upset Lynn, or do anything to jeopardise his pension. If Lynn's health declined at least it gave him the wherewithal to take care of her. He was too old to go charging round smashing in the faces of everyone who bugged him. The Police *Service* was more accountable now, couldn't afford to turn the same blind eye. There was an old Chinese saying; if you stood over the bridge long enough, the bodies of your enemies would float by underneath.

Shit floats to the top eventually.

All he had to do was wait.

CHAPTER 35

Last month it was drink. A month before that it was drugs. Now it was the turn of Britain's growing Knife Culture to indulge the public's need for a perpetual state of moral panic. Coupland should have been expecting it – the media frenzy over Ricky Wilson's murder. It had been two years since the last crisis over the supposed increase in the number of fatal stabbings, and now the Wilson case had been used to pick open old wounds just to boost flagging circulation.

Virtually every front-page headline dredged up the photos of victims whose lives had been cut down by the blade, making readers feel they were in the grip of an unprecedented wave of violence. In the less salubrious areas of the north west of England the use of knives had been endemic since the sixties, in fact so commonplace it barely merited a mention in most papers, remaining the weapon of choice for many ever since.

None of the headlines ever stated the less newsworthy facts: that across the rest of the country knife-related crime had remained stable for almost a decade, accounting for around seven per cent of violent offences. Coupland curled his lip in displeasure. Even though the problem was being over-stated, a solution was certainly required; he just didn't think much of the proposed solution.

Earlier, he'd returned to his desk to catch up on paperwork and answer emails that he'd avoided during the day – basically anything that had been sent with high importance. Sure enough there'd been the usual rain forest's worth of reports to be printed out and skimmed through before he could call it a night with a clear enough conscience.

DCI Curtis had sent a report detailing the Government's latest response to the 'upsurge' in knife carrying and related crimes that read like the policy-makers had finally lost the plot. A new awareness campaign was going to be launched throughout the city in the hope of encouraging young people to jettison their blades. Coupland grimaced at the words 'Initiative' and 'Intervention', buzz-words he'd been full of when he'd joined the force, before he had any experience of what it was like being on the front line.

The Government was pledging a headline-grabbing amount of funding – a dozen officers could have been recruited at a fraction of the cost, placed in problem areas where carrying a knife brought status. But this was politics and it was less about tackling the problem than it was about being seen to tackle the problem.

Benson, who'd seen more than his fair share of knife victims on his mortuary slab, had commented that many of his peers in the medical profession thought kitchen knives should be redesigned without sharp points, that the end of a knife wasn't used during food preparation anyway. Coupland frowned, could it really have been that simple to prevent Ricky Wilson's death?

Of course, solutions like that can't be unveiled at a conference, the approach just isn't sexy enough to grab media attention on its own, but until the whole knife culture was treated as a chronic condition rather than an emerging epidemic, it seemed to Coupland unlikely that any real progress would be made. He closed Curtis's report carefully before placing it in a desk drawer beside an out of date Kit-Kat and a banana that'd seen better days.

CHAPTER 36

It was 11am in the morning and Angus was already pissed. Whether from the night before or a brand new binge Coupland couldn't tell, but he recognised the clues: the place stank of vomit and a worrying dark stain had spread across the crotch of Angus's trousers. He'd slept – and urinated – in his clothes. He'd staggered to the door barefoot, emaciated and unshaven, the living embodiment of the word desperation.

'C'mon Angus, let's get you cleaned up,' Alex trilled. She'd asked if she could accompany Coupland when she heard he was going to speak to him again and if he was honest he was grateful for the backup. He was unsure how he was going to broach the topic that weighed heavily on his mind. Kyle had meant the world to Angus – what right did he have to rob the doting father of his perception of his family? He was thankful when Alex took control, didn't even wince when she started using the sing-song voice she saved for small children and the elderly, cajoling Angus into taking a shower whilst she made them all a cup of tea.

By the time Angus reappeared twenty minutes later he was clean, though little else could be said in his favour. He'd towel-dried his hair but not bothered to comb it and it stood up from his scalp in tufts. He hadn't bothered to shave; the stubble was more vagrant than designer and his previously troubled eyes were now drinkers' pink. Once more Coupland felt sorry for what he was about to do, wondering if it was really necessary. Adding insult to injury, Lynn would say.

They were seated in the room he'd questioned Angus in after making his grim discovery and his eyes homed in on the wedding photo taken in the back of the limousine, the one where both newlyweds were admiring the wedding band on Tracey's finger. Only this time Coupland saw where her other hand lay – across her slightly swollen stomach.

He decided to wade right in. 'Did you know Tracey was pregnant when you married her?'

Angus blew out air from his cheeks and perched onto the arm of the chair nearest to him. 'You don't pull any punches, do you?' he exclaimed. Coupland was conscious of Alex studying him, a practice that always unnerved him a little in case he didn't measure up to her expectations. Too tough or a soft touch, he wasn't sure how he least wanted to appear.

'Look,' he replied, sharper than he'd intended, 'I have to submit a report to the coroner to confirm whether or not there's been foul play.'

He saw the stricken look on Angus's face, held out his hand, palm outwards as though warding him off. 'Now I don't think there has been,' he placated, 'but several days into the investigation and I discover something that could be a material fact. I haven't got time to "pull any punches", as you say.'

Coupland got to his feet and walked over to the photograph standing proudly on the mantelpiece. He picked it up. Black and white in an expensive looking frame, it weighed heavily in his hands. There was something about the way Angus looked at his new wife. Oblivious to the camera, he seemed to project a desperate love onto Tracey that may have blinded him to some of her shortcomings. Now was the time to test how blind his love really had been. Coupland shoved his hands deep into his pockets and rocked back on the balls of his feet.

'Nice picture,' he commented, returning it to its pole position. 'The dress concealed her pregnancy well. Was that for you or your parents' benefit?'

Angus reddened. 'Look Sergeant,' his voice pained, drawn out, as though speaking to an awkward client, 'I work with numbers all bloody day; I'm not an idiot.'

'What do you mean?' Alex asked.

'I knew Kyle wasn't mine,' he said quietly. 'Tracey came clean with me early on. Told me she was pregnant.'

'Go on.' This'll be interesting, Coupland thought, deliberately not looking in Alex's direction.

'She'd had a fling with another student at the uni. It hadn't meant anything but then she'd found out she was pregnant round about the time we first started going out. I told her it didn't matter to me; I was already smitten by then, asked her to marry me there and then to show how committed I was. And yes, we hid it from my family because they would have disapproved. We told them Kyle came early though you can't really kid your folks when they're both in the medical profession. We figured that even if they worked out Tracey was pregnant when we married, it would never occur to them that the baby wasn't mine.

'Anyway,' he added defensively, 'it's none of their damn business.'

And so Tracey had managed to successfully blot out her old life. Angus had been so besotted he hadn't pushed her when she was reticent about her past. She'd told him her parents were dead – which was partly true – there was no reason for him to disbelieve her.

'I wasn't interested in her old life,' he persisted. 'She assured me there was no place in it for Kyle's father and, to be truthful, the thought of an instant family didn't worry me. My parents had a happy marriage. My sister and I grew up in a loving home; why couldn't I provide the same for Kyle?'

Angus was willing to bring the child up as his own, and the fact that there was no biological father on the scene to share the limelight must have seemed like a blessing. No one, not even his family, needed to know. And so, like all lies, after a while it became the truth; the subject of Kyle's paternity was forgotten.

Coupland decided to change tack. 'I understand Tracey had her handbag stolen a while ago but didn't report it. Can you tell me anything about that?'

The tension visibly eased from Angus's shoulders at the change of topic. 'She'd taken Kyle to the cinema. Put her bag down on the floor by her feet while they watched the film. When it was over she reached down to retrieve it but it had gone. She had to use a public phone box to call me to bring the spare car keys over.'

'Why didn't she report it?'

'You lot would've pulled out all the stops, then?' Angus challenged.

Coupland didn't respond.

'Look. She – *we* – didn't see the point. She wouldn't see her bag again, we cancelled all her credit cards, why add to the form-filling by involving the police?'

'So how come the journalist found her?' Coupland showed him the Evening News article.

'Oh Christ, him? He'd been roaming round the multiplex looking for quotes. Doing some sort of report on local crime. His timing couldn't have been better. Tracey was waiting for me to arrive and was mightily pissed off by the time he approached her. He was looking for comments from shoppers who'd been victims of theft at the retail park and she'd vented her spleen, told him what had happened and before she knew it the guy was taking her photo. I remember that by the time I arrived she seemed more upset about the photo than the actual theft. I wasn't happy either, didn't like the idea of these thugs knowing what she looked like, now they had our home address. I did look around for the journalist but by then he'd gone.'

His face paled. 'Jesus, you don't th—'

'No, Angus,' Coupland interrupted, quickly. 'Not for one minute. These kids are low level thieves, nothing more.' He pushed thoughts of Ricky Wilson from his mind.

Tracey's father had seen her photograph beside the article and decided to get in touch. A chance to make amends, clear his conscience, help him sleep better in his prison bed. Coupland could only imagine Tracey's shock at answering the phone one day and hearing Charlie Preston introduce herself, the terror she'd felt at being found. How would Angus react to finding out the boy he'd brought up as his own was the product of an incestuous relationship? Tracey's father had damaged her life once; now he knew where she lived he had the opportunity to damage it a second time. She couldn't risk the world finding out who her parents were, and she certainly couldn't leave Kyle alone to cope with the legacy of his mother's family. What if David started abusing Kyle?

Coupland wondered which event had had the most impact on the trajectory of the little boy's life. Being fathered by his mother's brother? Or being brought up by a kind man, unwittingly living a lie? He looked over at Angus standing defiantly beside his wedding photo. Even in his dulled state, his love for his wife was plain to see.

Coupland knew it was his duty to tell Angus the truth, to fill in the missing blanks before he heard it from the coroner's report or an over-zealous journalist. He knew by doing so he risked tainting the love Angus had for his wife and his son, but was it right to continue letting him believe Tracey had obliterated all they'd created for no reason?

Coupland didn't think so.

Who could have known that an innocent day out at the cinema would shake the young family to its very foundation?

Tracey had been terrified of her secret coming out. In her mind, her actions protected a man she loved dearly from humiliation and scandal. Hadn't she realised, Coupland mused, that the living hell she'd jettisoned Angus into wasn't any better, that given the chance he'd have chosen humiliation and scandal with his family beside him over the empty shell that his life had become?

It was terrifying, Coupland thought, the number of ways the human mind could delude itself. Despite everything Tracey had done they'd stumbled upon her secret anyway, thanks to the willingness of certain senior officers to come clean about the arrangements made on Tracey's behalf. He hoped it was possible to contain the news for a few days longer, to give Angus time to draw breath.

Coupland looked over at Alex and shook his head slightly; saw the relief in her eyes.

It would keep for another day.

Alex rummaged in her bag, placed Tracey's Filofax on the coffee table between them. 'There's a name in Tracey's contact list that I'm interested in, Angus: Ricky Wilson.' She studied his face as she said the name, he stared straight back at her.

'How did she know him?' she asked.

'Tracey used to arrange a lot of my business meetings, send out bills, annual Christmas cards, that sort of thing. It wasn't unusual for her to keep duplicate contact details in her address book,' he answered easily enough. 'Ricky is a client.'

'*Was* a client,' Coupland corrected.

Angus blinked at him. 'Sorry?'

Jesus, he didn't know. 'When did you last see Ricky?' Coupland cut in quickly.

'I'm not sure.' He shrugged. 'Couple of months ago. I'd need to check. I helped him with a council tender, gave him a bit of advice. That was pretty much it. Why, what's happened?'

'Ricky's dead,' Alex said as softly as she could.

'Murdered outside a local bar. It's been in all the papers.'

'If you hadn't noticed, so have I,' Angus shot back bitterly. 'Diane wouldn't let me read any in case it set me off again, you know?'

Alex nodded. 'How well did you know him?'

'I didn't know him socially, if that's what you mean. He'd been a bit of a rough diamond in his youth from what I gather, still liked to think he could handle himself. Went drinking in the types of bars I wouldn't dream of going into, but then he's a local, sorry, *was* a local, and I'm not. He was one of my business development clients. He'd needed help with marketing and advice concerning a maintenance contract with a local property developer. I'd helped him secure several large contracts across Salford which had virtually doubled his business.' Angus's neck seemed to sink into his shoulders. His face took on a bewildered look. 'Christ, poor Rick, he was a nice enough guy.'

'That's the problem,' Coupland observed quietly, 'they always bloody are.'

CHAPTER 37

Closing time at The Press Room bar brought the usual rowdy banter as colleagues stumbled out into the balmy night, back to waiting families if their shift was over, or the news-room if it had just begun. Some hesitated as the fresh air disorientated them – they'd been fine all the while they'd been sitting down. Now, standing outside, the stone flags beneath their feet seemed to move, take on a life of their own.

A man stumbled halfway across the road, dropping his car keys. The traffic was quiet along this stretch of road, a couple of taxis going to and from the airport, nothing major. He had time to stop, ponder where they might have got to before swooping to retrieve them when his eyes adjusted to the street lights above.

Coupland watched and waited; made sure the key had gone into the lock of the driver's door before quietly speaking into his radio. The patrol car was parked in a side street. The officers had only to coast the squad car around the corner; the flashing lights were really only put on for effect.

The man seemed to shrink when they asked him to blow into the bag. Cursed himself silently for not walking the short distance to his next meeting. He was a freelance. How was he supposed to do his job now if he lost his fucking licence?

Coupland lowered his driver's window and looked into the eyes of the journalist who had taken Tracey Kavanagh's photo and sold it on to the Evening News, changing the trajectory of her life in the flash of a light-bulb. He'd taken the bait greedily, barely concealing his delight when Coupland phoned to say he was willing to meet with him, give him the exclusive if he played his cards right. Coupland held the man's unsteady gaze for a split second before quietly pulling away. It was nowhere near as satisfying as the crunching of bone; even Coupland had to admit that. But, in the grand scheme of things the journalist had got his come-uppance, Coupland kept his pension and the traffic boys met their target for the night. Even DCI Curtis would have to concede it was a result all round.

*

There were times when Coupland would return to his home and crave a little silence. Amy and her girlfriends would set up camp in the living room, the stereo booming tracks he'd no chance of translating let alone enjoying. There would be talk of boys and whispers of men and he'd find himself listening out for names he recognised for all the wrong reasons.

Lynn, keen to put some distance between her own day and the evening ahead would zero in on him, bombarding him with questions even though some days were too awful to recount. At times like those he'd crave peace and quiet, an ice-cold beer and a read of the sports page without his opinion being sought or, worse still, his brute force required to unblock a sink or a toilet or put out the bin. He grimaced at his stupidity. Tonight Lynn would be home late; she was briefing her replacement in readiness for her operation in two days' time. She'd left him a casserole in the fridge, with instructions on how long to heat it up in the microwave. Amy, it seemed, was out on a date.

How he missed them. He had a family who welcomed him home every night, a wife and a daughter who gave a damn, on most days anyway, who were on his side no matter what, yet he'd had the audacity to resent it, craving a silence that now overwhelmed him. He wondered what the future held: him on first name terms with the local takeaway, nothing to look forward to other than the perfunctory visits from Amy when she was short of cash?

He looked out with shame onto the wasteland that was his garden. Lynn had been going on at him for years to get someone in to lick it into shape, neither of them were green fingered and the hours they worked made it hard to keep any sort of routine going. It struck him that in all the years they'd lived there he hadn't done anything to make the garden an enjoyable place to spend time in. The overgrown shrubs needed cutting back, what bit of lawn he could see beneath the overlong grass needed serious weeding. The state of it told him that it would be ball-breaking work but Lynn would love the transformation. With some decent garden furniture it might be somewhere peaceful for her to recuperate; they could potter about in it. Enjoy what time they had. He was struck then by an idea that was so obvious he wondered why it hadn't occurred to him before, and for the first time in two days he smiled.

Visiting hours were long since finished but the flash of his warrant card met with no resistance. Joe was propped up in bed sipping what looked like a smoothie through a straw. His face was a mass of different shades of skin held together by livid red scars. Only part of his chin would ever need shaving. Joe's eyes told Coupland he was pleased he had come. When he finished his drink he passed it to Coupland, who sniffed it before returning it to the table at the side of Joe's bed. 'Orange, mango, nutmeg?' He asked.

Joe shook his head slowly, 'I don't know what's in it but it's bloody good. See the auxiliary nurse over there?' He pointed to a large black woman with straight hair and shiny skin. She was carrying bedpans over to the sluice.

Coupland nodded.

'Her son was in Afghanistan,' he paused, 'didn't make it.'

The auxiliary turned, saw them looking over and smiled, a kind-hearted smile. 'She says I need feeding up.' Joe nodded again in her direction, 'Brings me this from home.' Coupland realised he hadn't brought Joe anything, but then his decision to come had been spur of the moment. Besides, living on the street had taught Joe the giver always wanted something in return.

'I've got a proposition for you,' Coupland began, helping Joe to his feet, 'now shut up and listen.'

They walked slowly into the corridor, Joe shuffling barefoot beside Coupland. As they neared the fire exit the auxiliary passed by them on the way to the staff room, raising her eyebrows knowingly in their direction. 'I'll tell sister ya stretching your legs,' she told Joe mock-sternly. 'You got five minutes.' She swept her gaze over Coupland, nodding her approval.

'You a fren'?' she asked him bluntly.

Coupland nodded shyly.

'Good,' she concluded before going on her way, 'him need a fren' right now.'

They stood on a balcony overlooking the car park; Coupland lit a cigarette and passed it to Joe before lighting one for himself. They stood silently, watching the traffic below: the ambulances racing in; the relatives' cars reluctantly driving out; Expectant fathers sitting on car bonnets wearing their clothes inside-out. Coupland told Joe his proposition.

'Kevin,' Joe replied, incredulous. 'I'm damaged goods.' His face, raw and stretched, belied the surprise in his voice, and Coupland was reminded of Hollywood actresses who spent a little too much time with their plastic surgeons, leaving them with permanently raised eyebrows, a trout-like pout. Joe's surgeon had made him look the opposite; his eyebrows were level and low, his mouth a thinly drawn line. He looked as though nothing could ever surprise him again. Yet Joe's voice conveyed surprise, and something else too – flattery? – at Coupland's suggestion. But he was pragmatic as ever.

'I'm a depressive, Kevin. Even when I'm sober I'm unpredictable. I'm not cut out for civilisation let alone trying to civilise your bloody garden.'

Coupland laughed. 'Then that makes two of us. If I'd wanted a poncey designer I'd have contacted Homes and Garden. Now are you up for it or not?'

Joe hesitated. He'd drawn the line at moving in, but was tempted by the prospect of casual work. Neither man spoke of the subtle therapy being offered: a man unable to look beyond the end of the day engaged in the seasonal cycle of the garden – an almost subliminal way to get him thinking about tomorrow.

'I suppose it means I could pay for breakfast now and again,' Joe reasoned, 'and show the sour-faced old sow in the Dockers' Bar I've cleaned up my act.'

'It's a deal then.' A flash of pain crossed Joe's face. Coupland wondered if it was his new smile.

'Now,' Coupland began tentatively, 'there's just one more thing I want you to do for me…'

Joe was right, as ever. The giver usually had an ulterior motive, and Coupland was no exception. They were treading the same path. Had common ground between them.

Joe listened to his friend's request, nodding sadly.

CHAPTER 38

Alex stared at her coffee as she forced herself to accept there could no longer be any doubt about Tracey's intentions. She'd had a reason – by God an unenviable one – and using the rope her father had trussed up his victims with showed her action was the result of rational planning rather than emotional meltdown. Was there some message to be interpreted in her choice of suicide? Throttling herself with a ligature she could at any time have stepped away from showed a determination to move on from this world. Was it also a punishment, a way to make her final suffering that bit more painful? Did it atone for taking Kyle with her, for the pain she'd be inflicting upon Angus? Had she ever managed to rid herself of the guilt she felt for the young girls who'd fallen victim to her parents' twisted desires? Maybe her choice of rope was her way of identifying with them. A nod to their plight. Could that have been the reason she'd kept it all those years – the one relic from her past that she'd carried into her new life?

A small suitcase under the bed in the Kavanaghs' spare room revealed paintings and sketches Kyle had produced during his short life; there could be no doubt he'd been an incredibly gifted child. Most parents would have been proud of his achievement and skill, yet Tracey saw it as a threat to the stability she'd created with Angus – a hint at Kyle's paternity.

It was unnerving, Alex thought, how Tracey had unwittingly become the focal point in so many men's lives: those of her father, her brother, her husband, her son. Yet all she could remember when it mattered was the wrong that had been done. It was hardly surprising, given what she'd been through, that not even Angus's love could light up the darkest corners of her soul. Alex thought about Carl at home with Ben, about the possibility of extending their family. There would never be a right time, she conceded, only a belief in the future and the hope that they would cope with whatever came their way.

She'd just finished writing up her report for Sergeant Coupland when he popped his head into the CID room, asking if she wanted another coffee. She wrinkled her nose. She hadn't finished the one she'd got, she told him, it had a metallic taste to it. 'I'll try a tea,' she informed him, before staring at the dregs in her cup.

Plonking the fresh drink onto her desk and spilling some of the contents, Coupland dabbed at the mess with his sleeve. He was animated, as though there was something he couldn't wait to tell her. He pulled a chair over to her desk. 'The lab's confirmed that prints belonging to Brooks and Horrocks have been found on the kitchen knife used to murder Ricky Wilson.' Tonight the two killers were enjoying the hospitality of the holding suite pending their appearance at the Magistrate's Court in the morning, along with several mates – including local ladette crimewave Dawson and Healey – who had given them a false alibi and were now charged with perverting the course of justice as well as the theft of Melanie Wilson's bag. He smiled as he told her, though it was a sad, tired smile.

'The toe-rags had had a successful little set-up, using both girls to steal from punters in the bar. They'd split the proceeds from selling on the stolen credit and debit cards; house keys and home addresses were passed onto local contacts for a fee. When Wilson kicked off after his wife's bag had been stolen he'd been pissing in the wind – the doormen weren't interested in his complaint for obvious reasons, didn't like it when he accused them of covering for the girls.'

'They couldn't risk him calling the police,' Alex concluded, 'drawing attention to their neat little enterprise.'

'It was the little runt, Brooks, who stabbed Wilson,' Coupland added.

Horrocks had spilled his guts in record time. So much for the band of brotherhood.

'When Wilson left the bar with his family both men slipped into the staffroom to change out of their suits and follow him. Horrocks claims he only wanted to scare Wilson, hadn't intended to finish him off. He reckons Brooks had been wound up all night, was just looking for an excuse…' He paused, took a large slurp of something that closely resembled hot water and milk, gestured for Alex to do the same. 'Horrocks masterminded everything that followed though… from hiding the knife to persuading the others to cover for them, conjuring up an alibi that placed him and Brooks in sight of the bar when the incident took place.'

Coupland pictured the pair calmly walking to their lockers to change before following Wilson. This wasn't the impulsive action of a nutter as Horrocks was trying to paint it – this was cold-blooded murder. He shrugged as he patted his trouser pockets for his cigarettes. 'I've done my bit. CPS pick up the baton from here.'

Alex nodded, took a sip from her tea, which tasted surprisingly good. She studied Coupland's wide, craggy face. 'Penny for them?'

Coupland had been thinking about Amy, who, all things considered, wasn't turning out too badly. An image of the track-suited Dawson and Healey flitted into his head. They were the same age as his daughter, though thankfully that's where the similarity ended. He gave an involuntary shudder.

'What is it with some young girls?' he asked, bewildered. 'Years ago their aspirations were getting pregnant underage and applying for a council flat, now they want to be as deviant as their gangster boyfriends. Is the prospect of doing time such a small price to pay?'

Alex shook her head, saddling up to climb onto her trusty high horse. 'Forget about the prospect of prison,' she reasoned. 'That's only a deterrent if it disrupts your lifestyle. Many of the kids we deal with are second-generation offenders, used to the people around them disappearing for long periods of time.' She shrugged, 'Having a conscience is an optional extra these days… C'mon, Kevin, look at their role models – female celebrities out of their faces on drugs and booze yet they still end up on the front page of all the magazines, even if it's for the wrong reasons. It's like their trip switch that tells them right from wrong is faulty.'

'Maybe so,' Coupland conceded, baring his teeth in an attempt at a grin, 'but it's all bollocks.' Trust Alex and her psychologist's view of everything. Coupland, like his father before him, subscribed to the belief that it was having rules in place that stopped the inmates taking over the asylum. He didn't give a toss if people didn't agree with the law or whether they even understood it; all they just had to do was bloody well follow it.

They'd just finished putting the world to rights when a civilian member of staff knocked on the glass partition before entering the CID Room. She handed Alex an envelope. Alex sighed as she opened it; she wanted to go home, start making inroads with Carl. She unfolded the A4 typed page and gasped.

She'd passed her sergeant's exam.

CHAPTER 39

Lewisham sat on his daughter's bed, his fingers trailing over the yellowing quilt. It was creased now, flattened in parts where he'd burrowed into it, searching for comfort in the scent of her, tear-stains long since dried into patches of sorrow. Her make-up sat dormant on her dressing table, the liquid eye-liner he had hated her wearing had dried, cracks visible on the surface like soil in a drought. Jewellery he'd bought her over the years lay scattered across its top.

In the second drawer of her dressing table, placed with care, a velvet box contained Sheila's engagement ring. It had been his wife's dying wish that Siobhan should have it, but in the melee that was the aftermath of their daughter's murder he'd forgotten, laying her to rest in the dress he'd bought her for her last school dance; her hands, placed carefully by her side, were unadorned.

He often wondered if Sheila knew that he'd failed her when it mattered most. First, failing to keep their daughter safe, then unable to keep his promise about the ring. He was supposed to give it to her on her twenty-first birthday or the eve of her wedding, whichever came first. Neither he nor Sheila had considered the possibility that neither of these events would take place, that the only time he'd accompany his daughter down the aisle was following her coffin.

It was the night of the funeral that he'd remembered. He'd been tidying away the cufflinks he'd worn when he opened the wrong box and found himself staring at the one piece of jewellery Sheila had specifically asked to be given to their daughter. He'd felt as though air was rushing past him and he seemed to lose his balance and all he could remember before his legs went from beneath him was stumbling into Siobhan's bedroom and placing it in the drawer, never wanting to set eyes on it again.

He pulled the drawer open just enough so he could see the offending ring-box. He had a niece getting married soon, he wondered if he should pass the ring onto her. He allowed the thought to stay in his mind, willing Sheila to send him some sort of signal, to let him know it was okay. He opened the drawer wide enough to lift the small box out, ran his thumb over the velvet cover.

The doorbell rang, breaking into his thoughts, and he allowed himself to turn the clock back and pretend – just for one exquisite moment – that Siobhan was outside waiting to be let in; red-faced because she'd forgotten her key.

She'd have been sixteen.

The sight of Coupland standing on his doorstep clutching a black plastic bin liner jolted him, and he didn't bother to conceal his surprise. 'Kevin?' he asked, unsure whether or not to invite him in. 'To what do I owe this honour?' His eyes fell back towards the plastic bag, already working out the answer.

'It's time, Roddy,' Coupland said simply.

During the journey across town Coupland had agonised over how to do it, how to start a conversation that was essentially telling his friend it was time to move on. There were so many concentric scenarios going on in his mind, from Wilson's family ripped at the seams, to a frightened young woman trying to protect the men she loved most in the world – both incidents bound by a tenuous link.

He'd called into the supermarket to grab refuse sacks and a

handful of cleaning products and set off to Lewisham's home before his courage deserted him. He hadn't got a clue how he was going to broach it, and before he'd had a chance to rehearse his words Roddy had flung open the door and he'd found himself spouting out something about it being time, and as yet his friend hadn't shut the door in his face.

Roddy stared at him. Slowly, he shook his head.

Coupland waited. Did he imagine it, or had there been a moment's hesitation?

'I can't do it,' Roddy said simply, with a shrug.

'You can. I'll give you a hand...' His words trailed away as he saw Lewisham's shoulders droop. He tried to read the conflicting emotions jostling for room on Roddy's normally impassive face.

He took a tentative step forward, paused.

'We're not going to *clear* it Roddy – you need to know Siobhan existed, but we can tidy it. Fold up her things and put them away, it'll help you understand that she won't be coming back.'

A breath, let out long, like a sigh. Roddy moved to one side to let him pass.

*

Hope is definitely not the same thing as optimism, it is not the conviction that something will turn out well, but the certainty that something makes sense, regardless of how it turns out.

-Vaclar Havel, Disturbing the Peace.

CHAPTER 40

It was normal for Coupland to attend the victim's funeral. It gave him the opportunity to pay his respects, to reflect on the relationship he'd built up with the deceased during the investigation, albeit a one-sided one. It signified closure too, their face relegated to the deepest recesses of his mind. Coupland knew that he would never look at a small boy again without thinking of Kyle Kavanagh.

Angus had chosen to hold a joint service for his wife and children, which meant that whatever way Coupland looked at it he was also attending the funeral of a killer. There was a first time for everything, he supposed.

He sat in silence on a pew at the back of the church, between Alex and Joe. Alex had been horrified when they'd arrived together; he could sense her wrestling with a desire to stare, for Joe's face was a mass of jagged scars, of which only a few would fade in time.

'You should have seen him before he borrowed my suit,' Coupland quipped, referring to the double-breasted charcoal jacket and trousers he'd encouraged Joe to change into. A suit that only ever came out for weddings and funerals, prising him away from his normal over-worn clothes. Lynn had had to get busy with a needle and thread, taking in the waistband, moving buttons across the jacket. She'd attacked the job with gusto, said it kept her mind off things, said she'd always liked a challenge.

'Reason I fell for you,' she'd joked.

In two days' time she'd be facing the biggest challenge of her life.

'But what happened to his face?' Alex had persisted when they were out of earshot, filing into the church. The truth was Joe's face was going to attract a lot of curiosity, even hostility, from now on.

'His face reflects the way he feels, Alex. It's not his looks we need to worry about,' Coupland reminded her, 'but the content of his mind.' The psychiatrist working with Joe had explained that it was a common misconception that people were most likely to harm themselves during their darkest hours. The reality was that it was during the recovery from depression that they become most at risk. At rock bottom it was impossible to sink any lower, but as their condition began to improve they became fearful of the future and what would happen if they suffered a relapse – for this time around they knew how bleak life could be.

Joe had simply wanted to blot out one form of pain with another.

*

Christ stared down from the stained glass above the altar. The indicator on the pulpit informed mourners of the hymn numbers to be sung during the service: *Abide With Me*, and *Morning Has Broken.* Coupland scanned the bowed heads of Angus's family: mother, father, sister. Angus sat between his parents, his head nodding to the reverend's words like a metronome. He wondered if Tracey and Kyle were watching, wondered what difference it made even if they were.

Alex couldn't tear her eyes from Tracey's coffin. Draped in a velvet cloth, photographs of her and Kyle had been placed on top of it. Inside the coffin lay a woman, a wife, a mother.

She and Tracey were the same age but only one of them was going to get any older.

As the mourners filed out of the church the wind rustled the cellophane around a flower arrangement and Coupland was drawn to the intensity of their colours: the red, white and black of Kyle's favourite football team vividly alive unlike the little boy they'd been bought for. A tag fluttered and he bent to read it:

To Kyle,

All my love,

Daddy.

It was the way it had happened, Angus explained earlier to Coupland, that kept people away. Friends kept their distance, told him they didn't want to encroach on his grief. The truth was, nobody knew what to say to him. He'd thought about holding the funerals apart, so mourners could pay their respects to Kyle and the infant without feeling they were being forced into paying respects to their mother. But it didn't feel right. Tracey had always been there for her son, and besides, he hated the thought of his kids being on their own.

'Whatever her reasons for doing what she did,' Angus reasoned, 'she was their mother, and I'd rather they had one of us with them,' he said simply.

And so three coffins had been carried from the back of three hearses along the aisle of the church.

Three coffins buried in one plot.

Tracey's father had been persuaded not to attend.

Coupland looked up at the clear blueness of the sky, the sun providing an almost holiday-like backdrop to the proceedings. It was wrong that the sun was shining. It should be hiding behind black clouds with rain lashing down and lightning flashes and rolls of thunder; a hint that God was angry. The sun symbolised everything that was good and happy; hope, even. And what hope could there be for anyone when a child wasn't safe with his mother?

Angus moved around the cemetery on auto-pilot, nodding at well-wishers, allowing himself to be hugged and patted. He hoped his memory would play silly beggars again and wipe out today, move it to the same padlocked place in his subconscious where his discovery of the bodies had been relegated. He wanted to forget every little detail:

The sight of the small white coffins. The muffled whispers of the mourners. The smell of freshly dug earth.

A displacement of air by his side made him turn. He found himself looking into the eyes of a horrifically scarred stranger.

Joe introduced himself and stuck out his hand.

'What the hell is he saying?' Alex whispered to Coupland, frustrated they were out of earshot of the solemn conversation.

'I imagine he's paying his respects,' replied Coupland, pleased his idea was going according to plan.

'But they don't even know each other.'

Alex turned to Coupland and, not for the first time, thought how they operated on very different wavelengths.

'No,' Coupland conceded, 'but maybe they can help each other. They have, after all, suffered similar loss.'

This seemed to silence Alex – but not for long. 'But I thought Joe was… homeless.' What little she knew of her sergeant's friend she'd gleaned from Turnbull but she didn't want to drop him in it. She felt sorry for what Joe had suffered, she really did, but wasn't he a drunk? A loose cannon? Although by the look of him he'd already exploded.

Instead she said: 'He's no job, no money, he's suffered from years of untreated depression – what kind of example is that?'

Coupland pulled a face. She just didn't get it.

'He's not an example, Alex,' he said grimly. 'He's a warning.'

CHAPTER 41

The news had spread. Word travelled fast about Alex passing her sergeant's exam and it was as good an excuse as any to stay behind and get tanked up. Carl had been subdued when she'd told him the good news the previous evening, even more so when she called him now to say she'd be late home again.

'I can't play truant from me own do, love,' she'd reasoned, and he'd accepted her logic, albeit begrudgingly, telling her they'd have their own celebration at the weekend. Grateful he hadn't gone into a sulk, she checked her make-up in a compact mirror before heading across the road with a couple of uniforms coming off shift.

There would be a time, a long way from now, when Alex would stop trying to rationalise Tracey Kavanagh's actions. She'd accept that it was pointless trying to fathom whether a young woman's childhood could excuse the murder of her son, whether it was an act of misplaced bravery rather than selfishness, a willingness to sacrifice Tracey's dreams for Kyle and all he'd become, to protect him from a knowledge that would tar him forever.

There would be a time when she stopped comparing every little progress of Ben's with Kyle, wondering if he'd have been at the same stage, wondering if Tracey understood just what she'd stolen from him. There would be a time when she'd stop thinking about Kyle and his mother, push thoughts of them into the corners of her mind, make way for other cases, other victims. She would learn to accept the things she couldn't change.

But not yet.

The nature of Alex's job had shaped the type of mother she'd become. In particular it gave her a stark awareness of physical peril. Ben was a sturdy, rough and tumble, *physical* boy, but the injuries she saw in her job made her realise just how delicate he was. At times she felt nauseous just thinking about how easily his bones could break, how easily his skin could tear. She felt nauseous now. She lifted a hand to wave at DCI Curtis, who was looking speculatively from his office window.

Alex coughed as she passed through the haze of smoke at the entrance to the bar. Not for the first time she wondered why smokers were fussy where they drank when they spent most of their time outside.

'About bleedin' time,' Turnbull called out to her, 'What're you having?'

A pint glass was already welded firmly into his hand. He'd spent the morning at the Magistrate's court; the gang responsible for Ricky Wilson's murder were now on remand. She'd watched them being escorted handcuffed from the holding cells at the station before being led into the waiting police van positioned at the side door.

She'd seen killers before: in the dock at the crown court and once, up close, with his victim still warm. Even now every nerve ending recoiled at the memory. Yet despite having met her fair share of bad people she still needed to look at these men and their stupid accomplices, *really* look at the thugs who'd robbed an innocent man of his future and tipped a young mother over the edge.

Four pairs of eyes stared ahead, shallow, devoid of emotion. The girls, Dawson and Healey, were focussed on some point in the middle distance, but Brooks and Horrocks, sensing Alex's attention, turned in unison to stare at her defiantly, meeting then holding her gaze. They were hard-looking men, the type you'd feel uneasy near unless they called you *Mum.* The thought of them being someone's sons made her shudder, and for the thousandth time she wondered what the trigger was, what had happened in their lives to turn them from mischievous little boys into killing machines.

She found herself thinking of Ben, prayed to God she'd never know.

The sound of thumping from the pub's jukebox jolted Alex back to the present. 'I'll get 'em,' she insisted, reaching into her bag for her purse. 'Tonight's my shout.'

'No need,' Coupland called out as he moved across the room to greet her. 'Boss's left money behind the bar.'

That silenced her.

'Jesus.'

'Close enough,' Coupland replied. He saw the look on her face and laughed. 'Turn up for the books, eh? Always thought Curtis had a soft spot for you.'

'Don't start,' she warned him, smiling. She'd been worried Coupland would see his backside over her passing her sergeant's exam. He'd been known to be touchy when peers overtook him and she'd wondered how he'd react with someone junior catching him up. She sighed happily. He'd made a point of coming over; taking the piss was his way of reassuring her everything was all right between them.

Someone placed a drink in her hand and when she tasted it realised the orange she'd ordered contained a double vodka too. She sipped at it slowly, already looking for a space on the bar where she could discreetly leave it. Robinson came over to join the group assembled round her, reunited now both the

Wilson and Kavanagh cases had come to a close.

'They told you where you're going?' he asked, already planning to swap desks. He didn't like being situated so close to the CID Room door; you got treated like the messaging service for the rest of the team.

'Staying where I am for the moment,' Alex replied. Her eye caught Coupland's but gave nothing away. Coupland wasn't sure whether HR had explained the reason for his leave, or if they'd even told her it was his job she'd be covering. From a selfish perspective it suited him just fine; if someone was going to step in his shoes, he'd rather it be someone whose judgement he trusted.

Alex excused herself and headed towards the ladies' toilets, passing small cliques who turned to congratulate her, slapping her back and ruffling her hair like she was back at school. She basked in the good cheer of her colleagues, conscious that those around her were getting more and more pissed.

'What you drinkin', Sarge?' someone called out, and it was only after a dig in the ribs that she realised the off-duty PC was talking to her.

'I'm okay, thanks,' she replied, her answer overshadowed by shouts of 'bollocks, get her a brandy,' and 'is there still a tab on?'

Alex ducked into the toilets and stared in the mirror while she caught her breath. She'd not been there an hour, yet she felt exhausted, realised that a quiet night with Carl was much more appealing. She looked at her watch; she had time to slip away, stop at the off licence at the bottom of their road and buy a bottle of something fizzy to take home. Still, there was something she had to do first, and now was as good a time as any.

Earlier in the day she'd bought a pregnancy testing kit and, ever since, it had been burning a hole in her bag. She slipped into a cubicle and took the white stick out of its packaging to read the instructions. The world wouldn't change because of a second blue line, she told herself. There'd still be robbers and rapists and murdering mothers and she'd still want to put them away. Maybe she'd have to do it differently for a while, but so what? What were plans anyway, except God's way of reminding us there was no such thing as a sure bet.

She undid her trousers and pulled down her underwear, crouching over the toilet seat so she could be sure the stream hit the predictor stick. When she finished she placed the stick on the cistern behind her. She heard a door open and unsteady footsteps followed by the sound of someone throwing up. Whoever it was hadn't made it to the lavatory. She wrinkled her nose and got to her feet, adjusting her clothes. Can't even spend four minutes contemplating in silence, she thought wryly. She flushed the toilet and opened the cubicle door, only to be met by a woman wearing a sparkly cowboy hat and t-shirt that announced she was on *Astrid's Hen Nite.*

'Christ I thought you'd got flushed down the loo,' she slurred, 'I'm dying to splash me boots.' Alex stood by to let her enter, noticed she didn't even lock the cubicle door before lifting her skirt. Trying not to look she washed her hands and shook them under the dryer before stopping dead in her tracks when she realised she'd left the predictor stick behind.

She approached the toilet door cautiously.

'Er, will you be long…?' she enquired self-consciously, keeping her eyes fixed on the broken Tampax machine by the mirror. The silence was punctuated by a series of small farts.

'Won't be long luv,' came the chirpy reply.

'...only I left something in there.' Alex persisted. The cubicle door widened and she found herself staring at the over-made-up woman as she strained to empty her bowels.

'Nothing a good curry won't fix, eh luv?' the woman informed her before holding out her hand. Alex held her breath as she took the stick from her, nodding her thanks. 'By the way,' the woman called out to her just as a couple of young WPCs swayed in, 'Congratulations, luv.'

The decibel level in the bar had exploded. Those still there were now on a bender, the excuse they'd needed to get a pass out for the night forgotten.

Lewisham, sat in the corner with a couple of colleagues, raised his glass to her as she caught his eye. Coupland was deep in conversation with the DCI, who'd been lured across the road by a pretty WPC when it emerged the bar tab was becoming dangerously low. No one would notice if Alex slipped out now.

It was quiet enough for a midweek evening. The shoppers and shoplifters had called it a night, would be home by now, showing off their respective hauls. The streets were empty bar groups of young men and women on the pull, cheap cologne choking the airways of passers-by.

It was a night of closure and new beginnings. Coupland's report on the deaths of Tracey and Kyle Kavanagh – and that of her infant – had been submitted to the coroner. Ricky Wilson's killers were at the start of a judicial process that would see them behind bars once more. Dawson and Healey, the girls who'd turned bag-snatching into a local enterprise, would soon be getting their first taste of life in a young offender's institute.

Alex doubted it would be their last.

It was a fine line, Alex knew that much, between aiming high and suffering disappointment or settling for what you've got and feeling you've been short-changed.

She was calmer than she thought she'd be. Happier too. A

thin blue line had altered her future but she was certain she would cope.

Well, as certain as you ever can be.

CHAPTER 42

The luminous fingers on the bedside clock pointed to twelve and six, although with the curtains shut tight and the room in darkness Coupland couldn't be sure it was half past midnight or six am. His mouth tasted foul, as though he'd been sick several times in succession. 'Fancy a cuppa?' he croaked, sleepily reaching an arm out to Lynn's side of the bed, but it was cold and empty. His eyes snapped open and he pushed himself into a sitting position. As he tried to make sense of it his thoughts began to shift in shape, flitting from one scenario to the next, images changing before he'd had time to register them, like a kaleidoscope in the hands of a toddler. For a moment he feared time was playing tricks on him, that Lynn was already in the hospital but that couldn't be right, her overnight bag was still by the bedroom door, a pile of magazines Amy had bought her balancing on the top.

Pulling on his dressing gown Coupland padded down the stairs. Relief flooded through him when he found Lynn sitting by the kitchen table, her chair turned so that she looked out onto the unkempt garden.

His heart sank.

'I'm sorry,' he whispered, placing his hands on her shoulders, berating himself for not getting Joe to start on the garden earlier. He'd had this notion of surprising her, seeing her face light up when he brought her home, at her realization that he'd been listening to her all these years after all. And so clandestine arrangements had been made: Joe was arriving at 9 am this morning, an hour after Coupland left for the hospital with Lynn. He'd been giddy with the planning of it, so consumed with getting every detail right it had almost taken his mind off the reason behind it.

Almost.

And then last night he'd begun to focus on the futility of it. What if Lynn never got to see it at all?

'Sorry for what?' Lynn asked, bringing him back to the present.

'For being a twat,' he grunted, 'For not realizing that something was wrong... for getting involved with that stupid bloody woman.'

'*Stop it.*'

'What?'

Lynn turned her chair to face him; her blazing eyes drilling into his own. 'Stop *dwelling*. Forget about the past, we can't change any of it but we can learn from it, can't we? I love you, Kevin. Isn't that all that matters?'

Coupland nodded. Moving towards the dishwasher he retrieved two cups and placed them in front of the coffee machine, which he'd left switched on from the night before. He opened the fridge door. 'There's just enough milk…'

'Kevin,' Lynn said softly, 'I'm nil by mouth.'

A pause.

'I knew that,' he said chirpily, though his hands shook all the same.

Two strides and Lynn was beside him, shooing him out of the kitchen. 'Go and get a shower, love, I'll cook you some scrambled eggs; it'll give me something to do.'

Coupland hesitated, shouldn't he be the one making a fuss of her? Yet instead here she was clucking over him, like his feelings fucking *mattered*. She was the one having the mastectomy. There, he'd finally said it. The word operation didn't even scratch the surface yet still she worried about how she'd look. *For him.* How could he show her that none of that mattered, that he loved the bloody bones of her?

'Give Amy a knock on your way up,' Lynn ordered, as though sensing he'd been about to protest. 'Be good for her to get some breakfast for a change.' Amy wasn't coming to the hospital; they'd talked about it and agreed it was better she go to college as normal, no point her moping when there were exams to prepare for. She'd given in reluctantly once Coupland promised to phone her the moment her mother's surgery was over.

He knocked on Amy's door, pausing for a couple of beats before entering. She was already awake, propped up in bed texting God knew who at that hour.

'Mum's making breakfast.'

Amy shrugged. 'I don't eat breakfast.'

Coupland stepped into Amy's room, tiptoeing over discarded clothing until he reached her bedside. He planted a kiss on the top of her head, taking in the sleepy smell of her. 'Perhaps today you'll make an exception?' he whispered, letting the question hang in the air. Maybe he did have a role to play after all. Maybe his job was ensuring Lynn got her own way today.

He left Amy's room and padded into the bathroom, removed his dressing gown and boxers and stepped into the shower. He stood beneath the jet of piping hot water for the longest of times, as though it could in some way wash away his fears, as though it were that simple. The water began to cool, but he remained there motionless, head bent, his forehead touching the cool tiled wall as the water ran over him, washing away his tears.

Amy joined them for breakfast, fresh-faced and animated,

providing a monologue that filled their own silence. Her date the other evening had gone well, it transpired, so much so that she'd agreed to see the boy again.

'Poor bugger,' Coupland grunted, winking at Lynn, the both of them remembering the dance she'd led him when they'd first started dating.

They drove to the hospital in silence. As Coupland approached the traffic lights at the junction they turned to red and he slowed to a stop. They were adjacent to the precinct where Ricky Wilson had been stabbed; a sign pasted onto the opaque window of the Sportsman's Bar proclaimed they were recruiting for new doormen.

Life went on.

Coupland grimaced, wondered if praying to a God he'd long since given up on made him a hypocrite. Decided to take his chance anyway. When the lights began to change he was already off, his hand resting against Lynn's thigh. 'Must've rained last night.' Lynn pointed to the glistening tarmac on the road stretched out ahead of them. There was no sign of rain now, although the air was noticeably cooler.

'Good day for gardening.' Coupland said simply.

THE END

FRAGILE CORD

READING GROUP QUESTIONS

1. How feasible do you think it is for someone to hide a part of their life from everyone around them for so long?

2. Why do you think Tracey didn't feel able to talk to Angus about her past once they were married?

3. Why did DC Alex Moreton feel so threatened by what Tracey had done?

4. Is DS Coupland right to feel the journalist is responsible for what happened to Tracey?

5. What is the significance of Joe's injuries to the direction of the story?

6. Have you ever hidden something about yourself? And do you think it made a difference to how your life unfolded?

Enjoyed FRAGILE CORD? Book 2 in the DS Coupland Series:

A PLACE OF SAFETY

is available to download now from AMAZON

Continue reading for the opening chapters:

A PLACE OF SAFETY

by
Emma Salisbury

Prologue

He always knew one day he'd get mixed up with guns. It was only ever going to be a matter of time, given the company he kept and the lifestyle he aspired to. You can't go about in the circles he moved in without needing protection, needing to defend your own corner once in a while, but what he hadn't expected was this.

'Go on,' a deep voice behind him urged as the car slowed down a second time, a hand snaking along his thigh in case further encouragement was needed.

He'd thought it was some sort of test, some elaborate initiation to prove he had bottle, could be trusted to follow orders. So he'd gone along with it, waiting for the moment they'd yank the gun away from him, pissing themselves because he'd been daft enough to fall for it, slapping his back and shaking their heads, telling him he'd had 'em going for a minute.

Only that didn't happen.

Instead a hush descended upon them as they watched him and waited. 'Go on,' the voice behind him repeated once more, the hand gripping him harder.

Sweat dripped between his shoulder blades as the car window lowered. His hands felt clammy and he wished more than anything he had the balls to say no.

Oblivious to the music thumping from the stereo, he swallowed, pausing just long enough to eyeball his target.

Then he fired.

CHAPTER 1

There was nothing quite like the anticipation of going out on a Friday night. Best day of the week, no question. Made sense of the endless shitty filing and data processing that filled Abby's working days since leaving school and joining the accountancy firm Rogers and Black as a trainee Finance Clerk. She looked at the time on the bottom of her computer screen and sighed; why did time drag when you had plans?

Through the office window the early rush hour escape had begun, workers pouring out of buildings onto the high street, eager to catch the early bus home, or failing that get a seat on the regular one. The evenings were still light, although cooler now; passers-by wore jackets and woollen scarves, young girls marking the transition by wearing thick tights under skimpy shorts. It seemed to Abby that Salford took on a life of its own once the offices had shut; the people milling around its centre over the next few hours did so because they wanted to, going out on a bender they'd slogged all week to pay for, a top night out in reward for keeping their heads down, going with the flow for another week.

Angela, a wiry bespectacled woman in charge of the firm's finance staff, smiled kindly in Abby's direction.

'You got your tickets then?' she asked. Abby nodded, trying not to let her eyes slide up to the wall clock above Angela's head.

'Queue was massive! They wouldn't let you buy more than two tickets at a time, so I had to text Dixie and tell her to get her backside down there soon as. But yeah, got mine and Becca's tickets okay.'

Angela pushed back from her desk to reach down for the elegant leather bag by her feet. 'I'll give you the money for Becca's ticket now,' she informed Abby as she rifled through the contents, 'she can owe it me rather than you.'

'You sure?' Abby asked, already on her feet as she made her way over to Angela's desk. Rebecca wasn't the best at settling her debts; good job she had a mother always willing to bail her out.

The older woman's eyes twinkled as she studied Abby. Tall and slim like Becca, but there the similarity ended. Whereas her own daughter was quite studious looking, some would even say plain, Abby's shock of red hair and dazzling smile catapulted her into a league of beauty that she seemed blissfully unaware of. Both girls had been best friends since primary school, virtually inseparable; she frowned as she remembered that was all going to change. She broached the subject once more:

'No regrets then, Abby, about coming to work here?'

'You mean regrets about not going to uni?' Abby corrected her. She paused, her eyes staring into space as though searching for an answer that would finally satisfy everyone; convince them all she was doing the right thing, that she hadn't been influenced by the situation at home. 'Look, I didn't get the grades, it happens. I wasn't prepared to do resits...' She smiled at Angela's concerned frown.

'…don't look like that, Angela,' she soothed. 'Becca was always the bright one. I just ambled by scraping through. But I don't want to carry on scraping through. A mediocre degree today is no good to anyone; besides, the graduate route isn't the only way into a career – you should know that – and who knows, if I get the experience here, maybe in a couple of years I'll study for the diploma, see where that takes me.'

Angela smiled sadly. 'You know, Becca was heartbroken at first, when you said you weren't going with her, wanted to turn Bristol down... if Salford had run a similar course...'

'I know,' Abby conceded, 'and I'm cool with it, really. The way I see it is it just wasn't meant to be. Besides, we'll have more to talk about when she comes home.' A further glance at the corner of her computer screen told her it was a quarter to five. If she didn't catch the next bus…

Tonight was a big night in many ways, the opening of a new nightclub in the centre of town and Becca's last night out before leaving for Bristol in the morning. It had to be special; Abby had choreographed every minute of it a thousand times in her head. They were starting out at her house for drinks at six, which left precious little time to get ready as it was. She turned her pleading eyes towards Angela. 'Haven't even made up my mind what I'm going to wear yet,' she confided impishly. 'Becca's bringing over a couple of tops…'

Angela glanced at her Longines watch. Stifling a smile, she made a wafting motion with her right hand. 'I can take a hint,' she said good-naturedly, 'off you go then,' her last words carrying over to Abby as she hurried towards the lift: 'Just don't do anything I wouldn't do…'

*

'You still gonna do this?'

'Yeah, I'm still gonna do this, what choice do I fuckin' have?'

'It's drugs though bruv, Mum brought you up better than that.'

'Like that stopped you from bein' sent down?'

Aston curled his lip, sucked air through his teeth and slapped his hand against his younger brother's shoulder. 'I'm only lookin' out for you, Earl, no need to disrespect me.'

Earl looked up at his older brother, wondered with a pang when it was he'd actually stopped looking up *to* him. Round the same time as Aston's stint in prison, he reckoned, leaving Earl to take care of their mother and sister. Their fathers were long gone.

'Look,' Earl reasoned, 'all I need to do is pull off this last job, then Pauly'll leave me alone and I can go back to school.'

Aston pulled a face and smacked his right hand against his own forehead as though he'd remembered something crucial, 'So that's how it's done…' he muttered slowly, 'shit man, why didn't you say? I can see now where I went fuckin' wrong…' He shook his head in frustration. 'Roundabout the time I used to believe what Pauly says and what Pauly does were the same ting…' he shook his head in disbelief, 'and to think we all thought you were the smart one in dis family.'

'I'm smarter than you man,' Earl retorted, 'I ain't been inside for handlin' stolen motors—'

'That was a long time ago, bruv, and I learned my lesson. Look at me, I've turned my life around, I got a girl, a job—'

'Yeah, under the thumb and always broke. Smart move, man.'

'I know what I want now. I don' wanna be lookin' over my shoulder for the rest of my life, and I don't want that for you…'

'Very touching.'

The temperature in the flat plummeted as a sinewy black man with a shaved head entered the room behind them. 'Why you here, Aston,' he drawled, his Mancunian accent peppered with third generation patois, 'dis is no place for a *pussy.*' Earl suppressed a smirk. Aston was bigger than him when all said and done. 'Why don'tcha run off back to your mamma,' Pauly taunted, 'leave Earl to take up where you left off.'

'Shut your mouth, Pauly.'

'Who you orderin' around, man?' Pauly moved forward with confidence; Aston might be taller and well built, but the older man had the benefit of his henchmen playing on the X box in the next room if needed.

Aston took a step back, tried a different approach. 'Just lookin' out for ma family, man, you know the score.'

It was hard not to notice Pauly's 'chib', a scar from a knife slash that ran from the right side of his mouth, curving down below his jaw line. A memento from a turf war ten years earlier, in the days when he travelled alone, fought his own corner. He'd moved on since then, got himself a reputation and the muscle to protect it.

Pauly stretched his lips into the widest smile; put his arm around Earl's slender shoulders, drawing him closer. The sight of the gangster pawing at his brother like that turned Aston's stomach but he knew how intoxicating it was to hold Pauly's attention. 'C'mon Pauly,' he placated, arms open to show he'd not give them any trouble, 'you can't blame me for watchin' his back.'

Pauly seemed to give this some thought. 'He's a big bwoy now,' he said in his defence, 'and if he wants to work for me that's his choice… but…' he paused as though working out how they could come to an agreement without him losing face, 'him do this last job for me and you have my word I'll leave him alone.'

'You sure?'

'I'm fuckin' sure man.' The grin was starting to slip. 'Now leave him, he's got work to do.'

Aston paused, looked back at Earl, who, at fourteen, was six years his junior. Fourteen going on forty.

'You okay with this, bruv?'

Earl nodded. 'Yeah man, just *go*.' Aston tutted; sucked his teeth once more before slamming out onto the tower block landing.

'Pussy,' Earl snarled after him.

Pauly patted Earl on his back, nodding his approval, his smile returning to its Cheshire Cat grin. At that moment one of his foot soldiers, all seven feet tall and shoulders as wide as the Hulme Flyover, entered the room carrying a package wrapped in brown paper. He paused in the doorway, waited for Pauly to grant right of entry before approaching them, stopping just in front of Earl. They both turned to look at Pauly, waiting.

'Empty your pockets.' Pauly instructed.

Bewildered, Earl did as he was told; removing the parcel of puff resin he'd been instructed by Pauly to pocket an hour before. A look of confusion flashed across his face.

'I thought you wanted me to deliver…'

'Tings have changed.' Pauly said abruptly, nodding at the Hulme Flyover to unwrap the parcel he was holding, careful not to touch the contents directly, holding the paper's edge so his prints didn't transfer onto it.

A 9mm semi-automatic.

He wrapped it up again before holding it out for Earl to take. Pauly's arm around Earl's narrow shoulders tightened in a vice-like embrace. 'An important job has come in,' he breathed low into Earl's ear, inhaling cheap body spray and teenage boy sweat.

'And when I heard what was needed, I knew juss de man for de job.'

*

The queue was already snaking round the block by the time the taxi pulled up at the kerb outside Ego, a long line of over-made-up girls in skimpy skirts and young men in knock-off designer clothing waited patiently to be let inside. Abby counted out the cab fare and included a tip, thanked the driver once more for waiting longer than was decent while she and Becca had run round the flat in a flurry of excitement collecting bags and purses, performing last-minute make-up retouches as they'd said their goodbyes to Marion, Abby's mum. The cab was Marion's treat; she'd given them money for the return fare too.

Won't have to worry about how you're getting home then – or if, ;) her typewritten note had read, hinting at a humour almost forgotten along with the sound of her voice.

'Seriously she's really cool your mum, Abby,' Becca gushed, 'bet she was a total honey when she was younger. I think my mum was *born* an accountant.' It was true that Abby's good looks had originated from her mother, going by old photos and the comments her dad used to make before the emphysema took him – and a stubborn streak to go with it. Sadly, two years into Motor Neurone Disease her mother's mobility had deteriorated, along with the ability to carry out most tasks – she relied heavily on Abby now to dress her, do her hair and make-up and help with her two younger brothers. Abby had been in the process of speaking to social services to ask for help with caring for her mother once she'd left for university, so in many ways not getting the exam marks she'd needed had been a relief; besides, she wasn't quite sure she was ready to leave home yet. In some perverse way she enjoyed being needed.

Findlay and Jordan, her younger twin brothers, were at that impossible stage – most days they did something that made her want to explode, like pouring her best perfume into their bed-time bath, or lathering themselves in her designer body lotion – a birthday present from Angela – but at the end of each day they would look at her with their big round eyes and little boy grins and all would be forgiven. She was like a second mother to them; how could she, in all conscience, leave them while she went away to study? Besides, there was another altogether selfish reason she was happy to stay put…

'What are you plotting now?' Becca giggled, already in the party spirit thanks to the bottle of sparkling wine they'd shared before leaving. Abby had wanted them to have some time alone, a chance to reflect on their friendship before they met up with the others and got off their faces. The first couple of hours after Becca had arrived at Abby's flat they'd stayed in her room, laughing and joking as they did each other's hair, swigging from bottles of Smirnoff Ice that Becca had brought with her. Afterwards, they'd shared a takeaway with Marion, the twins dispatched to their room to watch a film.

The taxi had arrived early and Abby still hadn't given Becca her gift, so hurriedly she'd thrust the simply wrapped parcel into her friend's hands. 'I'd got a speech prepared and everything,' she admitted shyly, 'but all I really wanted to say was good luck.' She waved her hands in front of her face as she felt the tears begin to well. 'I'll miss you,' she gasped, 'and whenever you wear it I hope it'll remind you of me.'

Becca tore into the parcel and opened the velvet jewellery box inside to reveal a silver chain with a small diamond chip pendant hanging from it. Lost for words, she rushed towards Abby to plant a kiss on her cheek.

'And don't go bloody losing it either,' Abby warned, 'I'll still be paying for it after Christmas.' The sound of a car horn beeping spurred them on, Becca handed the necklace to Abby to fasten around her neck, then with a flurry of hugs and handbags and a puff of perfume they were gone.

The blast of cool air and cigarette smoke as Becca held the cab door open for Abby in front of the nightclub brought her back to the present. Abby smiled as she answered her friend's question with a white lie. 'Just wondering if the men of Salford know what's gonna hit 'em tonight,' she replied, linking her arm through Becca's as they strolled towards the end of the queue.

'Here! Bex, Abby, over here!'

They followed the voices until the unmistakable shape of Dixie and Kristin came into view. Dixie, at six foot three, had always been the tallest girl in high school; Kristin, at four eleven, suffered from a growth hormone deficiency that resulted in her having rods inserted into her legs to stimulate bone growth. With killer heels she was a reasonable height, although forever overshadowed by her towering best friend who wore ballerina pumps to compensate. Waving, and ignoring the filthy looks and tuts from the crowd behind them Abby and Becca slipped into line some ten yards in from the back of the queue.

Later, Abby would look back at their decision to push in with regret. The defining seconds that formed a fork in their future, taking them on a path from which there could never be a return.

*

The car travelled south across the city, a heady mix of rap music and adrenaline causing the chassis to vibrate in time to the MC's lyrics. Earl wiped the front passenger seat window with his sleeve for the third time, his over-breathing causing it to steam.

'You sure you don't want some o' dis?' Pauly asked, taking

the reefer from Kester, his driver, offering it to Earl before taking it himself. Earl shook his head. Despite moving drugs around the city for Pauly, he'd never actually taken any, had seen up close what it did to the losers who bought from Pauly's men at the several trading posts across the estate, not long out of school but hooked on a substance that reduced them to nothing. Yeah, so it hadn't stopped him keeping the supply chain going but drugs would always be around, and while there were buyers there would always be someone like Pauly, ready and willing to cash in on other people's misery.

The stench of the reefer was beginning to make Earl feel light-headed. The atmosphere in the car was cloying, the leather seats giving off their own particular odour. He pressed the button on the passenger door to open the electric window.

'What the fuck—?!' Pauly kicked the back of Earl's seat, swore at Kester, his driver to close the fucking window, disable all the other fucking windows while he was at it.

They'd reached the main street that snaked its way through Salford's city centre, parallel to the new club that had once been a Casino, stripping the residents of hard earned money long before on-line gaming saved them the trouble of leaving their homes to be fleeced. Kester slowed, looked in his rear view mirror at Pauly, a baffled look on his face.

'Drive!' Pauly barked, pissed that Kester couldn't read his fucking thoughts, that he had to spell out everything. No wonder he was the main man, the one they looked up to, the rest of the crew couldn't find their arseholes with two hands and a mirror. Pauly sucked air through his teeth, leaned forward between the two front seats to turn the radio down. 'Round the block one more time, man.' He said to the back of Kester's head, and then, staring at the scalp between Earl's cornrows, instructed: 'I'll let you know when we're ready.'

*

It was the blast of loud music that caught her attention. The blare of Dizzee Rascal, full on and close up, that made her turn, glance at the car as it slowed down behind them before cutting the sound and moving on, foot down to beat the lights, engine revving, tyres screeching as it shot across the junction before turning left into the one-way system. Abby felt a flash of recognition, so quick she couldn't place it before it flew out of reach, moving deep into the corners of her mind where it evaporated, leaving a notion of unease in its wake.

At the start of the road leading up to the club Kester killed the engine, sat grim-faced, while Earl urinated in a side street. 'S'all we fuckin' want,' he moaned, 'im gettin' pick up for pissin' in public while we sit around in a stolen—' the nozzle of the gun at the base of his skull stilled his tongue. He stared solemnly at Pauly in the rear-view mirror, planning how to back-pedal. 'Look man,' he placated, 'I know he's cool, but he's young, s'all I'm sayin'.' He tried to laugh but it died in his throat.

'How ol' were you when you join' me?' Pauly asked.

'But that was different, man. I had nobody else, I had to look out for myself, I was hungry…' His words tailed off as he recognised the glint in Pauly's eye, felt he was back on comfortable ground. 'You were always hungry,' Pauly soothed, 'always willing to please…'

Pauly sat back in his seat as the car door opened and a sheepish Earl climbed back in. Handing him the weapon, Pauly removed his gloves, his hand dropping to the boy's thigh giving it a playful squeeze, leaving it there longer than was necessary.

'S'all right, pretty bwoy,' he drawled, 'everyone get nervous their first time…'

The moving line had picked up pace, the doormen letting

girls and couples enter without a second look, the groups of men held back, pockets patted, bodies frisked, questions asked and accusations made, pressing buttons until they got a reaction, refusing entry providing the only entertainment in the evening's proceedings.

They'd reached the entrance to the club. Dixie, after flirting outrageously with the man on the door had jumped the queue claiming she needed the toilet, dragged Kristin along with her, promising they'd get the drinks in. From where she was standing Abby saw the car that had driven past earlier approach a second time, pausing as it drew level with the club's entrance once more, no music this time as the passenger window lowered. From the corner of her eye she saw an arm, gloved, holding something steady.

Blink.

Her brain went into go-slow as she tried to make sense of what she was seeing, of what it could mean… the arm pointing out of the window… the boy in the passenger seat, the flash of gold around his neck, his face turned towards her, the fear in his eyes.

A gun.

Everyone around her oblivious, laughing, stamping feet to keep warm as they waited in line; the doormen, speaking into their mouthpieces as they jostled with a couple of chancers, unaware of the danger approaching.

Abby swung away from the gunman's aim, pulling Becca with her, but the force of her movement wasn't enough to remove them both from his range. Becca had an arm outstretched, as though she'd seen him too and was warding off the impossible. The shot when it came sent them reeling back, legs buckling beneath them, falling hard. The bullet entered Becca's neck, above the silver necklace Abby had given her for luck.

An arc of blood sprayed into the air turning everything red. There was a moment's hush, then pandemonium as the car sped off and the extent of Becca's injuries became clear. Abby's scream died in her throat. Her mouth tasted of metal. She bent double, swiping a hand over her eyes as she spat out clots of skin and tissue.

ABOUT THE AUTHOR

Born in Salford Emma moved to the Peak District as a child, commuting into Manchester's financial district as a consultant for HSBC. Spells in Birmingham beckoned (Selly Oak then Solihull) after winning a bank scholarship to Birmingham University before working out of bank branches in Castle Bromwich, Coleshill and Shirley.

Emma loved English Literature at school but studied Business and Finance in order to secure a 'proper' job. Other jobs have included selling ladies knickers at Grey Mare Lane Market and packing boilersuits in a clothing factory. 'I did try for waitressing work at one point,' Emma says, 'but restaurants seemed to think I wasn't capable of carrying plates from one room to another.'

After moving to Scotland Emma worked for a housing association supporting socially excluded young men which gave her plenty of material for her writing.

Widowed with two sons Emma writes from her home in East Lothian, which they share with their rescue dog, Star.

Find out more about the author and her other books at:

https://www.emmasalisbury.com

Visit Emma's Facebook page:

https://www.facebook.com/emmasauthor/

Follow Emma on Twitter: @emmasauthor

Printed in Great Britain
by Amazon